SCARLET REVENGE

Visit us at www.boldstrokesbooks.com

SCARLET REVENGE

by

Sheri Lewis Wohl

2013

ISBN 13: 978-1-60282-868-1

THIS TRADE PAPERBACK ORIGINAL IS PUBLISHED BY
BOLD STROKES BOOKS, INC.
P.O. BOX 249
VALLEY FALLS, NY 12185

FIRST EDITION: APRIL 2013

―――――――――――――――――――――――――――――

CREDITS
EDITOR: SHELLEY THRASHER
PRODUCTION DESIGN: STACIA SEAMAN
COVER DESIGN BY SHERI (GRAPHICARTIST2020@HOTMAIL.COM)

To my pal Vickie Gregory
I treasure your friendship, your encouragement, and that you
let Loba sleep with me whenever I come to visit!

Much wisdom,
much grief;
the more knowledge,
the more sorrow.

(Ecclesiastes 1:18, The New Jerusalem Bible Reader's Edition)

PROLOGUE

St. Louis Cemetery
New Orleans, LA
October 31, 1805

Victoria pulled her cloak tight against the wind that whipped and pushed her small, lean body. With her head down and her bag held tight, she hurried down the darkened street. The night was black as coal and the howling air unseasonably icy. The earlier storm had washed the air clear but left a chill in its wake. No warmth threaded through the wind to give her comfort. No stars guided her path.

More than just the frigid air made her shiver. Something else weighed heavy on the night, uncomfortably familiar in a way she didn't want to acknowledge, and she didn't like the feel of it. She'd been happy here, safe. Now a thread of something close to fear passed through her heart. She walked on, her senses on alert. Beneath the hanging boughs of a tree, she paused and listened. Was it a whisper? Was it calling her name?

No. It couldn't be. He couldn't be. He wouldn't dare. She touched the stake tucked into her belt, and the solid feel of the hardwood against her fingertips comforted her. He'd not get another chance. Even he had to know that. She was stronger than she'd been before, ready to do the distasteful though necessary task. This time, she wouldn't hesitate. With a deep breath, she stepped from the canopy of leaves and began to walk again, her step quick and sure.

The gate to the cemetery creaked as she pushed it open. It all but screamed its protest at her entry, as if telling her to turn and run far away. How she wanted to do just that. Instead, she stepped through the gate and hurried between the crypts, the stones uneven beneath her feet. No one else walked the ground this night, not that she expected to see anyone, alive or undead. She came in the deepest night to do what had to be done, what she owed him. She came because she loved him.

The door to the crypt was as yet unsealed, as she'd known it would be, the pounding rain of the storm making it impossible to set the mortar. In the morning, the workers would return to seal it shut, and none would be wiser for her visit. This was the only chance she'd have to make things right. Once her task was complete, she'd leave this place and the life that for a brief time had made her feel almost human. This would be the last night she'd walk the streets of this glorious city.

It wasn't fair, though not a great surprise to Victoria. Life had been unfair to her from the beginning. Why should this be any different? She should be grateful for the years of love and safety that he'd gifted her with. And they had been a gift.

In her heart of hearts, she'd always known it couldn't last. Her kind didn't belong in the human world. Never had. Trying to pretend otherwise always ended badly. The bitter reality of this night was how it all came crashing to an end. She never saw it coming.

Inside the crypt, she let her eyes adjust to the deep blackness, and the cloying scent of death filled her nostrils. The howling winds faded, blocked by the thick crypt walls, the near silence eerie. Within moments, she had her bearings and was as ready as she'd ever be to complete the grisly task. She stepped to the side of the coffin and slowly lifted the lid. Tears filled her eyes at the sight of his peaceful, familiar face. Though pale, he looked as though he was simply sleeping, and in a way he was. It wasn't the sleep she wished for him.

But delaying the inevitable wouldn't help her, and it surely wouldn't help him. With a heavy heart, she pulled from her bag the salt, the herbs, the tools she needed to cast her circle. Slowly, carefully, she began calling up from memory the power that a witch had taught her so many years ago.

Once it was done and the words spoken to protect his soul, she once more stood at the side of the coffin. Only one thing remained for her to do. From her belt, she pulled the stake she'd carved from a branch of the tree behind the parsonage. The wood was solid, cold against her palm…powerful. Tears blurred her vision as she held the stake in trembling hands, high above her head, and aimed right at his heart.

She dared to take one last look at his beloved face, so familiar and comforting even in this place of death. If only things could have been different. If only she could have given her life instead. But it wasn't to be, and now she had to do the one thing she could to protect him. Tears fell from her eyes as she brought the stake down with all her might, and as she did, he opened his eyes.

CHAPTER ONE

New Orleans, LA
November 10, 2005

It was easy here—easy to blend in, easy to be part of the night. Not a soul even gave him a second glance as he came and went in darkness.

Yes, it was easy here.

Easy to be a vampire.

The hurricane that freed him from the grave also served up sustenance in endless quantities. Within a fortnight, his body was healed and his strength restored. Nothing could stand in his way now. He was back and ready to rule the world.

As the city emptied, he had helped himself to whatever he wanted, whenever he wanted it. When the press reported a total of 700 bodies recovered as of last month, he'd laughed. Authorities classified all of them as victims of the levee breaches. Only he knew how inaccurate those reports were. Just thinking about the incredible feast brought to him by an act of God had him licking his lips. What was a disaster for the city was a grand coup for him.

Things had changed while he slept, and he approved—so much better than when a black eternity had shrouded his entire existence. Once the roaring waters of Hurricane Katrina had set into motion the perfect conditions to free him from the confines of the crypt, he acclimated quickly and took only a little more time to establish a financial base from which to work.

He'd considered himself successful in life before, but nothing like this. A personal catastrophe had put everything into perspective, and a natural catastrophe had given him an opportunity to put this life back together. All he'd needed was a little time and imagination. Fortunately, he was blessed with plenty of both.

At last he was ready.

Through the curtain of rain, he peered into the darkness and smiled. The night was so like another many years before, and it seemed only appropriate. Things did have a way of coming full circle. He smiled and tipped his head to the starless sky.

"Come out, come out, wherever you are," he whispered.

CHAPTER TWO

Washington, DC
Present Day

Tory Grey left the Metro stop at Union Station and began to walk south. The daytime hustle and bustle was long gone, and quiet had settled over Capitol Hill. Her bag slung over one shoulder, she strode briskly. She didn't worry about danger on the streets of the city but didn't feel the need to linger either. If trouble came her way, she'd deal with it as she always did. Better for everyone involved if she didn't have to.

As she crossed the street, a figure huddled in layers of dirty clothing almost blended into the shrubbery that bordered the park. Tory reached into her pocket and pulled out the twenty-dollar bill she'd tucked there before leaving her house. Instead of avoiding the obviously homeless person, she walked close.

She crouched and touched the bundle with the tips of her fingers. "Hello, Belle." She kept her words low and gentle.

A throaty voice, nearly inaudible, came from beneath the folds of cloth. "Go away, I'm invisible."

Tory kept her voice even. "Yes, Belle, you're invisible. I can't see you at all."

"Invisible." The bundle of thrift-store clothing quivered and seemed to draw farther into the shrub.

Tory waited and, after a moment, a hand with broken nails and spotted skin snaked out from beneath the pile. She pressed the bill into the trembling, dirty palm. The odor of unwashed body and clothing caught on the air, but Tory didn't wince. "Go get something to eat, all right?"

"Can't...the food...poisoned. Danger."

She held Belle's hand when she tried to snatch it back and gently stroked until the trembling subsided. "Belle, you have my promise the food will be safe. I've made sure of it just for you. I talked to them before I came here tonight." Belle never inquired who *them* might be, which was good. The important thing was to get her to eat.

"Truly?" Her voice sounded old.

"Yes, truly." Some nights it worked. Some nights it didn't. This appeared to be one of the good nights.

Helping Belle to her feet, Tory watched her amble down the street. In the darkness, Belle moved slowly, her gait uneven and hesitant. When she disappeared around the corner of Union Station, Tory sighed and began to head up the street again. It was all she could do for the moment, even though she worried that one night she'd reach the park and Belle wouldn't be here. The thought sent a chill up her spine. To worry about one mentally ill homeless woman didn't really make sense, but she couldn't help it. Belle touched her heart for whatever reason, and in her lonely world, it was enough. She didn't have to come this way each night. It was a long and convoluted way to her office, yet she did, always looking for Belle.

Tory's path tonight took her up First Street past both the Russell and Dirksen Senate Office Buildings, where lights still glowed in about half a dozen windows, past the Supreme Court, and across the street to the Library of Congress. She continued around to one of the employee entrances and waved her keycard in front of the small gray pad next to the door casing. A tiny light on the pad changed from red to green. When she heard the click, she pulled the door open and stepped inside, inhaling the scent of old books and polished wood. God, she loved this place.

It was funny how things worked out even when someone was technically dead. Before walking down the hall, she looked up and gave the security camera a wave. The night crew was relatively small and hence they'd become pretty tight-knit. Well, except for one little secret she kept to herself. What woman didn't have a secret or two?

Downstairs in the outer office, Tory grabbed a pair of white cotton gloves from a supply box and slipped them onto her hands. Though she preferred to wear them, they weren't required for her work. The rare books she dealt with daily wouldn't suffer harm from the touch of human hands. It was one of those better-safe-than-sorry things for her. She didn't need her fingerprints left behind. Too many questions would be asked that she didn't feel inclined to answer. That little secret thing and all.

She didn't know when it would happen, only that it would. Discovery was inevitable, and when the day came, she'd have to move quickly and leave as little of herself behind as humanly—or rather inhumanly—possible. By now she was getting pretty damned good at imitating a ghost. Of course, she'd had a fair amount of experience.

As she crossed the threshold into her private office, the lights flicked on automatically, thanks to the nifty little sensor installed by the General Services Administration a couple years earlier. If she was gone from her office or simply failed to move for more than ten minutes, the lights would go out. More than once, she'd had to wave her arms like a crazy person to catch the sensor's eye and get the lights to come back on. A little annoying, but who was she to complain about energy conservation? Besides, she still remembered all too well when the only light was a single candle. Lights that turned themselves off and on beat candles any day of the week.

In the middle of her desk someone had placed a nondescript cardboard box. She couldn't recall ordering anything or even being told that something was coming to her. It'd be nice to know where it originated, but no one was here to ask at this time of night. These days anonymous packages could be scary—way too many people with misguided ideas they put into things like mail bombs. Still, even with no return address, the package had gone through security, so it was probably fine.

It was a real coup to land a job here at the LOC. The work was interesting and treasures were plentiful, even if they did come unannounced. She clicked on the desk lamp she used to examine books and opened the box. An unpleasant odor drifted up as she began to remove layers of packing materials. Okay, maybe something *could* slip through security. She wrinkled her nose and tried not to inhale too deeply. The acrid smell reminded her of the underground crypts of old Europe. She'd honestly rather not remember those.

The old books, on the other hand, were a different story. Some brought back incredible memories, including reading first editions… when they came out. Though it would be fun to be able to share that tidbit with someone now, she had to keep that knowledge to herself.

Just like she'd have to enjoy this treasure all by herself. Anticipating the find, she folded back the last layer of packing. Nestled in a bed of cushioned foam and wrapped in a final protective paper was a fifteenth-century New Testament produced by the Brethren of the Common Life, maybe eight inches wide and eleven inches long. Her hands trembled as she picked it up and turned it over. She didn't have to open its pages to know it was written in Latin. With a hiss, she dropped it back into the box.

It isn't true a Bible would scorch a vampire's skin. In fact, most folktales about what would harm a vampire were pretty much a crock. Take holy water. If Tory wanted to, she could take a bath in the stuff and it would only make her wet. She dropped the Bible now and jumped back from her desk as if it had indeed scorched her palms because the Bible had been a gift from Tory to her father—or, rather, her surrogate father.

Even that wasn't the worst part. No way in hell should it be here on her desk. Over two hundred years ago, she'd personally buried him with this very book. By all accounts, the book should be locked inside a beautiful black casket with whatever was left of the body of Roland Lyle.

How then did it end up on her desk?

She ran her hand over the cover, and the rough feel of the old leather against her fingertips sent chills up her arms. Published around 1435, it looked pretty much as it did the night she left it on his chest and closed the casket cover. A dedicated bibliophile even back then, she had felt pain to see the fantastic medieval book locked away forever. Given how he'd died, Tory'd believed it the right thing to do. She still did. That long-ago dark night, she'd said good-bye to both the man and the fifteenth-century New Testament, never expecting to see either again.

For the tenth time tonight, she inspected the package it had arrived in—a simple heavy-duty brown box with her name printed on a white label in bold crimson letters. Nothing special. Though security had scanned it, they hadn't detected anything to flag it as dangerous. Books came to her routinely. It was her job, after all. They went through security, were checked for any obvious threat, and then sent her way. No one gave it a second thought.

Of course, since she worked at night she didn't have anyone to ask. It was one of the beautiful things about the Library of Congress. In the current economy, they were all too happy to have her, even if she insisted upon graveyard working hours. Her job didn't require the presence of others, and so they granted her unusual request. Their sole concern: get the work done.

The folks responsible for receiving the incoming packages were long gone by the time Tory arrived, and she'd be long gone by the time they showed up again. As with everything else in her life, she was alone in this. She'd have to solve the mystery another way.

Her mind whirling, she sat and turned to her computer. First things first. She e-mailed the entire staff asking for any information about the mysterious package. By the time she returned tomorrow, she might have an answer. Somebody had to know something, right?

The mass e-mail done, she returned her attention to the book. Not only was it a mystery how the book came to be here, so was its provenance. This was not a cheap volume. She knew her books well, and this one would fetch close to or even more than a hundred thousand dollars in a rare-book auction. She also knew all the collectors and who had what. That had been her job for a very long while. If this book had been in the hands of a serious collector any time during the last two hundred years, she would know. So, who'd sent it to her?

And why?

❖

How he liked this city. It possessed a totally different flavor than New York or Paris or Rio. Oh, he liked those places a great deal too, but the good old District of Columbia, it was a completely distinct beast and loads of unbeatable fun. The trail that brought him here had been long and full of twists and turns. When he'd begun his journey he'd believed it would be a short one. The complications of it surprised him, but the sheer adventure of it was exciting. The end would be that much more thrilling.

Streetlights sent butter-yellow light to cut through black night, while clouds covered the stars, making it a perfect setting for tonight's masquerade. No one paid too much attention to him as he sauntered the streets in his Goth ensemble. It was so intoxicating. Here he was a vampire pretending to be a Goth pretending to be a vampire, and everyone bought into the charade. The irony was simply delicious.

So were the people. He'd just left Ruben, a tall, well-muscled black man, back in the alley behind a brick apartment complex. Ruben was a real looker who turned out to be a bit of a fighter too. No doubt he could have been a great deal of fun if he'd been so inclined. Unfortunately he'd not had the time to indulge in foreplay, so to speak. First, he'd had to deal with dinner, and Ruben was handy.

But he was still hungry. He'd picked Ruben because of his size and thought he'd be a full-meal deal. Didn't work, his hunger still gnawed at him, sending an edge of tension zinging along every nerve. Long trips had a way of doing that to him, and though Ruben was a fine first course, no meal was complete without dessert.

Leaning against a tree on the Mall, he wasn't surprised when a man walked up and said, "Hi." Confident. Assertive. Not someone making idle conversation.

Giving the guy a once-over, he licked his lips and all thoughts about big old Ruben disappeared. "Hi." Dessert had just been delivered to the table.

"What's your name?"

The lie rolled easily from his lips. "You can call me Vlad." He smiled, but only a little. Didn't want his fangs to frighten away his final course.

"As in Dracula?" The guy smiled back with perfect white teeth. Some dentist had made a load of money off him.

"Definitely." The fictional character wasn't where he'd drawn the name from. No, he liked the real guy, the Vlad Dracula who'd impaled his enemies on wooden stakes and dipped his bread in their blood. The man had possessed the kind of style he admired.

"I'm Warren." He stuck out his hand. On his right pinkie he wore a sterling-silver ring with an intricate design. Good thing he wasn't a werewolf. It was a nice bit of bling. He might have to keep it. Warren wouldn't need it much longer.

Warren wasn't quite as bulky as Ruben, though it was clear he did some work in the muscle department. He was maybe thirty, with dark hair long enough to curl over the collar of his charcoal-gray suit. Not a bad suit. Looked custom-cut and designed to flatter his physique. The shoes were none too shabby either. Made him wonder what he might have in his wallet. He wasn't a thief, but it didn't make much sense to leave perfectly good jewelry or cash lying around for just anyone to pick up. Waste not, want not.

"What's up, Warren?" Vlad winked.

Warren's smile widened, his teeth so straight and pearly they almost glowed in the dark. "My cock, how about you?"

Ah, how easy the humans made this game. It didn't matter what century it was; they never really changed much. He'd met many Warrens in his time—guys who walked the straight and narrow when under public scrutiny, pretending they were so much better than everyone else. Yet, when the lights went out and they knew no one was watching, they were all about doing the nasty with another man. In crappy hotel rooms, in dark alleys, in the backseat of cars—it didn't matter as long as they got off. He'd heard it. He'd seen it. He'd lived it.

Even a vampire had his dirty little secrets.

"Could be." Vlad hedged, one eyebrow raised.

"So, Vlad, you want to go somewhere and grab a drink?"

"You have a place in mind?"

Warren held a hotel keycard out. The silver ring sparkled in the glow of a nearby streetlight. "I sure do."

Vlad stood up and straightened his long black leather coat. "Lead the way."

❖

This time of the day, or rather the night, was always her favorite. Something about the shadows as they danced on the walls never failed to make her smile. Probably all the years of working while most slept blissfully unaware in their beds. Or maybe it was because she shared an affinity for the night with those born to it. Some people would say it was creepy. She thought it was inspiring.

Inside the huge church, tranquility reigned, and for Naomi Rand it provided a time to seek harmony with her God. She could kneel at the altar and allow her spirit to soar free in a way she couldn't when others were around. Despite knowing it could never be, she continued to hope one day God would grant her forgiveness and take away the burden weighing heavy on her shoulders.

But the dream had no chance of being fulfilled. Even someone irrefutably damned could hold on to hope. It kept her going even when she knew better.

From the first night the church allowed her to begin midnight services, she'd been here for every one of them. At one time she'd flirted with the thought of becoming a full-fledged member of the clergy, though only for a little while. It didn't take her long to realize she was more suited to a different calling in the church rather than as a bona fide ordained pastor.

The church was very open and encouraging to all, including those whose place was in darkness. In fact, it was those very souls to whom they were reaching out to now with the midnight services. Still, even as accepting as the church was, she couldn't in good faith close the gap between her calling and the path of the clergy. She had cast her lot a long time ago, and trying to pretend otherwise couldn't change who and what she was. She had to be content with where she was right now. It was—had to be—enough.

Twice a week, the cathedral was all hers for about an hour. Well, that wasn't technically correct. True, she was the first one here each week to open up and prepare for the midnight service, but she wasn't completely alone. Armed guards were on duty twenty-four seven, though for this service, they didn't exactly provide protection. For most of the congregation during this very special hour of worship, the guards were little more than window dressing. The impressive sidearms the guards carried would stop few who came to pray with her. And while that might concern the guards, it didn't worry her. She left her fate in God's hands and would accept whatever came her way, good or bad.

Her footsteps echoed softly in the nave as she walked toward the altar. At one station, she stopped, said a quick prayer, and lit a candle in one of the red votive cups. The gesture didn't change what she'd once done, but it made her feel better, which was the best she could ask for.

At the altar, she dropped to her knees and bowed her head. Her sins were many and forgiveness elusive, not just for her actions but for the thing in her heart that led her to do all that she'd done. No single action had pushed her beyond redemption, though her final act was unforgivable. Nightmares continued to haunt her sleep, and she often awoke to the sound of her own screams.

From the direction of the huge entry doors, footsteps were soft, almost silent. Almost. She finished her prayer, rose, and turned to see who had arrived early. Most who attended this service were regulars and she knew them by face, if not by name. She also knew what they were because all understood their secret was safe with her. This was not a place for judgment or discrimination. All were welcome here regardless of who or what they were.

Now, instead of seeing a familiar face, she spotted a lone woman sitting far in the rear, her head down, her hands in her lap. An air of loneliness seemed to surround her like a dark aura. If she was looking for comfort, she'd come to the right place. Naomi did what she could to help those who had to find a way to exist in two very different worlds. Werewolves, witches, psychics, and so many others came because she offered a safe place. This one would find her secrets safe here too, though what she was wasn't clear from this distance.

When Naomi reached her the woman looked up, the deep intensity of her gaze taking her aback. Lovely, with long auburn hair that fell to her waist, she had dark-brown eyes and full lips. No, lovely wasn't right. Stunning was more accurate, even with the pale skin.

Vampire.

Briefly, Naomi paused, but not because the woman was a vampire. Very few still existed, as far as she knew, and that made her unique amongst those of Naomi's congregation. No, the mysterious woman's identity made her curious. Naomi knew everyone who came to the midnight services, yet she didn't know this woman.

Logically, that didn't really mean much. It wasn't like every preternatural in the city attended the worship services. A great number did, probably an equal number did not. Far too many felt abandoned by God and couldn't bring themselves to step inside. She just tried to be here for whoever, whenever, and liked to think she had a pretty good feel for the preternatural community. Once she'd sought to destroy them. Now she tried to save them.

"Welcome." She reached out. "I'm Naomi Rand."

For a long moment, the woman studied her outstretched hand almost as if she'd never seen one before. She finally looked up and said, "Good evening, Bishop Rand." Her hands stayed in her lap.

Naomi wasn't offended. People came to the church for a host of different reasons, most of which were intensely private. She never pushed to uncover those reasons. She wasn't that big a hypocrite.

With a smile Naomi told her, "It's simply Rand, no Bishop. But please, call me Naomi. Everyone does." She didn't stand on formalities and, more important, never wanted to misrepresent her place in the church. In a hundred years, she'd never be clean enough to approach the role of bishop. This quasi-role was enough.

A single eyebrow arched. "My apologies, Ms. Rand."

Well, she knew a line drawn in the sand when she saw it…or rather, in this case, when she heard it. The stranger didn't want to be friends. Everything about the woman screamed *back off, bitch*. So she did. It wasn't wise to push humans when they weren't ready for the offered solace of the church. Pushing a preternatural? That was just plain stupid.

"I hope you enjoy the service." Maybe once the woman experienced the inclusiveness of the services she provided for her special congregation, she would understand that here they were all friends.

She wanted to ask about the book that lay in her lap beneath her small, folded hands, though she instinctively knew it wasn't a topic for discussion. It was a very old Bible that looked suspiciously like a few in the exhibits here at the church. Valuable items like historical Bibles were housed in alarmed cases, and to date they'd had no issues. Even so, that didn't mean someone wasn't capable of bypassing security, particularly if that someone possessed preternatural abilities.

"I'm sure I will."

Dismissed by both word and a turn of her head, Naomi left the woman sitting alone and continued her preparations for the evening's worship service. As she walked back toward the pulpit, she heard the front doors open and footsteps on the stone floor. She didn't have to turn around this time to know who'd come in; she recognized the heavy step of a regular. She didn't think much more about the mysterious woman until the service was over, and by then, she was gone and so was the Bible.

CHAPTER THREE

Her feet seemed to have a mind of their own. Only an hour after she'd arrived at the library, Tory had left her office and hopped on the Metro. The next thing she'd known, she was getting off at the Woodley Park station and, thirty minutes after that, climbing the steps of the National Cathedral, where she walked right on through the massive front doors. For the flash of a second, she'd wondered if she would burst into flames. After all, wasn't she the devil's child? She'd been called that and much, much worse through the years. But as she stood motionless at the threshold, no flames erupted and no bolts of lightning sliced down through the night sky to destroy her. Thank the Lord for small favors.

Roland had always insisted she was as much a child of God as anyone else, despite what she was. After some time and at his never-wavering insistence in her inherent goodness, she'd finally started to believe him. At least until *that* night when what she'd done proved him so very wrong. She hadn't placed so much as a single toe inside a church since. Safer that way.

Why now was the big question roaring through her mind? Why was she compelled to be in a place God didn't want her? Or anyone else, for that matter. In all truthfulness, she had *no* place on this planet. This world was for humans, not the likes of her. Sadly, she lacked the courage to end this miserable thing that passed for her life.

Before entering, she'd paused. The exterior doors with the intricate scenes carved in metal had seemed to beckon to her. Even the gargoyles high on the stone walls looked as though they winked and smiled as if to say *come on in*. Had to be hallucinations. Had to be. Nobody in their right mind would want her to walk through those doors.

Maybe. Even in the face of every instinct screaming at her to turn around and run as far away as possible, she wasn't able to retreat. Instead, she'd reached out, opened the door, and stepped inside. The draw was as invisible as it was strong. Unbreakable. Sometimes, she just didn't have the strength to fight.

Inside the cathedral, the soaring ceilings were aglow with light from the pendant fixtures. The air held the suffocating scent of jasmine, probably from the sprays of so many flowers just inside the doors. Candle flames flickered in the tiny red votive cups that lined the exterior walls, and the murmur of a voice floated disembodied through the chapel like a whisper from Hades.

Turning around and running back to the Metro stop would have been her best response. She had no more place in a church tonight than she'd had years ago when Roland had stood at the pulpit. He'd wanted her to feel at home in God's house, believed she could. Except she simply didn't belong. Not then, not now. What in the heck was she thinking? Vampires and religion didn't mix. Period.

When Naomi Rand stopped to talk with her, she'd wanted to scream *go away*. To hiss and show her fangs. She'd come here hoping she wouldn't be noticed. She'd wanted to sit in silence in a place that could bring her closer to the spirit of Roland and simply think. If she could capture him anywhere, it would be in a magnificent church like this one. Her grand plan lasted all of about thirty seconds. Certainly, Naomi had the best of intentions. Wasn't that what the clergy was all about? She didn't need it and sure as hell didn't want it. Her not-so-subtle message got through, and Naomi left her to return to her church duties.

The doors opened and closed behind her as one after another trickled into the cathedral. No one spoke, just quietly found their places and sat. Tory'd sensed and smelled the presence of other preternaturals, not just vampires. An earthy scent just below the pervasive aroma of jasmine let her know at least one werewolf sat among the small crowd, along with several of a variety she couldn't quite catch. It was a most unlikely and unexpected blend of worshipers.

Even amongst those of her own kind, she'd been unable to stop the feeling that at any moment God would see her sitting beneath the incredible stained-glass window and destroy her where she sat. Actually, that might not be such a bad thing. After a while, immortality became a burden capable of breaking even the strongest.

Thankfully, the service began, the sounds of music floating beautifully throughout the room. About halfway through, she was able to slip out without causing distraction or attracting notice.

Now, out on the church steps, she paused and gulped in the crisp night air. Her hands were shaking as she clutched the New Testament close to her chest. The smell of the old leather brought tears and a flood of memories. She didn't want to remember and sure as hell didn't want to feel emotions she'd managed to keep buried. The numbness she'd wrapped herself in for decades, even centuries, was her safety net. Letting in emotion only complicated her life, and that's exactly what had gone wrong with Roland. Back in his time, she'd managed to delude herself into thinking it would all work out—a terrible mistake impossible to undo. She'd vowed not to let it happen a second time. With the back of her hand, she wiped away tears that she tried not to let fall. She didn't need some kindly soul to see her crying like a baby and rush over to offer her comfort. Not only did she not deserve comfort, she didn't want it.

Back under control, she glanced around to make sure she was alone, then hurried down the steps and took a left toward the gardens. Nobody in their right mind would be in the gardens alone at this time of night, which practically guaranteed peace and quiet.

The path wound through the trees, plants, and flowers, and Tory walked slowly along, letting the solitude calm her. The fragrance of blooming flowers filled the night, and, unlike the cloying heaviness the sprays inside the church created, the scents out here were lovely on the gentle breeze. At a bench beneath a tall tree, she sank to the hard granite.

She touched the cover of the New Testament, the leather rough and dry against her fingertips. Thinking about the last time she'd held this book, she closed her eyes and took deep, steadying breaths. The impossibility of holding it now pressed heavy on her mind. Her world no longer made sense, and that pissed her off. Even when she spent a lot of time and effort creating a very secluded existence, somebody found a way to mess it up.

The smell reached her before she saw anyone. A human. Blood rushed through the human's veins, though interestingly Tory sensed no fear. A woman, and she knew what Tory was. She wasn't afraid. She knew and understood the night. It wasn't a stretch to figure out who it was.

"Why are you following me?"

Call-me-Naomi stepped around a tall flowering shrub and onto the path. Her worship attire was gone, replaced by black slacks and a silky button-down shirt with long sleeves. At almost six feet tall with long black hair pulled into a ponytail, she studied Tory with dark eyes. Pretty conservative was her first thought. Pretty nice was her second. She'd always been a sucker for a woman with long, dark hair.

Not quite the time or the place to get the hots for someone, though. She had others to worry about, even if she didn't exactly know who—or what—they were. She clutched the New Testament to her and returned Naomi's steady gaze.

Dark eyes met hers. "Following you? No, not exactly."

"Then why are you here?" Not for a second did Tory believe the encounter was accidental. Maybe Naomi hadn't followed her here, but a coincidence? Not a chance.

Naomi raised an eyebrow. "I needed to drop off some things for the gift shop." She pointed to the small building on the edge of the garden. "I noticed you sitting here and so I took a slight detour. No stalking, I promise."

She looked up and noticed that she was, indeed, carrying a sack. Possibly Naomi was doing exactly what she said. It was also possible she'd come looking specifically for her. Tory hadn't been born yesterday—far from it actually.

"I'm fine. You can go on to your car."

With one hand stuffed in a pocket and the other still holding the bag, Naomi examined her for a long moment. "It's after one o'clock in the morning and you're sitting in the dark, in the gardens, alone."

"So…"

"So, I'd be a piss-poor person if I simply walked by and pretended not to see you."

Piss-poor? Not the kind of language she'd ever heard from a woman of the cloth. "I'm fine," she said again.

"I don't think so."

Tory took a deep breath and then let it out slowly. "I really am all right." She tried to keep irritation out of her voice. Why wouldn't she just leave her the fuck alone?

"You do realize this is Washington DC in the middle of the night, in the dark? Right?"

No shit. "Yes, of course I do."

"Then you also have to know that it's dangerous to be out here all alone. Right?"

As if punctuating the gravity of the word *alone*, several cars drove through the driveway, and when Tory looked up not a single car remained in the outside parking lot. A few minutes ago, it had been almost full.

Tory turned her gaze back to Naomi. "I appreciate your concern. The thing is, I'm aware of my surroundings and, trust me, I'm perfectly capable of defending myself if need be."

"So, say I buy that you can defend yourself, would I be any less derelict in my duties if I walked on by without inquiring what brought you to this lonely place in the middle of the night?" She gave Tory a half smile, which did something quite nice to her face.

As much as Tory craved solitude at the moment, Naomi Rand was doing a pretty good job of chiseling away at her defenses. Who would have guessed? Probably nothing more than long-buried emotions that the appearance of the New Testament had brought up. Yes, that's what it was. It wasn't attraction or anything stupid like that.

"Okay, would it make you feel better if I went back to work?"

Naomi's dark eyes looked startled. "Back to work? What are you? A nurse or a doctor or something like that?"

Something, all right. Tory stood and, as if in slow motion, watched the centuries-old New Testament tumble and hit the ground with a solid thump. It lay there on the gray stone path, its cover riddled with spiderweb cracks, the by-product of its age and having spent two centuries sharing a casket with the body of her friend. She bent to retrieve it. Naomi beat her to it.

"Wow," she breathed, turning it over in her hands as she studied the age-darkened leather cover. "This is really something."

Tory took a menacing step closer, intruding on Naomi's personal space. She touched the spine of the book. "I'll take that."

Naomi didn't release her grip or step away to restore her space. Instead, she ignored Tory and began to riffle the pages with a very soft touch, stopping here and there to recite a passage in perfect Latin.

Tory was intrigued, but not enough to get sidetracked. "Give it back." It took some effort not to show her fangs, though the menace in her voice would be hard to miss.

"Tell me." Naomi's face underwent a subtle change. "Why exactly did you bring such a valuable book to our rather special services? Or did you steal this from the cathedral?"

"Excuse me!" Shock and insult made her words sharp. The idea that someone would think she stole the book had never occurred to her.

Naomi shrugged, her gaze intent on Tory's face. "Legitimate question. You come to our services while security is down, look like you're in the middle of an inquisition when I stop to say hello, and then bolt before the service is over. To top it all, I find you hiding in the gardens with a very old and probably very rare Bible. You'd have had plenty of time during the services to sneak into our facility and snatch something like this. My question is far from being out of line."

As Naomi spoke, Tory bit the inside of her lip so hard she drew blood. The metallic taste on her tongue brought an unwanted jolt of electricity to her body. It was time to get the hell out of here, except she wasn't leaving without her book. The woman needed to give it up or Tory wouldn't be responsible for what could happen.

"I didn't steal anything. Now give me back the fucking Bible before I do something we'll both regret." Her voice was low and controlled, but with a dangerous edge.

Naomi tilted her head and studied Tory for a long moment. Slowly, she offered up the New Testament. "I'm going on faith here. Please don't make me a fool."

Tory took it and said quietly, "You'd have been a bigger fool not to give it back to me."

She turned to leave, intending to waste no time putting distance between them. As the blessed darkness closed around her, Naomi's voice cut through the night and made her pause.

"You never told me your name."

CHAPTER FOUR

B lood was everywhere—on her clothes, on her hands, on her face. She tried to wash it away, but the harder she scrubbed, the more it increased. Her heart began to beat so fast it stole her breath. Was she going to die at long last?

In the distance thunder pounded and the air thickened. She couldn't get away. She could barely breathe. Run. Run. The pounding grew louder, louder, LOUDER.

Naomi bolted upright in her bed, shoved the hair off her sweat-covered forehead, and tried to bring her breathing back to a normal rhythm. Sweet Jesus, that was the nightmare from hell, and she'd had some terrible ones to compare it to. Her terror was so real she was surprised she hadn't had the big one.

All of a sudden it dawned on her that part of it wasn't a dream. The nightmare hadn't manufactured the pounding. It was real. Someone was knocking on her front door so frantically she wondered if the house was on fire. No smoke, so probably not.

Daylight tried to sneak in through the closed blackout blinds, and a glance at the clock told her she'd at least managed a few hours of sleep. Not enough. She wanted to lie back down, pull a pillow over her head, and try for long, peaceful slumber. Wasn't going to happen. The assault on her front door was not abating.

With a groan, she slid her legs over the side of the bed and stood up. After slipping on a pair of sweats, she pulled a T-shirt over her head as she headed to the front door. When she looked through the peephole, she groaned. Maybe the nightmare wasn't so bad after all.

For a second she gave serious thought to turning around and going back to bed. Then she slid the safety chain free and swung the door open. "What?"

"Yeah, and a fucking good morning to you too, sunshine."

Naomi leaned against the door frame and waited. For Nathan to show up at her house at this time of day meant one thing: bad news. The only real question was whether the visit was personal or professional. The odds, unfortunately, were on professional, which sucked.

"So, sis, you gonna ask me in or make me stand outside?"

She was tempted to just shut the door, except years of experience told her it wouldn't make any difference. Her twin brother wasn't the kind who would take a hint. Not that he didn't get it—he just consistently chose to ignore it, at least when it came to her.

She opened the door wide enough for Nathan to step inside, and he immediately headed to the kitchen. She tried to think if he'd ever come here when he didn't inventory her pantry and refrigerator. Not in recent memory. Too busy to buy his own groceries or always starving, she was never sure. She'd lost her appetite years ago, and even being out of the hunt didn't bring it back.

"When the fuck are you going to get a coffeemaker?"

She rolled her eyes. "I don't drink coffee."

He rolled his eyes back at her. "That's pretty un-American, cupcake."

She was about *this* close to pinching his head. Call her cupcake one more time and there'd be some pinching going on. "Deal with it. What do you want?"

He looked up from her refrigerator where he'd been rummaging around. Her eating habits and his usually didn't mesh well, yet when he stepped back he held a bottle of orange juice. "There were two particularly gruesome murders last night. One close to the Hill, one on the Mall."

Like murder didn't happen with some degree of regularity around here? "What does that have to do with me?" A sinking feeling deep in her gut told her she knew what he was getting at. Even so, she was going to make him spell it out. If he had the nerve to drag her out of bed, he could explain in detail.

Nathan tipped his head back and took a long draw of the juice before he wiped his mouth with the back of his hand. Women seemed to fall all over themselves for him, and she couldn't figure out why. Maybe his table manners were better with the ladies. She really, really hoped so. Around her? Slob was one of the nicer descriptions.

His dark eyes that looked so much like hers were serious. "One of yours did them."

Crap. "They're not *mine.*" Not technically, anyway. She knew what he meant, but she wasn't going to make it easy for him. He was supposed to be impartial, to look at everyone the same. She'd give him a few points for minimal effort. He could do better.

He smacked the orange juice down, some of it slopping over the rim to the counter, where it pooled on the clean white tile. The mess would still be there when he left. "You know what I'm getting at, Meme."

When he used her childhood nickname these days, she hated it. The name should have been a term of endearment, but coming from Nathan lately, an endearment was about the last thing it was. The way they butted heads, it was hard to believe they were once inseparable. When they were growing up he always had her back. Even if he never said it, she now figured she was on her own. Not that she blamed him. They were in different places without a bridge between the two.

Still, it pissed her off when he got so high and mighty. Her eyes narrowed and she clipped her words. "No, I don't. Why don't you spell it out for me, *bro*?"

He gave her the same look in return. "Fine, you want to play it that way. How about this? One of your goddamn bloodsuckers picked up a big-time lobbyist, fucked him, and then drained him dry. Not just the lobbyist either. The same kind of hit was made on a bodybuilder after he left his gym. Clear enough for you? Two, Meme, two in a single night by one of those monsters you protect. When are you gonna learn they're not on your side?"

The reality of what he said made her sink to one of the tall stools at the kitchen bar. Running a hand through her hair she sighed. She hated the way he thought about her congregation, how he assumed they were all evil. She knew they weren't and, at the same time, understood where he was coming from. She'd been there once too…before she'd learned the hard way how wrong she'd been.

"Are you sure?"

Nathan dropped to the stool beside her and let out a breath, the anger of a moment before evaporating. His shoulders slumped and his dark eyes were haunted. When he wasn't being a macho ass, he could be an okay guy. Too bad she didn't see that side of him much lately. "Yeah, I am."

"How bad?"

"It's not good. The one guy had some serious clout and shit is going to start rolling downhill. We need to find whoever did this and get him shut down before the good citizens of the District get riled up again."

The thought gave her chills. The relationship between the humans and the preternaturals was tenuous at best. Something like this could blow the precariously balanced truce to hell in a heartbeat. A decade ago, a vampire turned a gang member. He showed his gratitude by turning his whole gang. By the time they were put down, at least a hundred were dead and blood literally ran in the streets. She was there and remembered it all too clearly. The tragedy still lingered in the city's collective memory enough that nobody wanted to see something like that happen ever again, especially her.

Her brother wasn't being unreasonable, even when he was angry and bitter. Nonetheless, he had a firm grasp of the real dangers of a preternatural serial killer. Too many deaths and it could get out of hand in a hurry.

"Let me see what I can find out," she told him, her thoughts turning to the beautiful and mysterious woman at last night's service. Did she know something? Could she be involved? Her gut said she wasn't the killer, but her gut had been wrong before.

He squeezed her shoulder lightly. "Appreciate it." He headed to the front door, pausing before he stepped outside. "Meme?"

She met his dark eyes. "Yeah?"

"Make it quick."

Their eyes locked and she nodded. "I'll call you tonight."

The door had no sooner closed behind Nathan than her cell phone trilled from the kitchen counter. So much for going back to bed for a little more R&R, not that she'd be able to sleep after her brother's visit. His warning had her wound up tight.

She grabbed the phone and tried not to sound as grumpy as she felt. "Hello."

"Where is your lazy butt?"

"What…oh, Karen." The familiar voice cut through the fog.

"I'm waiting…"

Naomi walked to the window and looked out. Sure as the world, Karen was standing on the sidewalk leaning against the streetlight pole, dressed in workout gear and holding her road bike upright in one hand. In the midst of all the chaos, she'd forgotten their once-a-week morning bike ride. She really was out of sync. They'd ridden together for the last couple of years.

She stifled a groan. The last thing she felt like doing at the moment was riding. Then again, the physical exertion might be exactly what she needed. "Give me five."

Karen gave her a thumbs-up and put the phone into the zippered pocket of a light jacket. It actually took six minutes to throw on clothes, slip into her biking shoes, and grab her bike from the rack in the hallway. Even if she didn't feel like going out, Karen wouldn't accept any excuses. The woman took her workouts seriously and showed up at her door with frightening punctuality each and every week. Naomi, on the other hand, was not quite so serious. Truthfully, she exercised only because it kept her in shape and she liked the high that came at the end of a long, hard workout. When she was a hunter, keeping in top condition was critical to battle survival. These days it was more to win the battle against the slow creep of age. Today, it would be a good way to clear her head.

"Saw tall, handsome, and grumpy as he left your place," Karen said once Naomi was in the saddle, her shoes clipped into the pedals. They started out at an easy pace for warm-up. Like Nathan, Karen was a police officer. While he was a detective with the DC force, she was a street cop with the Capitol Police.

"Yeah, Mr. Sunshine came with more good news." The sun on her skin felt good, the air clear and nice. Despite her reluctance this morning, she was glad she'd come out. Anything that might help unblock her mind and help her think was probably a really good idea.

Karen nodded and picked up the pace. "I know and I'm worried."

"That makes two of us."

"If my secret gets out..." Karen powered up a hill at a pace that made Naomi's thighs burn as she tried to keep up.

With close-cropped red hair and sharp features, Karen was a powerful necromancer, capable of raising the dead. Few would guess it, though now and again her law-enforcement confidants called on her skills to help solve cases. Didn't make it any less of a secret because people in general were scared of someone who could literally bring folks up from six feet under. Only the very trusted knew of Karen's special ability.

Karen didn't need to finish the sentence. The reality of what could happen pressed at Naomi's heart and soul. At the top of the hill, she stopped, got off her bike, and bent over to catch her breath, her hands on her thighs. Karen sped ahead to a trail with paved paths and plenty of tree cover. Once she realized Naomi wasn't right behind her, Karen backtracked to where she'd stopped and dismounted as well.

Naomi straightened and pulled Karen close. The tough policewoman trembled.

"I won't let anyone hurt you."

Karen hugged her back. "You have a great heart, but you're no match for the monster out there now." Her voice trembled and Naomi hugged her tighter. "None of us are."

If she could have argued with Karen, she would have. The problem was, Naomi was deathly afraid she was right.

❖

Wind slapped her face while rain bit into her flesh like slashes from a hundred tiny sharp knives. Victoria raced through the night, stumbling only when she tripped on a fallen tree, catching herself before crashing to the sodden earth. She didn't have time to pause for even a moment.

In the distance, the sounds of terror filled the air. So did the sounds of laughter. God, how she hated that laugh. So many years ago, she'd run from it, hoping she'd never have to hear it again. Here in this new land and with a new life, she'd believed she was sheltered from the dangers of her past. No one knew her here and, more important, no one knew her secrets.

Except for Roland.

The only way to be safe was to keep her secrets buried. She had never intended to confess to him, yet it had happened as though it were the most natural thing in the world. Her words had streamed out in a torrent until she thought he must surely hate her to her soul; yet she'd been wrong. It wasn't hatred she'd seen in his eyes that night but compassion and, more surprising, tears. Reverend Roland Lyle had cried for her—for what she'd been, for what she'd lost, for what she'd become.

On that night, she found the father she'd never had, and her loyalty to him had been sealed for eternity. In her heart, she believed that nothing would be able to come between them. Again, she was wrong.

Now she heard his words, barely audible in the throes of the building storm. She could feel the beat of his heart and hear the slight, thready breath that passed between his lips. Most frightening of all, she sensed that the life in his body was beginning to slip away. She ran harder, her skirts pulled high, her feet barely touching the damp earth. Nothing else mattered excepting reaching Roland's side.

At the rectory, she wrenched open the door, rain blasting inside as she flew across the threshold, the soles of her shoes slipping on the wet stone floor. She nearly lost her balance, barely managing to stay on her feet. The smell was like a slap in the face. It wasn't the stench of hot, human blood that made her gasp.

"I told you what I'd do."

Pierre stood, straddling Roland's body, blood dripping from his fangs, his smile triumphant. Tall and lean, he was as beautiful as the first time she'd seen him, the night he'd turned her. Even the blood flowing across his full lips did nothing to dampen his raw sexuality and handsome face. That was one of his most dangerous weapons, and he used it again and again to seduce the unwary. She'd fallen victim to the smile and sexy voice only to learn what was beneath the smooth façade. How easily he hid pure evil behind beauty.

The hate she'd tried several lifetimes to let go of roared to the surface, and her howl of rage cut through the storm's power. The church's lessons told her to forgive Pierre for what he'd done to her, and she could...almost. She couldn't forgive him for what he'd done here in this place and on this night. Not in a thousand lifetimes.

"I'll kill you."

His smile grew as one long finger swiped away blood from his bottom lip. "Too late, my sweet, someone beat you to that one." He winked.

She hissed, her gaze steady on his face. She wanted to scratch his crystal-blue eyes right out of his skull. She wanted to make his face as ugly as his soul. "I'll destroy you."

"Tsk, tsk, is that any way to speak to me? You know what I want. Give it to me and this all ends." He waved his hand in the air, seeming to encompass the death and destruction that lay around them: the man prone and motionless at his feet.

"Go to hell." Her fingernails cut into her palms as her hands curled into fists at her sides, while her fangs dropped and her blood roared in her ears.

Pierre stepped over and away from Roland, brushing by her where she still stood close to the doors. His finger trailed across her cheek as he passed, his touch icy against her flesh. "You first."

Then he was gone amidst a gust of rain and cold wind. She spun and nearly raced into the darkness after him. She didn't, stalling at the door as a terrible sense of fear threaded through her heart. Behind her the interior of the church was eerily silent.

Victoria turned away from the doorway and ran inside to Roland, dropping to her knees at his side. She pressed her fingers against the soft flesh of his neck, probing, feeling. Nothing. Not even the tiniest flicker of life. Tears blurred her vision and she thought her heart would surely break. Then she saw it, and once more her scream filled the night.

Tory came awake with a start. She touched her cheeks, not surprised at the wetness she found there. That the dream had returned again after so many years troubled her. Not too shocking but troubling nonetheless. Even after centuries, she was never free of that night. Never would be. Guilt did that.

Now it was even worse. How could she not think about Roland and that horrible night when she held the New Testament? The past was being thrown, literally, into her face. She couldn't escape the biggest mistake of her life, no matter how far she ran or how many oceans she crossed.

She swung her legs out of bed and headed to the bathroom, where she stepped into the large shower and let warm water pour over her. It didn't chase away the chill but it helped. When the water began to cool, she turned it off and reached for a towel.

Dressed, her long hair in a single braid down her back, she went to the refrigerator and pulled out an elegant crystal pitcher. She poured the dark, crimson liquid into a glass and drank. She didn't even think about the taste any longer; she'd grown accustomed to it. Once she weaned herself away from the taste of human blood, all she was concerned with was surviving, and the crystal pitcher held what she needed.

Showered, dressed, and hunger sated, she repeated last night's exercise: she sat and stared at the book. What she wouldn't give for a good old-fashioned psychic right now. She was getting nowhere and wondered if someone with a touch of second sight might be able to tell her what she needed to know. Secrets were beneath her fingertips, if only they could be coaxed out.

Why not? Picking up her cell phone, she hit speed dial and waited as a classic rock-and-roll song played on the other end. It made her smile, just a little, remembering another, more happy time, and a concert filled with loud music, dope, and a hell of a lot of wine. Those were some wild days. Even a vampire had her moments.

"Hey," a cheerful voice said when the call connected.

"Hey to you too."

"Vampira! What's up?"

Tory smiled. In her mind, she could picture Sunny O'Neill with her short red hair, emerald-green eyes, and lithe body holding the phone to her ear and smiling. She seemed to always have a grin on her face, and it reflected in her voice. Truth be told, Tory was a little in love with Sunny and had been since the first day she'd met her. Under different circumstances, Tory would have made a run for her, except Sunny preferred men, which left friendship as the only the option. That was enough for Tory, who was grateful to have a friend she could confide in. Thus, Sunny became one of the elite few who knew her secret.

"Got a strange one for you, Sun. Do you happen to know anyone with real psychic abilities? I mean someone who really has the sight."

Sunny's laughter was light and bright. "Damn straight, girlfriend. My buddy Viola Juve is a bona fide real deal. She's helped the five-oh on lots of cases. Don't know if she's ever read another mistress of the dark before. No biggie if she hasn't. If I tell her you're okay, you're in like Flynn."

Tory ran the name over in her head and came up with nothing. "I've never heard of her."

"And you wouldn't, sweetie. One of Viola's conditions is that her name is kept out of everything. She doesn't do it for money or recognition. For her, it's one hundred percent about getting assholes off the street. You gotta understand, she only gets brought in when people are dying and the cops got nothing. She's their candle in the dark."

"Exactly what I'm looking for. Do you think she'd see me?"

"Sure, if I ask her to. We've been pals since the fourth grade. Like I said, I can vouch for ya. Besides, I know you'd only ask if it was real important, speaking of which, what is this about anyway, Vampira? You don't usually need help from anybody else of the otherworldly persuasion. You're more of the lone-vamp kinda girl, if you know what I mean?"

Tory knew exactly what she meant. "I do and you're right. Asking for help isn't high on my list. Problem is, I'm in a real dark corner on this one. It's a book."

"Uh? Why would you need a psychic about a book? They're your cup of tea, sister. You're like this incredible walking encyclopedia on cool books."

"This one is special and I know what it is. I just don't know why it is."

"Kinda cryptic, sister."

"I know, and I'm sorry I can't give you more right now. I promise I'll explain it all when you bring your friend over."

"Okey doke. Let me give her a call and I'll get right back to you."

"Thanks, Sunny."

"No problem. Besides, you never know when I'm gonna need a favor from She of the Darkness!" Sunny's laughter was as bright as the woman herself.

When Tory flipped the phone shut, she felt better. Maybe just talking to Sunny did it. Her taste for life and continual optimism always lifted Tory's spirits, and after the reappearance of the dream, that was precisely what she needed. She liked her world ordered and without surprises. For nearly two centuries she'd kept it that way, providing her with a comfortable, predictable life. Until, that is, that damned brown box showed up on her desk. Sunny's offer of help meant a lot and would go a long way toward restoring order to her existence. Yes, she felt so much better…at least until she looked down.

USA Today lay on her desk, in the same place Jenni put it each day before she left the office. Tory picked it up and read the headline, not once. Not even twice. No, she read it three times before dropping it as though the paper singed her fingers.

Impossible. Yet there it was for God and everyone to see. Her aunt, the true daughter of Henry VII, sister to the infamous Henry VIII, and a vampire, was pictured on the front page under the headline, SERIAL KILLER STOPPED BY LOCAL ME. Dr. Riah Preston, apparently the name Catherine Tudor now claimed as her own, along with the assistance of three others, was credited with stopping a serial killer who left bodies all across the United States. Once again, she thought, impossible.

Nearly two hundred years had passed since she'd seen her aunt in the flesh. Those had been happier days for Tory, a time when she'd believed she might actually have a chance to live in harmony with humans. Hope had bloomed in her then, but she'd been so very wrong about everything.

Her heart ached as she looked at the picture of Riah, and she longed for a time when her world was peopled with friends and family. She had been full of love and laughter and, most of all, hope. Until the moment Pierre had walked in and robbed her of everything that was precious. Not once, but twice. First he took away her humanity, and then he snatched away the only father she'd ever known. After he took Roland from her, she had embraced an existence of darkness and solitude because that way she had nothing to lose. She made occasional friends, like Sunny, but kept everyone else at arm's length. As long as nothing and no one mattered, she couldn't be hurt.

Tears dropped onto the paper and the face in the photograph blurred. It wasn't fair. So much time, so much heartache. If only she had the courage to be more like Riah—to be bold and walk among humans, to take the curse and use it to do something important with it. How different would her life be if she wasn't such a coward?

CHAPTER FIVE

Waiting was beginning to get on his nerves. In the old days, he'd had the patience of Job, but not right now. Of course it had been a good many years since he'd let the lessons of Job guide him, and the influence of those teachings was long gone. Or maybe he was just grumpy.

Bottom line: he didn't like waiting. He didn't possess much of anything that even remotely resembled a calm demeanor these days, and for good reason. After what he'd endured, he was entitled to immediate gratification. He wanted what he wanted, when he wanted it. And he wanted her this instant.

Then again, he did so like to play games. There was much to be said for the classic game of cat and mouse…as long as he was playing the cat. Like now.

His little mouse was impressively quick. So far in the week he'd been in this nation's capital, he'd glimpsed her only twice. She moved swiftly through the darkness and, from what he'd observed, steered clear of the daylight. She was getting old enough that the sun wouldn't destroy her. Still, she shied away. Just as well. He preferred the night himself, an acquired taste that he embraced completely.

He was standing deep in the shadows when she walked past him, her stride quick and sure, heading tonight in the opposite direction and toward Union Station. She only stopped when she stood beside a dirty old woman dressed in rags and huddled inside a bush near the edge of the park. As he'd seen her do the first night, she pressed money into the old bat's hand.

Armed with acute senses, he nearly gagged when he detected the odor drifting from the rags that completely covered the old woman. He didn't get it. Why would Victoria even bother? People like that didn't matter; they simply took up space. Diseased, filthy, and smelly, they didn't even make a decent meal. He wouldn't waste his time or soil his hands. Only the very desperate would look twice at the worthless thing. Considering how well-fed he was at the moment, she wouldn't rate a second glance. Even if he was starving, he'd hesitate to feed on her.

Of course, Victoria wasn't feeding on the filth. In fact, she seemed to be taking care of her rather than scoping out a good meal. She might be altruistic in her actions toward the beggar. She wasn't thinking dinner. Made him wonder where she did feed in this pretty little world she'd created for herself. So far he hadn't seen her approach a human. The thought of animal blood made him shudder. Why would anyone in their right mind give up the sweetness of a human for an animal? Nothing compared to the ambrosia of the blood of a well-bred human.

Hard to say what she was up to in this incarnation. She'd changed after the attack at the parsonage so long ago. Not for the better either. She'd had some kind of break with reality, and that break had cost him dearly. Now she had to pay. He'd lost time she could never give back to him. Still, there was something to the old saying about a pound of flesh. He intended to get what was coming to him, and she was going to be the one to give it to him.

As he watched Victoria turn away from the old woman and begin to walk once more in the direction of Union Station, he had a sudden wicked though delightful thought. Brilliant, if he did say so.

He watched the old woman as she lumbered away from the park and down the street. Yes, it was distasteful but it might very well give Victoria the kind of push he'd find endlessly entertaining. So far, his first gift hadn't riled her up as much as he'd believed it would or should. How could she not sense both kills had been for her? Was she that far gone? It was time to ratchet the game up a notch or two and see what she was made of.

When Victoria disappeared from view, he slid out of the darkness and began to walk in the same direction as the dirty old woman. Her stench grew stronger as he closed the gap. Perhaps he should come up with a different, less nauseating plan. But he kept following. It was too perfect to ignore, even if it was disgusting.

The woman shuffled as she walked, the swish of her coat melding with the sound of her voice as she held a conversation with some nonexistent companion. Though her mental limitations and physical state repulsed him, Victoria seemed to have some sort of connection that made the old woman not just interesting but irresistible. He closed the final few feet that separated them.

He quietly moved next to her and tilted his head toward hers. "Good evening," he cooed.

The old bat started and then put several feet of distance between them, shuffling her feet as fast as she could. "Go away," she rasped, a fine spray of spittle nearly hitting him. "I'm invisible."

He smiled, even though the sensation of her saliva on his flesh made him want to snap her neck. Taking a breath, he buried his rage and kept his expression friendly. Out of the range of any more flying bodily fluids, he said, "Of course you are. So am I."

Her head rose and the remnants of a surprisingly once-pretty face tipped toward him. Now instead of beautiful, it was lined and sallow, framed by gray, matted hair. Her lips were cracked and dry, a line of dried blood across the bottom lip. A breeze blew, carrying with it a fetid odor that hit him full in the face. It took massive self-control not to let the overwhelming repulsion show on his face. He needed to end this before he lost it.

Holding out his hand, he forced his smile to grow. She would come, they always did. Persuasion was a skill he could wield at will. Time hadn't taken it away from him or dulled its power. "Come, let's watch the night together."

She seemed to study him for a long time, her brow wrinkled.

"It's so beautiful with all the stars and the glowing moon. I would be honored to share it with you."

Perhaps he was losing his touch. She didn't move, only continued to stare into his eyes. Then just about the time he thought he might have to use force, her expression cleared and she put her hand in his.

❖

The last thing Tory meant to do was go back to the National Cathedral. She had work to do, not the least of which was figuring out how the New Testament had showed up on her desk. The only bit of information she'd confirmed so far was that Katrina had not destroyed Roland's crypt, and while there had been some vandalism, it was still intact. Of course even if vandals had taken it from Roland's final resting place, there was no way to connect it to her. For all the world, she'd ceased to exist hundreds of years ago.

She needed to trace the journey of the book to her desk, sooner rather than later. The answer was there. That equated to time at her computer digging into all her resources to find the trail leading to her desk. But was she doing that? No. Instead, here she was, back in the gardens by the same statue, sitting on the same bench, and staring into the darkness. Hoping for what? Answers? God's voice?

Or was it something else she sought?

The wisest thing would have been to head to the office, do a little research, and wait for Sunny. As usual, she couldn't do the wise thing. As usual, she tended toward the crazy, like hanging out in the gardens where security guards would be patrolling and see her lurking. Oh, if only she could have inherited some of her mother's grace. Life would be so much easier.

Just as last night, Tory had smelled her before she was close enough to see. The nearby traffic and the pounding in her ears had muffled the sound of her footsteps. Though she'd deny it if asked, the church wasn't the only thing that drew her to the gardens now. She told herself she was just looking for a sympathetic ear, someone who could relate. That's all.

Tonight, Naomi Rand was dressed casually in blue jeans, a white button-down shirt, and black boots. Her long black hair spilled over her shoulders in a way that softened her broad shoulders. Her skin was smooth and unadorned, her features striking with full lips and strong cheekbones. Last night in her formal attire, Tory hadn't noticed how attractive she was, but now it struck her in a rush of awareness. She pushed aside the emotional response to a lovely woman. Not interested.

"Hello," Naomi said as she leaned against a tree, arms crossed over her chest. "What brings you out here yet again?"

"What brings you out?" Tory countered, not quite sure how to answer the question anyway. A hint of vanilla made her want to press her face into the beautiful black hair.

Naomi shrugged. "I work here."

"In the middle of the night?" There wasn't a service tonight. She'd checked. She should have been blissfully alone.

"Let's just say my hours aren't exactly nine to five. I'm a bit more flexible than your average pastor."

"Back at ya."

Even in the darkness, Tory could see the raised eyebrows. Still,

Naomi's voice was even as she replied, "You never said what it is you do or, for that matter, what your name is. Feel like sharing now that we're on our second date?"

Her words were soft, as though she was talking with a child. Not condescending—more patient and kind, with a touch of humor. Tory studied her face, the light of the moon bathing the gardens with a warm illumination that chased away all but the deepest shadows. Under different circumstances it would be romantic. If only...

"Tory—" she offered, "and I'm a rare-books expert over at the Library of Congress."

The small smile that pulled up the corners of Naomi's mouth softened her features in a wonderful way. No longer was she simply attractive. That little smile turned her into beautiful. God, what on earth was the matter with her? She had far more important things to think about right now. Of course, it had been a very long time. Top that off with the emotional turmoil shaking up her life and it sort of made sense. Even an old bat vampire could succumb to stress.

"That's why you had the old Bible with you last night?"

Tory nodded and focused again on what had brought her here in the first place: trying to find a place where the essence of Roland's spirit might exist. She needed to understand the path of the Bible since that long-ago night, and this was as close as she could get to a place where she might feel him. "New Testament, actually."

Naomi's gaze never wavered. "Doesn't the Library of Congress frown on their books leaving the building, or is it your SOP to bring rare books to church with you?"

Not in about a hundred years. "No," she said. "No standard operating procedure with that one. Let's just say last night was, well, unique." A bit of an understatement, but Naomi was on a need-to-know program.

Naomi studied her before uncrossing her arms. "May I sit?" She motioned toward the empty space on the bench next to Tory.

Her first inclination was to say no. She didn't need the woman up close and in her personal space. The attraction was hard to deny, though she fully intended to do just that. She didn't trust what she was feeling. The arrival of the book had turned her quiet existence upside down. Everything was in turmoil, including her perceptions. She couldn't afford to misinterpret a single thing, especially something like attraction.

"Yes" finally passed her lips. At times her brain and her mouth lacked simple coordination, and once that single word was out, she sure as hell couldn't unsay it.

Naomi came close, lowering herself to the bench very close beside Tory. After a minute or so of silence, she asked her, "Do you want to talk about it?"

"It?" She wasn't trying to be obtuse; she just wasn't putting it all together. God, she was way too messed up.

"Whatever brings you here in the middle of the night." Naomi prompted her in that same patient voice.

"I work nights." Simple explanations always seemed to work the best. Most people didn't need details. The majority of the time, they didn't want them anyway.

"I didn't know the library was open at night."

Well, so much for keeping it simple. Didn't seem to be what Naomi wanted. She found that intriguing, even in the midst of turmoil. "It's not. I requested special hours, they agreed. Suffice it to say, I'm very good at what I do and the library is willing to accommodate me for the most part."

Naomi shifted and Tory could feel her gaze. "You're a vampire. I'm usually pretty good at knowing, even though I see very few vampires these days."

Tory ran a hand over her eyes. "Yes," she said slowly, debating how much to tell a relative stranger. With Naomi's body only inches away, the heat of her washed over Tory. It was like a warm blanket surrounding her entirely, and the strength of its sensual heat nearly took her breath away. The attraction was strong. The fear was even stronger. Something about that woman sent a whisper of caution through her.

"But I'm different." That was the best she could offer. No way to put her backstory into a sentence or two. Not that she really wanted to try. The less Naomi knew about her, the better for her and everyone else.

"Okay…" Naomi drew out the word. "Different how?"

Tory stood and looked out into the distance. "It's a long story that I don't have the time to get into right now."

"I won't judge, you have my word."

Her laugh was far from amused. "Judgment is the least of my worries but if you want to hear the ugly truth, here it—" Tory turned her gaze to meet the other woman's eyes and saw truth in them. She checked the bitter words ready to tumble from her lips. In a softer voice she said simply, "I'm a vampire and that pretty much says it all." She took one step away from where Naomi still sat on the bench.

She expected to see repulsion or disgust in Naomi's eyes. She didn't. Instead, the other woman stood and stopped her retreat by putting a hand gently on her arm. The touch was like a shot of electricity that almost made her jump. She managed, with effort, to stay in one place.

"Don't go. You didn't just happen here. Something brought you to my church, so please don't go."

"I have to." She started to walk swiftly toward the shadows. Distance was very appealing at the moment. Everything was messed up and this woman was complicating things even more. She couldn't think. Didn't know what to feel. Just knew she had to get away.

"Tory?"

Against her better judgment, she stopped but didn't give in to the strong urge to look back.

"I'm here when you need me."

CHAPTER SIX

If she could have done something for Tory, Naomi would have felt better. Obviously it wasn't the right time. Distrust and stress seemed to pour from the other woman's body like water spilling over open dam gates. Naomi longed to reach out and hug her, if nothing else, to just offer her the solace of another woman—someone with empathy and understanding for what she was going through.

Hell, that was a lie and she knew it. Oh, distrust and stress where there all right. Who could blame her? Hadn't she all but accused Tory of stealing from the church just last night? Offering comfort was the only decent thing to do for someone in her position. But it wasn't just comfort foremost on her mind; it was something a little more self-serving. Naomi was one hundred percent attracted to the petite beauty with her lovely curves and long, shiny hair—too bad it wasn't the right time, place, or person, for that matter.

Cold storage was a strange beast. Here she'd been, minding her own business for years and finally feeling like her world was on the level again. Then a strange woman, a strange beautiful woman, walked into her church and bam, all her carefully constructed serenity flew out the window! All of a sudden she was thinking about things better left in that cold storage.

The inappropriateness of her feelings wasn't the only issue. She simply didn't have time for this. She'd promised Nathan she'd ask around about a murderous vampire, see if any of her regulars might know something helpful to his investigation. His needs were far more important at the moment than her awakening libido. He was trying to save lives while she was thinking about getting into Tory's pants. With a quick prayer for guidance, she turned her attention back to the moment.

Thoughts of this particular vampire had to go on the back burner. She wasn't the one Nathan sought, even if Naomi had nothing to base her conviction on other than gut feeling. She'd been around the preternatural community long enough to know the good from the bad. This vampire was very much in the good column.

Though there were no services tonight, the weres always sensed when she was here, kindred souls even if some of them were human and some of them were not. Focusing on gathering information for her brother was a much safer road, despite that road being populated by weres. She didn't need to let herself get sidetracked by a beautiful woman...ah, vampire.

She was in the courtyard listening to the water spill over the sides of the fountain and sipping a cup of tea when she heard the first footsteps. He was a shadow in the open doorway, a shadow she recognized.

"Good evening, Darin."

Darin Reed, a tall, handsome man, looked like he couldn't possibly be older than about twenty, twenty-five tops. His curly brown hair framed a strong face, and his dark eyes were sensual and mysterious. Naomi always found his hands fascinating. A ceramics artist, he had hands that were broad and strong, with long fingers made for an art. At first glance, Darin appeared to be a talented young artist living in a vibrant city. Always paid to look deeper than just the pretty face.

He was indeed an artist—in this life. Forty years ago, he'd been a milkman in a working-class neighborhood in London. Early one morning while making his rounds, he'd been attacked by what he'd thought at the time was a dog. Turned out to be a werewolf.

Darin came to her like so many others. The whispers on the street about her services reached him at a time when he needed support and understanding. He wanted to find a place of peace where his secret didn't have to stay buried and where it didn't matter if he was no longer completely human. She offered him what she did to all who walked through the doors, unconditional acceptance.

"Pastor." He greeted her, his voice low and serious.

"Darin, I've told you a hundred times, it's Naomi."

She took particular notice of his unsmiling face, mainly because it was so unlike him. These days, Darin was always cheerful. Despite having his life forever changed, he'd found inner peace and created an existence that not only worked for him but seemed to flourish. That he was deathly serious tonight sent an uncomfortable flutter through her body. She'd give anything to see his normal boyish smile right now.

He folded his hands and his head dropped. "Naomi," he said quietly. "Trouble is coming, I feel it here." He tapped his chest.

Naomi sat up a little straighter. "What have you heard?"

He brought his gaze up to meet hers and his eyes, usually so full of mirth, were almost black. "Nothing. It's something I feel. Someone or something is out there and it's bringing death."

The chill that washed over her skin had little to do with their surroundings. This was a beautiful place with paved walkways, lush bushes, and trees with boughs hanging full and green. The sky was filled with stars that blinked and shone like thousands of candles flickering above. The air carried the scent of the flowers that bloomed in the many tended beds. Any other night, she'd be filled with peace and contentment as she chatted with parishioners.

The way he talked, Naomi thought he had to know something. "Two men were killed by a vampire last night. Do you have any idea who it might be?"

He shook his head. "No, though I'm aware of the murders—we all are. I'm telling you, whoever it was, it was none of us."

She knew what and who he referred to by "us." She considered them hers as well. She'd been a lay minister at the midnight services since they began. Every face was familiar to her, as were most of their stories. There were witches, werewolves, even a couple of vampires, and many others who made their homes in the shadows. Her congregation of preternaturals was small in comparison to the total population of the District of Columbia. That minority status was part of what made them such a tight-knit and very protective group. They watched over each other as though their differences didn't exist. In other times, they would have been bitter enemies, but in this life they were allies. Far too often, it was the humans against the preternaturals. Preservation forced them into an alliance that, in this day and age, worked. No, if it were one of them, they'd know it.

A second voice joined in from the arched doorway, echoing Naomi's thoughts. "It's not one of us." Dressed in her police uniform, with a gun and handcuffs at her belt, Karen Carter leaned against the stone wall studying Naomi and Darin. She so often saw Karen in casual cycling attire that it stopped her every time she saw her in full-out cop mode.

"I know, I know." Naomi muttered more to herself than her late-night companions. "It worries me."

"Yeah," Karen said. "Worries the shit outta me too. It's definitely fucked up and it's gonna cause some serious issues for all of us if we're not careful. I'm not the only one who can't afford to have my secret out in the daylight."

Enlightenment as to what Karen meant by "issues" wasn't necessary. Naomi was all too aware of the delicate balance existing between the human population and the preternaturals and those, like Karen, who possessed powers few understood. Uneasy was an understatement. Something like murder by a vampire could throw uneasy right out the window and usher in something akin to the villagers storming the castle. She didn't want to see that happen, again.

❖

Colin Jamison picked up his ringing cell phone and studied the display. Area code 202? That was Washington DC and he didn't recognize the number. He looked up at the clock. Midnight, meaning it was three in DC. Who the hell would be calling him and at this time of night? Once upon a time there were several from that area who would think nothing of calling him any time of the day or night. Not anymore. Bridges had been burned and phone numbers right along with them.

He shot a glance at Ivy, who was busy working on a book she was writing on the connection between folklore and medical anomalies. Once a brainiac, always a brainiac…alive or undead. Some things just didn't vary despite the impossible changes that now defined each of them.

On a stormy night a year ago when both of their lives were forever altered and while they were still finding their way, Ivy had been the coroner in the town of Moses Lake, Washington. He'd been a vampire hunter. Not a likely coupling in any universe.

Everything had changed that strange night. Ivy literally died in the battle to destroy a vindictive five-hundred-year-old vampire and her violent minions. Though he'd never have believed it before that moment, he'd been the one to beg another vampire to turn Ivy—to make her into the very thing he'd sworn his life to destroy. Riah Preston, herself a medical examiner in Spokane, Washington, and also a vampire, had saved his beautiful, intelligent Ivy by giving her immortality.

He'd never been happier.

The phone in his hand continued to ring. They weren't giving up whoever *they* were, and he had an uneasy feeling about the incoming call. Nothing good ever came at this time of night. Not in his line of work anyway or, rather, his former line of work. Somehow living with and loving a vampire kind of undermined the motivation he possessed in his other life to walk dark streets and turn creatures of the night into dust. Not that he didn't still smoke the occasional vamp, but only when it was a very, very bad vamp.

Before the phone went to voice mail, Colin finally gave in. Bad news or not, he couldn't in good conscience just ignore it. "Yeah," he said, not able to keep the snap out of his voice. If that didn't warn someone off, nothing would. He'd been called a bastard more than once. He could live with that.

"Colin?"

A voice he hadn't heard in at least five years and really never expected to again made him straighten up. Shock took all the bite out of his question, and the annoyance of only a moment before evaporated. "Naomi?"

"Yeah, it's me."

He ran a hand through his brown hair that was in dire need of a trim and closed his eyes. He could see her in his head, tall and dark-haired with a kick that could send a preternatural into next week. She'd always been beautiful, powerful, and focused on her job as a hunter totally in tune with the church's goal of eliminating every vampire on the planet. He'd liked Naomi and, at the time, was shocked when she'd left the hunters. He'd never known why, though the rumor mill posited all sorts of stories. He figured the truth was buried in the rumors somewhere but liked Naomi enough not to try to guess. He'd figured if she ever wanted him to know, she'd tell him.

Even though she was no longer a hunter with the church, there was only one reason she'd reach out to him. "This can't be a social call."

"I'd like to tell you I'm only calling to say hey, but you'd know it was bullshit. Never could lie worth a damn."

"Not to me anyway."

"You were always like another brother. Always there when I needed you."

Friend or not, quasi-brother or not, he might as well cut her off. Didn't need to waste his time or hers. "I'm not a hunter anymore, Naomi."

She didn't even pause. "I need your help anyway."

He didn't pause either. "I can't." Despite the fact that she'd left her calling as a hunter behind, he didn't delude himself that she'd call and ask for any other kind of assistance. She probably didn't know the extent of his defection.

"You have to. You're the only one I trust." A note in her voice pulled at him. She could have said a hundred other things and he'd have been able to hang up the phone without guilt. She said the one thing that kept him on the line.

Colin rubbed his temple with his free hand, and glanced again at Ivy. "Tell me."

"Thank you." She said it on a sigh. Her words came in a quiet rush as she explained the reason for her call.

When her voice trailed off a few minutes later, he told her quietly, "I'll come as soon as I can." He didn't have to think about it or run it by the others. Going wasn't a question.

Ivy looked up when he put the phone down. "What is it?"

He met her gaze and tipped his head slightly. "An old friend. She's in some trouble."

"She?" Ivy raised an eyebrow and folded her hands on top of the book she'd been reading only a moment before. "Do tell me more. An old flame?"

"Hardly." He smiled and ran a hand down her glossy black hair. "Naomi Rand is a retired hunter."

"A pretty hunter?"

He laughed and appreciated how Ivy's question made him feel. "Don't worry, love, I'm not her type."

"Oh, you're sure about that?"

"One hundred percent." He kissed her ear and whispered, "She'd be more interested in you."

Ivy laughed. "Well, then I think I like her already. She's obviously got good taste. When do we leave?"

"We?"

Surprise had her brow wrinkling and her lips pursing. She pushed back in her chair, her dark eyes studying his face. "Of course, we. You go, I go, real simple. What's the problem?"

"Ivy, this is a cross-country trip. Naomi is in Washington, DC."

"And your point would be?"

He knelt next to her and took her hand in his. Her skin was smooth and smelled of something sweet. When she turned those sexy, smoky eyes on him, it was hard to tell her no on just about anything. Then again, he would never knowingly put her life in jeopardy, and that's exactly what he'd be doing if he took her cross-country.

"It's too dangerous for you and I won't put your life at risk. I almost lost you once, and I have no intention of doing it again." Just the thought made him sick to the stomach.

She pressed her lips to his hand. "I love it when you get all knight-in-shining-armor on me. Sexy." She kissed him on the mouth. "But not to worry, handsome. I have a plan."

He rocked on his heels and laughed. "Of course you do."

❖

Despite her hasty retreat to put distance between herself and Naomi Rand, Tory took her time walking back to the Woodley Park Metro station. It was quiet this time of night, the residential neighborhood shrouded in darkness. It was a lovely area with older homes spaced closely together and surrounded by tidy fences and tiny yards. Large trees formed a canopy over her head, blotting out the majority of warm moonlight trying to shine through the boughs heavy with leaves. If she ever could have had a regular life, a home in a neighborhood like this would have been wonderful. Even though it could never be, she didn't stop dreaming of it.

She could theorize that she returned to the church again and again because she was so fond of the area. The theory was crappy and untrue. That she kept returning to the National Cathedral unsettled her. Like the church was going to magically reveal the answers to her. Not a chance. Whatever was going on with the New Testament making its way to her had nothing to do with the National Cathedral and everything to do with her past. Nobody associated with the church could help her, nobody alive anyway.

If Roland was still around, he'd know what it all meant. He had a way of cutting through the bullshit to reveal the truth. Better yet, he'd know what to do. Of course, if Roland was still alive, the book wouldn't be a mystery. It was like a big circle that kept going around, everything connecting to each other but never really revealing a single thing that might help.

At the Woodley Park Station, she hopped on the Metro and made her way back to Union Station. Only a few other people were on the Metro this late at night…or rather this early in the morning. It was a nice ride and she sat back, her head against the window. She even liked the smell. Somehow it made everything feel real, as if she was still a part of the human experience. It was an illusion, of course, but she liked it anyway. Selective denial was a great tool for maintaining long-term positive mental health.

The LOC was a short walk and she didn't bother to look for Belle. She'd be off to one of her hidey holes by now, tucked away with her treasures and, hopefully, some food. She tried to look out for her but she could do only so much. For whatever reason, she was drawn to the troubled woman. Throughout the years, she'd encountered hundreds of the mentally ill. Until Belle, she hadn't felt compelled to protect a single one. She didn't dig too deep to find out what was different about her. Suffice it to say she was unique and Tory wanted to keep her safe. As she walked toward her office, she prayed Belle would stay out of harm's way.

Still, as she passed Belle's favorite hiding spot, she couldn't help but look. It was empty. No sign of her. A twinge of unease rippled through her, and for just a moment she paused, thinking about what she might be able to do. That equated to a big fat nothing. She had no way of knowing where Belle might be and no way to track her down. Rather than dwell on something she had no control over, Tory hurried up the street. Plenty of work was sitting on her desk, with only a few more hours left before she'd need to return to her beautiful brick house. Maybe she couldn't control much else, but she could take charge of the work she was hired to do.

Sounded good, except she didn't feel like working, especially after her encounter with the lovely minister over at the cathedral. Naomi Rand intrigued her. Well, intrigued her and pissed her off. She still bristled when she thought of the passive/aggressive accusation about the New Testament. To even think she would ever steal a book was absurd. She revered books and had never once in her long life considered appropriating one that didn't belong to her or her employer.

Then again, in Naomi's defense, it was pretty weird to show up at the church holding a centuries-old volume. She didn't know what she'd been thinking when she took off with it in the first place. Well, that wasn't quite true. The fact was, she hadn't been thinking at all. Pure reaction had propelled her and the New Testament out the doors of the LOC and across town to the cathedral. Everything after that had just sort of happened like an avalanche that couldn't be stopped.

Tonight was a bit of the same thing. Despite everything sitting on her desk, she kept losing her concentration. She couldn't get her head in the game no matter how hard she tried or what deadlines were staring at her from the calendar on her wall. When she left her office, she'd fully intended to simply take a walk and clear her head. A bit of fresh air was a common-sense approach to improving her focus. Why she'd headed straight back to the church again mystified her. Her feet seemed to have a mind of their own.

Even when she was standing on the steps of the cathedral, she figured it didn't matter where she went to puzzle things out as long as she did. The cathedral was as good a place as any. Right?

So far, however, it wasn't going so well. She wasn't any closer now to finding answers than she'd been an hour ago. Bottom line? Whoever was screwing with her was doing a damn fine job. Throw in the distraction of the gorgeous pastor who kept popping up and things got that much more convoluted. So, running away from Naomi like a scared cat wasn't as much a coward's way out as a head-clearing option. Except wasn't that why she'd stepped away from the LOC in the first place? To clear her head? Oh hell, she couldn't win. She didn't like it.

As soon as she'd stepped out of Union Station, the wail of sirens filled the night air. Not unusual and, with the pervasive police presence on the Hill, a frequent occurrence. A person—a vampire—simply grew accustomed to the sound. She started walking, hands stuffed into the pockets of her pants. The closer she got to the LOC, the louder the sirens became.

As she crested the rise at Constitution Avenue, at first she thought something was happening at the Capitol Complex. Not too terribly unusual there either. People, especially the disgruntled or unbalanced, often focused their aggression on the beautiful, but secure, complex. Typically, the problem was handled quickly and efficiently. Another half block down she realized the problem was somewhere beyond the Capitol Complex and on the other side of the street—the same side of the street where the Library of Congress was located. The twinge that she'd first experienced at Belle's empty hiding spot returned. This wasn't one of those quick or easy situations. Too many lights. Too many cars. Way too many uniforms.

Tory walked briskly, her eyes focused on the flashing red and blue lights that cut through the darkness like lasers. After all this time, she should be accustomed to the violence that was an unfortunate part of the city. Not yet. Hopefully never. And tonight, the sight of those flashing lights brought a sick feeling to the pit of her stomach.

In front of the Library of Congress, police and emergency vehicles fanned out to create a wave of pulsing light and sound. Her step quickened. Despite the dread pooling in the pit of her stomach, she hoped to slip by unnoticed and get back to her office. Or, for that matter, slip in and back out without attracting attention. She didn't want to find herself stuck in her office all day. She could survive it; she just preferred to keep her schedule intact and be long gone by the time the nine-to-five bunch showed up. Safer for everyone, particularly considering she didn't keep a supply of blood in her office.

At the corner, Tory started to turn in the direction of the employee entrance and then paused. Something wasn't right here. It wasn't the *standard* crime scene she was accustomed to seeing. She gazed up, focused her eyes, and caught her breath. For a minute nothing registered and then it hit her. She trembled, her knees nearly buckled. Some sick bastard was making a statement, and she had a terrible feeling the statement was directed at her.

Slowly, she backed away. Her breaths were so short and shallow it was all she could do not to lose it. Her only hope was to blend into the shadows before anyone noticed her or she did something really stupid like pass out.

By the time she got to the employee entrance, she was steadier on her feet but tears streamed down her cheeks. She managed to pass her badge over the keypad sensor, open the door, and slip inside. In the hallway, she leaned heavily against the wall and pressed her hands to her face. As tears continued to fall, she wondered if she'd ever be able to erase the sight of Belle's lifeless body stretched out on the steps of the library.

CHAPTER SEVEN

Finding Nathan in her doorway yet again didn't surprise Naomi. He blew through her door, spilled coffee from the paper cup in his hand all over her floor, and made a halfhearted attempt to clean it up. Mopping the floor hadn't been on her to-do list for today until now. At least it wasn't carpet and he did manage to keep most of the coffee in his cup. Small favors.

His face was pale, serious. "Meme, you gotta give me something."

And that would be what? She turned away from him to stare out her window. "I can't give you something I don't have." She would help him if she could. Protecting her congregation was important, but so was stopping a killer, whether human or not, and frankly, the pressure he was putting on her wasn't helping.

"Shit, this is going to get ugly."

A shiver rippled through her body and she closed her eyes. That was a mistake. It blocked the sight of the setting sun but not the visions of red that filled her mind. "I know," she whispered. "I just don't know how to stop it."

People were getting nervous. Worse than that, angry. In a city this size, anger was a very dangerous emotion. Once before, she'd witnessed firsthand what happened when that kind of mood blanketed a city. She didn't want to see it again.

When she was a hunter everything in her world was black and white. She knew who was good and what was bad. Made her life simple and her decisions easier. These days, all that black and white was long gone. It seemed that all around her were shades of gray, and that's where she found so many generous souls who deserved her respect and protection. Unfortunately, she was among the minority, and those who were growing restless with the lack of progress toward capturing a killer had the potential to be as dangerous as the killer they sought. The mere thought of what could happen sent waves of apprehension surging through her body.

"Don't any of them know who it might be? Anything about someone or something going off the deep end?" His words were sharp.

She shook her head, opened her eyes, and turned around to stare at her brother. The story about the homeless woman left on the steps at the Library of Congress had been on every channel and on the front page of the newspaper. The words *vampire* and *serial killer* punctuated just about every sentence of the various newscasters. It wasn't good for a whole bunch of reasons. In the old days she'd be gathering her weapons and heading out for the hunt, jacked up and ready to kill. Now, she worried about how to protect those who looked to her for salvation. They put their trust in her and she didn't want to let them down. She'd done that once and she vowed never to do it again.

Naomi tried to explain to him. "I asked everyone that I know well and even some I don't. No one has a clue and they're as scared as you are. As I am. Nathan, everyone knows what this means and what could happen."

"Yeah, Meme, but do you?"

Was he serious? Her shoulders stiffened. Nathan, of all people, should know better than to ask her that question. "That's a stupid thing to throw at me. Trust me, I have a much better idea than you what this could mean. I've seen it up close and personal."

"Maybe that was true at one point. But—" he said very softly as he laid a hand on her shoulder, "you walked away a long time ago. You're not exactly on the front lines anymore."

She twisted to dislodge his hand. That he was able to so accurately zero in on her weaknesses irritated her. She'd think her own twin would be a little more diplomatic. "You're right. I'm not on that particular front line anymore. I gave up the sword, literally, but the damage had already been done. Years of memories can't be washed clean or prayed away. They're with me every day and every night. I see the damage I caused in faces of the preternaturals every time I look at them. I have to live with my sins, but I'll be damned if I'll stand by and watch others be victimized by ignorance or fear."

He sighed and stuck his hands into the pockets of his jeans. He looked haunted and she suspected she looked exactly the same. "And despite all of the years of seeing with your own eyes the destruction caused by vampires and other unnatural creatures, you have this sort of Pollyanna attitude that the preternaturals can be trusted. Or even worse, that they're the same as we are."

Would he ever…ever…understand? "They are and they deserve the same respect and shot at redemption." She believed that with every fiber of her being. She had to, because if they weren't worthy of a chance at redeeming themselves, where did that leave her?

The haunted expression fled, replaced by hardness. "They aren't the same as humans and never will be. You can preach all you want, try to bridge the gap between humans and preternaturals, and it's not going to change a damn thing. Vamps are going to feed on human blood and werewolves are going to snack on human flesh, and that's only two of these creatures. This rash of murders is putting this city one hair's breadth away from setting off a war. Too many will die if that happens."

"I won't let it happen," she told him, tears beginning to form in her eyes. Why couldn't she ever reach him? More than that, why was his heart closed? So long ago, he'd been different, happier, loving. Along the way somewhere, he'd walled up his heart to everyone, including her.

Nathan shook his head, refusing to meet her eyes. "You can't stop it." He snatched his jacket from the chair he'd tossed it on when he first came in, then headed to the front door. "You couldn't stop it when you carried weapons at your sides, and you sure as hell can't stop it now with your words of God and forgiveness."

"You're wrong," she said to his back.

At the door, Nathan stopped and turned to look at her once more. His eyes were dark and angry as they met hers. It was a look she knew well and tried to avoid whenever she could.

"Don't do anything stupid. You might have God on your side, but without that sword you tossed aside, you're just another meal to this monster. I don't want to have to positively identify your body because you end up as a midnight snack for the bastard. You're still my sister, and while I respect what you do, if I have to choose between human and preternatural, you know which side I'll come down on."

The slamming door made the pictures rattle on the wall and the vase Darin had made for her start to tumble off the bookshelf. Catching it before it crashed to the floor, she held it, running her fingers over the surface. Like the artist who created the piece, it was beautiful inside and out. That Darin had given it to her had made it all the more special because he was special.

Setting it gently back onto the bookshelf, she turned and for a long time stood staring at the closed door. Things were so messed up. Not just the murders but with her brother too. She didn't know where it had all gone off-kilter. Didn't know why. Just wished it could be different but didn't suppose it ever would be again. They were two very different people these days who managed to irritate the hell out of each other day in and day out.

She was still simmering about Nathan's holier-than-thou parting words when she hit the sidewalk half an hour later.

"What's got you looking like you want to start a fight?"

Angie Oberman was leaning against the same light pole Karen had used as a prop only a day before. With her arms across her chest, she studied Naomi's strained face. Dressed in a running skirt, figure-hugging top, and running shoes, Angie looked like any other young, tall, and athletic Beltway professional. In fact, she was an up-and-comer in the Capitol Police, but what Naomi knew and not many others did was that Angie was also a wereleopard. Unlike Karen, who walked the streets of the capital, Angie had long since given up her uniform for plain clothes and a big salary. It would stay that way too as long as everyone believed her to be human.

Angie was the second of her two workout partners. If Naomi wasn't out here with Karen, it was Angie. The two of them ran together at least once a week, although saying they ran together was a bit like saying a wolf and a turtle run together. Angie could do six-minute miles without breaking a sweat while Naomi had to work hard to maintain ten-minute miles. Having to always push to keep up with Angie was good for her, though, and more than that, she enjoyed her company. Angie was smart and funny, and a good friend to have. Especially on days like today.

"My brother," Naomi said, without any further explanation.

Angie laughed. "Should have figured as much. He's about the only one who makes you look like you want to punch somebody."

"I don't look like I'm going to hit anyone."

Angie pushed away from the light pole and shrugged. "Whatever you say, Rev." She was laughing again as she took off.

Naomi was too as she tried to catch up.

❖

Tory met Sunny near the luggage carrousel at Reagan National Airport. Sunny smiled the second she caught sight of Tory and ran to wrap her in a big hug. It was like being surrounded by sunshine, or what she remembered of sunshine.

"You're looking gorgeous as ever," Sunny said as she stepped back to study her. "Cut your hair? I like it."

She laughed. Sunny was like a whirlwind of energy and laughter. It didn't matter how bad she was feeling, the minute Sunny walked into the room, everything felt better. Even now with the horror of last night still fresh in her mind, just being around the dynamic woman wrapped her in a blanket of hope. There was no escaping her aura of positive energy.

"No." She hugged Sunny. "I didn't cut my hair." It was futile even if she did because it grew back so fast, it was as if the trim never happened. So she left it long and dark, just as it had been the night she'd been turned.

She shrugged. "If you say so. Hey—" Sunny yelled at the same time she started to wave energetically at a tall, heavy woman who walked in their direction pulling a bright-orange rolling bag. "Vi, over here."

"Good grief," the woman exclaimed as she reached them. "I swear to Lord, your hair gets redder every time I see you. I could've picked you out from the gate. Oh no, I could have picked you out from the window on the airplane!"

"Of course it is. I say if you're gonna go to all the work to dye your hair, do it up nice and big. The redder the better. I look stunning, don't you think? I was born to be a redhead." Sunny turned full circle, her arms held out before she did an exaggerated curtsey.

Both women burst out in boisterous laughter that had everyone within earshot turning to stare. The scrutiny made Tory a little uncomfortable. It didn't seem to faze either of the other two.

When Sunny's laughter sputtered out, she laid a hand on Tory's arm. "Tory Grey, this is my dear, dear friend Viola Juve. All-around good chick and psychic extraordinaire."

Viola stuck out her hand. "Good to meet you, Ms. Grey."

Like Sunny, something about Viola radiated vibrancy and, more important, friendship. Tall, and nowhere near slender, she was a large woman who carried herself with incredible grace. No one in their right mind would call her obese. In fact, Tory suspected Viola's sculpted arms were the product of either weight lifting or regular swimming. Not bad. Her handshake was firm. Tory liked her immediately.

"Please, call me Tory."

Viola studied Tory, her eyes narrowing, a smile still pulling up the corners of her mouth. "Sunny didn't tell me."

"Never do," Sunny said with an even bigger smile. "How else am I gonna sneak in little tests?" Sunny cut her eyes to Tory. "Like she thinks we're just gonna take her word that she's the world's best psychic?"

Tory barely heard Sunny. She was focused completely on Viola and her cryptic words. For a second, she didn't get it and then it hit her. "How?" Tory sputtered.

She blended incredibly well with the humans. After all, she'd had a great deal of experience pretending she was still human. People rarely figured out she wasn't one of them, and yet this woman did in less than thirty seconds. If she wasn't the world's best psychic, then she was pretty damned close.

Viola laughed boisterously and good humor glowed from her eyes. Once more, faces turned in their direction. Viola didn't seem to notice or, if she did, didn't care. "I'm a psychic, babe." She gave Tory a nudge with one elbow that was powerful enough to nearly topple her.

She'd run into many self-professed psychics in her time, and just saying it was so didn't mean much. Viola was different…in a good way. "I'm impressed."

"Oh, girlfriend, you haven't seen anything yet. If you've got secrets, Vi will know!" She put an index finger to each side of her forehead and said in a low, lilting voice, "Madam Viola, mind reader, psychic extraordinaire, here to reveal your deepest, darkest desires." She dropped her hands and winked at Tory.

"Great," Tory muttered, though a small smile turned up the corners of her mouth. "I need a secret or two uncovered, but I was really hoping they wouldn't be mine."

"Come on." Sunny broke in, patting Tory on the arm. "Let's get out of this place. I think some good wine on your dime would be fantastic, and then we can talk about those dark, dangerous secrets you want to keep so close to the vest."

"Fabulous idea." Viola grabbed the handle of her bright-orange suitcase and headed in the direction of the exit. "I've been on planes all day and I could use a little vino. Oh, hell, I could use a lot of vino.

Besides, I'm still on Pacific Standard Time, and it'll be hours before I'm even close to getting tired. Good thing you're a night owl."

Tory liked Viola already. She started to follow the two women. They were right. What they needed to talk about would be better hashed over in a private setting. They'd already gotten more than their fair share of attention here at the airport. Time to take it a little more private. Her house with a nice cabernet sounded about right.

Before she'd taken more than ten steps, she stopped. It couldn't be. She was seeing things. Had to be because it didn't make sense. Viola had her shaken up with her uncanny accuracy, and that's what made her see things now. Yes, that's all it was. Still, her feet didn't move and she continued to stare. Four people were walking toward the same set of doors they were. One tall, handsome man, one lovely Hispanic woman, one attractive black woman…and one ghost.

❖

Naomi was standing just outside the security area watching as passengers from incoming flights filed through. It was very late, and most the people coming down the hall looked haggard and drawn out. She knew that feeling far too well, particularly during her days as a hunter. A hunt could take days, even weeks, and the physical toll had been immense. It wasn't uncommon to go two or three days with little to no sleep. She sure didn't miss that. These days, the physical side of her job was much easier, though the mental fatigue tended to drag her down on occasion.

She kept watching as people pulling bags of various sizes and colors moved toward the taxi signs or climbed the steps to the Metro stop. When she finally caught sight of a familiar face, she breathed a little easier. Until this moment, she didn't realize how anxious she was to see an old friend and ally.

The first thing she noticed was how refreshed Colin appeared. Retirement seemed to suit him well. Still tall and handsome, he stood out from the surrounding throng. Or maybe she could still pick a hunter out of a crowd in under sixty seconds. Some skills stayed sharp no matter how long out of the game. At first, she didn't realize he wasn't alone.

His face broke into a smile as he caught sight of her. "Naomi," he all but yelled, wrapping her in a bear hug when he reached her. "Damn good to see you."

Tears welled unexpectedly in her eyes as she returned his embrace. She had no regrets about the way she lived her life these days, and yet Colin's touch made her feel like she'd come home after a long cold night alone. "I'm so glad you came," she murmured into his chest.

"I told you years ago, I'd always have your six. I didn't mean only when we were hunters." He hugged her a little tighter.

Her emotions unexpectedly fragile and barely under control, she stepped away and looked up into his face. "You did and I believed you. It's just that I've been out of the fold for such a long time and don't really trust very many people these days."

He studied her face, his eyes intent and serious. He'd changed very little in the intervening years, and she was glad to see that darkness hadn't taken him down like it had done to so many others before them. "That makes two of us, Naomi. I wasn't kidding when I told you I'm not a hunter anymore. I'm out of the game and I'm not going back. Ever."

Boy, did she get that. Walking away was never quick or easy. Few did it. Fewer still stayed away. Colin was not the type to make a move he wasn't behind all the way. He would never go back.

"I didn't think for a second you were, and I didn't call you to try to convince you to jump back into the fold. That phone call was for entirely selfish reasons. You're the only one I can talk to who might understand, and I didn't know what else to do."

"Yeah, I get that, I really do, and that's why I'm here, with reinforcements no less. Naomi Rand, this is my better half, Ivy Hernandez."

A lovely Hispanic woman stepped forward and offered her hand. Compared to Colin, she was tiny. She had wavy black hair, smooth skin, and intelligent dark eyes. Not hard to see why Colin would be attracted to her. The "better half" comment was interesting. Never thought he would be the kind of guy to settle down. Not that he was ever a player. No, it was more about the way he was driven that had always made her believe he would keep everyone at arm's length. His heart was off-limits. Apparently, she'd read that wrong and she was happy she had. He deserved more than loneliness and a whole lot of memories no one should have to live with.

"Nice to meet you, Naomi."

Naomi took her hand, surprised by the cool flesh. "A vampire?" It slipped out before she could stop it. At least she didn't snatch her hand back. It wasn't that she thought Ivy was evil. She rarely jumped to that often-mistaken conclusion these days. It was more the shock of a hunter actually being *with* a vampire, carnally speaking. She turned a puzzled look his way.

Colin laughed as he stepped away from Naomi to put an arm possessively around Ivy. "It's a very long story and I promise to tell it to you real soon, but first, I'd also like to introduce you to my friends, Dr. Riah Preston and Adriana James." He held up a hand. "Before you say it, yes, Riah is also a vampire."

She stared at the two women—both petite, one pale and gorgeous with long dark hair, the other dark and sultry with close-cropped hair and black eyes. They were an attractive couple—yes, definitely a couple. Their body language screamed it. A streak of jealousy hit her as she studied the two couples. Once upon a time she'd hoped for that kind of relationship in her life. Not these days. She'd had to accept the reality that for some people it wasn't possible.

Not wanting to let the past intrude, she returned her attention to Colin and his friends. The reality that Colin had brought not one, but two vampires across the country to a city that was under siege from yet another vampire sunk in. What had he been thinking?

"No offense, ladies, but are you out of your fucking minds? I thought I made it clear to Colin that the problem we're having is a rogue vampire. This is about the worst time ever for you to be in the city. You're putting your lives in danger just by being here."

Colin walked over and put an arm around Naomi once again, hugging her to his side. His arm was strong, his body warm. The simple gesture gave her a boost of confidence, though it did little to relieve her concern over the safety of the two vampires.

"Trust me, Naomi, it'll be all right. What you see here is one kick-ass team, a strange sort of group that works and travels together. You called me to help and that means you get all of us. We're a package deal."

Sounded good, but she still had a bad feeling swirling around in the pit of her stomach. A package deal wasn't a bad thing as long as it was made up of those of the human variety. She had enough on her plate already without adding the responsibility for the safety of two more preternaturals. Colin, on the other hand, didn't appear apprehensive in the least. She'd certainly like to know his secret.

"You're sure?"

He pressed a kiss to her head and gave her another squeeze. "One hundred percent. Trust me, Naomi. You've got a hell of a team watching your back."

Hopefully he knew what he was talking about. Then, of course, there was the tiny detail about Colin being the best hunter the church had ever trained. The day he walked away had to have been a very black one for Monsignor and his church. Would have been interesting to be a fly on the wall that day.

She crossed her fingers that Colin still possessed the same skills that had set him apart from every other hunter. She'd bet he did, but she'd been wrong before so she'd keep those fingers crossed—just in case.

"Well, then..." She let her gaze sweep over all four. "Let's get out of here and I'll fill you in on my story, after which you all have some explaining to do. Four of you..." She shook her head and started toward the exit doors once more.

They were almost to the doors when Naomi stopped. Flanked by two women, Tory stood only a few feet away. She was surprised to find her here and equally surprised to see Tory's gaze locked onto the woman Colin had introduced as Dr. Riah Preston. Or maybe surprised wasn't quite the right word. By the look on Tory's face, shocked disbelief might be more accurate.

CHAPTER EIGHT

"Catherine?" Tory said the name on a breath. She couldn't believe her eyes. Talk about seeing a ghost. First the New Testament. Now this?

"Victoria? Tell me I'm not imagining you." Riah's words were as disbelieving as Tory's.

Tory shook off her shock, smiled, and wrapped her arms around her aunt. She'd lost touch with Catherine a few hundred years ago. Then she'd heard through the vampire grapevine that Catherine had been destroyed in a fire that also claimed a master vampire known only as Rodolphe. Catherine's maker, if the rumors were to be believed. Since she'd never laid eyes on Catherine again, she'd been inclined to believe the fire report. Until the picture in the paper. Knowing she was still somewhere in the world had been comforting, but still Tory had never expected to see her again.

"For years and years I thought you were dead." If she wasn't touching her right at this moment, she wouldn't believe her eyes. For centuries, she'd thought herself alone in this world, and the sorrow of it never left her heart.

Catherine smiled, lighting up a heart-warming, familiar face. "Not a chance, little niece. I'm like a cat. You know, nine lives and all that. Haven't begun to use up even half of them."

Tory was still confused. If she hadn't been destroyed in a fire, then where had she been? "But Rodolphe? The fire? Until I caught that article about you helping catch a serial killer, I was convinced you'd been torched."

She touched Tory's cheek. "Don't believe everything you hear. It'd take more than a puny fire or that ass, Rodolphe, to kill me. Let's just say I've been under the radar for a spell."

Tory stepped away and studied her only living relative. Well, sort of living relative. "I can't wrap my head around the fact it's really you. How is this possible? How are you here?"

She squeezed Tory's hand. "It's me all right, though I go by the name of Riah Preston these days. Catherine has been gone for eons. For all intents and purposes, she died alongside Rodolphe."

That she understood. Victoria had likewise been gone from what had become her life since that long-ago black night that changed everything. "Rodolphe?"

Catherine or, rather, Riah shook her head. "Dust in the wind, I'm pleased to say. But that's another long, long story I'll have to share with you later."

Tory wanted to say halleluiah to confirmation of the end to an evil being that never should have been allowed to survive. He'd been a bastard of epic proportions. The stories about his trails of destruction were legendary and still whispered about in certain circles. She didn't say any of it because she wasn't sure how much or how little Catherine—Riah—might have already shared with her companions. Instead she opted for neutral ground and changed course. "What are you doing here?"

"We came to help." She motioned in the direction of her companions. Tory's eyes met Naomi's.

"This is a surprise."

"Back atcha, Tory. We can't seem to stop running into each other. I wonder what that means?" Naomi pondered out loud.

"Tory?" Riah's question made them all look her way.

Tory shrugged. "You go by Riah, I go by Tory. Gotta keep up with the times or…well you know what I mean, auntie."

Naomi looked from one to the other, her gaze appraising. "You're related?"

Tory shrugged. "Sort of. My grandmother and Catherine…I mean Riah, were sisters. She's my great-aunt." From the time she'd learned of Riah's existence, she'd found it amusing that while Riah was technically old enough to be her grandmother, the two of them looked to be barely a couple years different age-wise.

Riah held up a hand. "Could we talk about this somewhere else? This is a little too public for my tastes, if you know what I mean. It's bad enough for Ivy and me to be here, but two former hunters could be a problem too. Better for us all to fly under the radar."

Two former hunters, what exactly did that mean? Then it hit her and she stared at Naomi. Now she understood what it was about the preacher that had seemed just a touch off. Naomi looked away first without saying a word. Now wasn't the time to get into it.

Tory scanned the terminal and had to agree that Riah had a point. Even at this time of night, there were way too many people. She dug into her pocket for a scrap of paper and a pen. Quickly, she jotted down her cell number and handed the paper to Riah. "Call me."

Riah took the offered number and nodded. "As soon as we get to where we're staying, I'll be in touch."

Tory watched the group leave and still couldn't believe it was real. She'd been alone for so long, how could this be possible? While it was certainly true her family's blood lived on in Great Britain, this was different. Had they not each been turned, they might have known each other. As her grandmother's sister, Catherine would have been an important member of the family, someone to look up to.

Except Catherine's life, like Tory's, hadn't been that simple. Far from it. Their shared heritage was the very thing that had made both of them outcasts, both during their mortal existence and as vampires. When human, neither had ever been truly safe. Instead, both of them began life amidst complicated webs of lies. It was the lies probably more than the blood that had drawn them together when they discovered each other. In a strange sort of way it was fitting they both ended up living in darkness.

As surprised as she was about Riah, she was stunned about the discovery of what was beneath Naomi's façade of righteousness. A hunter? It figured. Her life was so screwed up, why not fall for a hunter? Fate was so messed up.

"Shall we head out as well?" Sunny asked.

She'd all but forgotten about Sunny and Viola. Neither had said a word during the exchange with Riah, though they'd watched it with undisguised interest. Not that she blamed them. It wasn't often that people encountered two descendants from the famous Tudor line, and even fewer knew that Lady Jane Grey gave birth to a daughter before she was beheaded. No, she didn't blame Sunny or Viola for their open-mouthed interest. She and her aunt were definitely not garden-variety vampires.

Tory apologized. "God, I'm so sorry. That was incredibly rude of me. I was just so shocked to see Catherine, I mean, Riah, after so many years. Not every day you run into the aunt you believed dead for the last couple hundred years."

"Ah, honey, happens to us all." Viola laughed and put an arm around her shoulders. "You'll have to fill us in,"

Together they walked outside the terminal and waited in line for a taxi. This time of night the wait was short and within a couple of minutes, the three of them piled into a yellow cab. Tory gave the driver directions and they were on their way, the lights of Ronald Reagan National Airport growing dim behind them. The night was clear, the sky filled with stars and the moon bright.

They headed to Tory's house on Second Street, directly behind the Supreme Court. The street with its close-together historical homes was beautiful even in the darkness, and soon, the cab dropped them at Tory's tiny front yard. The minute she stepped through the gate, she felt better. She was smiling as she opened the door for Sunny and Viola, following them inside.

Leaving the bags in the entryway, they all settled in the front room. Viola was planning to stay with Sunny, so it made sense to get right to it. Viola already had a feel for the lay of the land; might as well have her go for the jugular. No better place for that than home sweet home.

The house in the middle of the block was large for a Capitol Hill home and had undergone a complete historic restoration a few years before Tory purchased it. The hardwood floors gleamed and the furniture was comfortable and stylish at the same time. Outside, the small front yard was simply landscaped and enclosed by a sturdy wrought-iron fence.

Though she preferred to think of herself as not materialistic, she'd made some wonderful friends through the years and was lucky enough to have their gifts scattered throughout the house. They made it feel like a home and not just a stopping place in a long life. She ran her hand over the smooth marble sculpture that her dear friend Camille Claudel had given her just before Tory left France for the United States. It was a beautiful yet haunting piece done right before Camille's three decades of commitment. She and Camille had been great friends, and her heart was still heavy over the sad turn her life had taken.

Over the fireplace was an oval painting Angelica Kauffman had created during the years Tory lived in Rome. The depiction of a woman reclining against a tree, her dress slipping off one shoulder to reveal her smooth, white breast, had spoken to Tory the moment she'd laid eyes on it. Talking Angelica into selling the painting had taken a great deal of heartfelt pleading. In the end, Angelica relented and Tory prevailed. The painting had been with her for over two centuries.

When the time came to leave here, she'd be sad. During her lengthy lifetime she'd lived many places and few ever felt like a real home. This house did. This city did, and she'd leave with both a heavy heart and much regret. She wished it could be different and knew it wouldn't be. Leaving was inevitable no matter how much it would hurt.

"Can I get you anything?" She snapped on the gas fireplace and the room brightened with a warm glow. That was better.

"Wine would be fabulous if you've got it," Sunny said with a smile.

"Make it two." Viola grinned, her face lighting up. She kicked off her shoes and curled her toes into the thick rug. "Hmm, feels good."

In the kitchen, Tory opened a bottle of wine and set it on the counter to breathe. From an under-counter refrigerator faced to look like just another cabinet, she pulled a package of blood. She popped it into the microwave for thirty seconds, just enough to take the chill off.

By the time she finished the packet of blood, the wine was ready to be poured. She didn't usually drink alcohol, but tonight was anything but usual. She filled three glasses, set them on a tray, and carried it into the living room.

"Well, ladies, shall we get this party going?"

Viola took a sip and nodded. "Yum," she drawled, then looked into Tory's eyes. "Let's do this. I've never read a vampire before, and I'm anxious to find out what's inside that pretty little immortal head of yours."

That made one of them. If Viola could reach something that might help unravel the mystery of the New Testament, great. The rest of the not-so-helpful stuff inside her head should really stay there. No one needed to know. She didn't need to remember.

❖

Word on the street said Whispers was the place to be for the bright, ambitious, and beautiful LGBTQs in the District. The way he figured it, she'd put herself firmly in the middle of bright and beautiful, so hanging out there was bound to pay off. It was also a win-win for him. He could send her another pointed message and get a little for himself all at the same time. Fun, fun, fun.

Dupont Circle was alive as he strolled through the streets on his way to Whispers. Such a lovely mix of people, sights, and smells. It wasn't quite as enticing as the melody of life found near his New

Orleans home, but it wasn't bad. Here there were far more suits and overpriced haircuts. At home, it was all about the culture of the bayou and the sheer joy of living. Here, it was about living the see-and-be-seen life of pedigrees and knowing the *right* people. The game was okay to play for a little while, but when it came right down to it, he preferred the culture of his own home.

Then again, the package didn't matter so much. It was the contents that were important. Blood was blood regardless of what it came in. As for what was to be found beneath the suits? Well, it was pretty much the same for a good fuck. Some of the best ones came in the most surprising packages. A conservative suit and tie might scream proper, but sometimes the freaks hid just beneath the expensive tailoring. He hoped he'd have the luck to find some of those freaks tonight. He was up for some nasty fun.

Despite the political incorrectness, he pulled a cigarette from his pocket and, lighting it, took a long drag. The sweet smoke filled his lungs. The surgeon general's warning didn't give him as much as a second thought. He loved the taste of tobacco. Besides, it wasn't like he was going to die…again.

By the time he dropped the butt to the sidewalk and put out the last glowing ember with the toe of his boot, he was wound up and ready to go. Time to party.

An interesting parade of patrons had entered Whispers as he'd leaned against the building smoking. So far, two held the top spot on his list. The woman was a winner, with red hair cut short to frame her pretty face. Tall enough to look him in the eye, she had broad shoulders and wide hips that appealed to him. While he found beautiful women alluring, he often found himself far more attracted to those women with a hint of masculinity. Something about the blend of butch and babe made his dick hard. That, and the challenge of convincing her to come with him when she obviously had her sights set on the fairer sex. He rubbed his hands together and grinned.

The other winner was a black-haired hard body. In designer jeans and a black sweater that didn't hide his muscles, the guy was on a very obvious troll. Yeah, that completely worked in the big scheme of things, especially considering the hard-on straining at his jeans and impossible to miss. Just what he needed to catch the attention of tall and hot. It was fantastic when a plan came together.

Music played loud enough to be interesting but not enough that it forced patrons to scream to be heard. Dirty martini in hand, he surveyed the room. Lots of potential in tonight's crowd, and before long he'd settled on his soon-to-be companions. His initial picks were still perfect for his evening plans. Getting to both of them would require some finesse, his particular strong point. Smooth was his middle name, and he could work it no matter which side he was swinging from. The challenge was far from daunting. In fact, quite the opposite. It energized him.

He put his empty glass down, grabbed a couple of full drinks from the bartender, and started in the direction of handsome and muscled. In an hour or so, he'd be back for his redhead butch.

❖

"Well, that was pretty fucking wild," Riah said once they were all in the car.

"You two are family?" Seriously, what were the odds of that? One in a million? A billion?

"A couple of generations removed but yes," Riah said. "I'm as amazed as you are. I thought she'd been destroyed a long time ago. I guess she thought the same about me. We are so busy protecting ourselves, we lose others who are important. It's the sad reality of the vampire existence."

"Damn it," Naomi spit out from between clenched teeth.

Colin put a hand on her arm. "It's not a bad thing. These are good people, I promise."

Naomi shook her head at the same time she put the car in park. She'd pulled into her driveway behind another car not normally parked there. "I'm sorry. That had nothing to do with Riah or Tory. That—" she pointed to other car, "is the problem. My brother is here again."

"Should we stay here?" Riah asked from the backseat.

"No, it's not that. He doesn't have a huge problem with vamps as a general rule. Don't get me wrong, he's not pals with vampires…"

"But?" Colin prompted her.

"But right now is a bad time. He's a detective in the District and these murders have him on a very precarious edge. All vampires are suspect in his mind, as well as shape-shifters or weres of any ilk. He sees protecting humans as his number-one priority."

Riah put her hand on Naomi's shoulder. "Honestly, it's not a problem to make ourselves scarce for a while. We don't want to put you in an uncomfortable situation, particularly with your family."

Naomi shook her head. "I appreciate it, but really, Nathan meeting you isn't what has me so twitchy. It's the mere fact that he's here. Something's got to be wrong again. Let's just say casual visits for a brotherly hello are few and far between, despite the fact we're twins. Lately he's here about every day." She took a big breath and then let it out slowly. "All right, ladies and gent, let's get this over with. Putting off the bad news isn't going to make it any better."

When she swung the front door open, Nathan was waiting in her living room, a scotch in one hand, his cell phone in the other. From the sour expression on his normally handsome face, things were not going well. And why would she expect anything different?

She waved her guests in and walked right by Nathan and into the kitchen. A scotch had a really nice sound to it. Colin and Adriana joined her, although Riah and Ivy declined. Nathan kept talking in a voice too low to be able to make anything out. She wasn't sure she really wanted to know anyway. Of course, the way things shook out lately, he'd tell her whether she wanted him to or not.

After he ended the call, Nathan was silent as he looked from face to face, his gaze lingering on Riah and Ivy a little longer than anyone else. Not much was lost on Detective Rand. She liked that about her brother. She also hated that about her brother.

"Yeah," she said before he could open his mouth. "They're vampires."

"Why?" The single word was brittle. He sounded as close to the edge as she felt. Not good.

She shrugged as if none of this was a big deal. "It was time to call in the professionals."

He put one hand on the gun at his belt. "I'm a professional."

Nathan was in full police mode. She knew the tone of voice and the stance. It screamed law enforcement without ever saying a word. It might work on lots of other people, but she wasn't intimidated.

"Yeah, but you're not the kind of professional this city needs at the moment." He had to know it too. The training he'd had at the police academy and during his classes at Quantico didn't mean a damn thing when it came to the current problems. This was outside his area of expertise and right smack in the middle of hers, Colin's, and the others'. Nathan knew about her years as a hunter but he didn't really *know*.

He removed his hand from the gun and ran it through his shaggy hair. "You're playing a dangerous game, Meme," he said quietly.

She held his gaze. Did he even remember what she did before the cathedral? If so, he'd understand that she had a far better idea than he did what the hell was going on. "Been there, done that, bro."

He let out a harsh laugh and shrugged. "Yeah, you have." His shoulders seemed to relax a little and he slid his gaze toward her guests. "So introduce me to the vampires et al."

She'd braced for a fight. Nathan was always up to spar with her, especially when he decided he was on the side of good and righteous, and she was in league with evil. His retreat was as surprising as it was appreciated. An ugly sibling fight wasn't the show she wanted to put on for her guests. At this moment, she loved her brother, a lot.

When she completed introductions all around, Naomi turned back to Nathan. "You haven't told me why you're here."

"Two fresh kills."

CHAPTER NINE

By the time Sunny and Viola got into a taxi and drove away, Tory was shaking. What Viola had told her seemed impossible, yet at the same time, she believed it completely. After all the years she'd been around, little surprised her. Tonight, she'd been surprised.

Holding the New Testament in her trembling hands, she pulled it close to her chest and, for the first time in decades, allowed the tears to fall. She remembered that long-ago night as if it had happened just yesterday. Year after year, the horror of it haunted her sleep and guilt crushed her heart. If not for her, Roland would have lived a long and important life. He'd had so much left to give. His life had been taken violently only because he'd embraced her as if she'd been his own daughter...as if she'd still been human. The important work he had been doing came to an abrupt end.

His death nearly destroyed her too. If not for a few trusted friends, both human and preternatural, she'd have stopped running then and there and let the hunters catch her at last, put a stake through her heart and a sword to her throat. It wasn't until word came that Pierre's luck had run out and he'd lost the battle with a particularly vicious werewolf that she gathered her strength and continued.

Tonight, the old feeling of despair washed over her like a tidal wave. For years, she'd believed Pierre was gone, reduced to ash and scattered in the autumn wind. She'd believed wrong. Somehow it seemed he'd survived the werewolf attack. She didn't know how. She didn't know why.

There was no mistake. Viola's description of the tall, dark-haired man with the regal bearing she saw when she touched the book was so like him. Even today, she could picture the way he moved, his black hair shining as it caught the light of the fire. He was a beautiful man and a charismatic vampire. The combination made him a dangerous hunter, easily luring in the unwary. When that didn't work, he still took what he wanted…like her…and he didn't like losing what he considered his. So now Pierre was back, and she knew one thing with a terrible certainty: he was here for her.

Wiping away the tears with the back of her hand, she glanced up at the clock. Plenty of night left. Pierre might be back for her, but she wasn't going to make it easy. Stronger and smarter than the last time they were face-to-face, she also had tools not even imagined at their last meeting. She planned to be ready. Putting the book on the desk, she turned to the computer. Her fingers flew over the keyboard until it coughed up the information she sought. Had to love computers and the Internet.

It took only thirty minutes this time of night to make it to the lovely little home six blocks from the cathedral. The neighborhood was quiet, with old-growth trees and parked cars lining both sides of the street.

The house she sought was actually pretty easy to find because it was one of the few with lights still burning. Plenty of neighborhoods in the city where things happened all night long. This wasn't one of those. Here, people worked during the day and slept during the night. Except in this house.

As she stood and studied the place, the front door opened and a man walked out, although walked might be a stretch. More like stormed out. When he passed under the light, she got a good look at him and was surprised how much he resembled Naomi. Didn't have to be a genius to figure out the two were related. His step didn't slow until he reached the unmarked District police car. He got in and drove away, perhaps a bit too fast for the tight residential street. Then again, who was going to pull him over in that car?

Dragging her gaze away from the rapidly disappearing police car, she took a deep breath and went up the steps to the front door. Old habits were hard to break, and walking face-first into a hunter rather than turning and fleeing took every ounce of will that she possessed. Of course the fact that Naomi Rand was on the other side of the door didn't hurt. She wanted to see her as much as she needed the help of a hunter—or former hunter, as the case might be.

Her hand shook as she reached up to knock on the door. She paused. Could she really go through with this? Ask a hunter for help? Didn't want to ask anyone for help, least of all a hunter. She knocked.

Right at the moment, all she had to go on was faith. Roland instilled in her the belief that faith was the one thing she could always count on. He'd never let her down and she prayed his lessons held true today.

Something about Naomi promised trust, and Tory desperately needed that right now. Even though she felt a little betrayed to learn of her former profession from someone other than Naomi, she still couldn't shake the feeling that she was different. Yeah, there was that the little attraction element too, but it wasn't the primary draw tonight. It would be stupid to ignore the truth, and she wasn't a stupid woman. For the first time in a really long time, she needed help, and she was going to ask for it. Beg, if she had to.

Naomi opened the door and stared. "What the—" From inside the house the low sounds of conversation drifted out.

"Hello," Tory said. "I'm sorry to bother you but…I need help."

"I'm sorry." Naomi sputtered. "Forgive me. It's just I'm so surprised, no, shocked, to see you. How did you know where I live?" She stood, blocking the doorway, her expression mirroring her words.

Tory shrugged. "I Googled you." Truth was the best explanation she could come up with.

"Googled me?" Naomi laughed softly and her face cleared. "I love it. Come in." Naomi stood aside to let her in.

Not waiting for her to change her mind, Tory took three big steps off the front porch and into the entryway. Tension crackled in the air the second she stepped inside, and Tory had a split second when she almost turned around in retreat. She actually started to and at the same time heard a distinct click. Naomi stood with her back against the heavy locked door. Her exit path was blocked. Naomi put a hand on Tory's shoulder and the electricity that shot through her body at the contact nearly made her jump. The little "oh" that escaped Naomi's lips let Tory know she wasn't the only one who felt it. It was a small measure of comfort to know that.

"Maybe this isn't such a good idea." As if the whole situation wasn't weird enough, this *thing* happening between her and Naomi was disconcerting. She needed help but maybe from someone she didn't want to haul up and kiss.

Naomi squeezed her shoulder lightly. If she sensed the direction of Tory's thoughts, she didn't let on. "Don't be silly. Come in."

What choice did she have? Well, short of picking Naomi up and throwing her out of the way. She shrugged and said, "Lead the way."

Naomi waved her into a room on the left. "In here."

In the living room, Colin and Ivy sat close to each other on a pale-green sofa while Riah and Adriana shared an overstuffed chair, Riah on the cushion and Adriana perched on the arm. Riah jumped up when she saw Tory, rushing over to gather her up in a hug. Tory loved the solid feel of her body and the sweet scent of her perfume. Even after all these years, it was achingly familiar.

"I'm so glad to see you," Riah said as she pressed a kiss onto Tory's cheek. "I thought you were dead."

"Back at ya, auntie." She hoped no one heard the catch in her voice.

Riah stepped back and studied Tory. "Tell me what's wrong."

That was a loaded question. What wasn't wrong right now? "Besides a rampaging vampire here in the District?"

"Yes, besides that. I know all about the rogue. What I don't know is what's bothering you."

Her legs felt suddenly weak. Everything was bothering her. The New Testament. The reappearance of Pierre. Her attraction to Naomi. Most of all, the way her life was suddenly whirling out of control. Yeah, pretty much everything was bothering her right at the moment.

Naomi seemed to sense her near crumble and took hold of her arm. "Come on," Naomi urged. "Sit here." Her hand was warm, comforting.

She took the chair gratefully and wouldn't have minded at all if Naomi continued to hold her arm. She didn't and Tory didn't make a fool of herself by being clingy. She turned her attention back to her aunt. "What's bothering me? Okay, here it is in the down-and-dirty version."

"My favorite way," Ivy said from the sofa, one eyebrow raised and a tiny smile on her lips.

Riah looked at Ivy, rolled her eyes, and said, "Don't listen to her, she's always horny. Can't you do something with her, Colin?"

Colin slung an arm around Ivy's shoulders and hugged her close. "I'll see what I can do. Now quiet, you," he said to Ivy right before he gave her a quick kiss.

Naomi grabbed a dining-room chair and sat in it next to Tory. Once more she laid a hand on her arm. "Tell us."

Yes, it was better with that touch on her arm. That and the light, easy way they all talked to each other helped put her at ease. It felt somehow normal in a time when she didn't have a clue what normal was. Even so, her voice still shook a little as she started to talk, her eyes on Naomi's face. "It began that first night."

Naomi nodded and then turned to the others. "She means two nights ago when Tory came to the special service at the cathedral. I noticed her there before the service started and walked over to introduce myself. I try to do that anytime someone new ventures into the church."

"Right," Tory said. "It was a nice gesture I really didn't appreciate at the time. Sorry." She gave Naomi a small, wry smile.

Naomi's return smile was warm. "No problem. Go on."

Tory took a deep breath. "When I got to work that night, I discovered a mysterious package on my desk." She went on to explain about the New Testament, the box it came in, and her inability to discover anything about how it got to her desk. When she was done, everyone was quiet for a moment. She got the impression they were each rolling over the possibilities in their minds.

"I don't understand why the book threw you into such a panic," Naomi told her. "You haven't explained much about it, and since you work with old books every day, it doesn't make a lot of sense. It's an old Bible. Big deal."

"I get it." This came from Riah, who until now had listened to her fragmented story quietly.

Tory looked away from Naomi and over to Riah. "I thought you might."

"It was your mother's"

Tory nodded. "Yes. Unfortunately, that's only a tiny part of it. About two hundred years ago, give or take, a lovely Episcopal minister befriended me at a time I was ready to have it all end. He became like a father to me, and when he died, I buried that book with him. I had to do something for him, and to leave my mother's New Testament with him seemed only right."

Riah seemed to be following. "That was in New Orleans, wasn't it?"

Tory nodded again. "He was buried in a crypt in one of the oldest cemeteries in the city. Just leaving it with him made me feel a little bit better. His death never should have happened. It was one hundred percent my fault."

"You didn't kill him, did you?" Riah was giving her a puzzled look.

Tory was actually shocked Riah would think that. She loved

Roland and even on her darkest days never would have hurt him. Never. "Absolutely not. It was Pierre. He killed Roland because he was important to me. It was the ultimate way to punish me. It worked. God, how it worked."

Even now so many years later the pain was sharp in her heart. From the day she was born her life had been one long sea of movement from house to house. Good-intentioned, it was designed to keep her safe, and though it did keep her alive, the feeling of isolation was her constant companion. Then she was turned and the nomadic nature of her life ratcheted up another notch, until she freed herself from Pierre and met Roland. Finally, she had a real home and a real family.

"Pierre?" Adriana asked. "Who was this Pierre guy?"

"My maker." One thing about this group, those two words were all the explanation they needed.

"I'm so sorry." Naomi touched her hand.

"If he'd just killed Roland it would have been a terrible tragedy I'd have learned to deal with. But that wasn't good enough for Pierre. It didn't hurt me quite enough. No, he took it further and turned Roland, leaving him for me to find. He knew I'd be forced to do the unthinkable. I destroyed Roland and left him sealed in that crypt, the New Testament on his chest. I hoped it would send his soul to heaven where it rightfully belonged. It was all I could do for him. I thought he'd be safe forever."

Colin spoke up at last. "But Hurricane Katrina dredged up all kinds of things. Nothing and no one was safe from that hell-born storm."

She closed her eyes and images of the hurricane that destroyed the city she loved flashed through her mind. Water, destruction, heartbreak. "True, but it wasn't the hurricane that brought the book to me."

"What or who do you think it was?" Naomi rubbed her shoulder lightly.

She thought about what Viola had told her. The words had chilled her soul, only to be replaced a few minutes later when the embers of a fire ignited almost a century earlier took flame. She saw the crypt as it had been that night—strong, beautiful, solid. She imagined the destruction created by one with the power of an immortal.

"I don't think, I know. Pierre Babineau."

❖

He had to hand it to the DC police, they were certainly Johnny-on-the-spot. His perfect gifts were barely cold by the time the police were there with their yellow tape and evidence bags. With lights on tripods illuminating the bodies, it was like his work was center stage for all to see. No one would ever accuse him of understatement.

Leaning against a nearby building, he blended in with the curious crowd. What was more fun than watching them scurry around like busy little ants and feeling the tension ripple through the night? It was on every corner and down every street, out in the open and behind locked doors. The line between the human and preternatural communities was growing more solid and defined with every passing hour, thanks to him.

In this city where diplomacy and cooperation were a hallmark, coexistence had been not only tolerated but embraced. The capital wanted to be seen as the example of peaceful coexistence for the country, and perhaps the world, to follow. What a load of crap. In his mind, the need to all get along was unnecessary and so he was changing that all by his little self. The early returns pleased him. How he loved to stir the pot.

Actually, it wasn't quite correct to say he was doing it alone. If not for his precious flower, his beloved Victoria, he wouldn't be here at all. She had set everything in motion, and to be honest he still didn't get it or, more accurately, her. He'd given her everything he'd had, including the most important of all: love. She'd turned her back on all of it, including his love, and tried to destroy him in the bargain. Talk about an ungrateful bitch. He'd had such high hopes for her.

In her defense, the rich and powerful had been after her soul from the moment of her birth. Until the night she received the gift, she'd had to hide who she was for fear someone would take her life. Her true identity was always shrouded in secrecy, and she never got to be the princess she should have been. With immortality, no one could threaten her with death again, but it had left her alone and lonely.

He was the one to change all that. He shared his home with her, even gave her a family of sorts, and was totally devoted to her. He'd been there for her through thick and thin, yet how did she show her gratitude for all he'd done and the sacrifices he'd made? She'd tried to destroy him and then she ran without ever looking back. Some kind of princess she turned out to be. He'd been fooled by her pretty face and big words. Behind it all was a coward who took the first opportunity she had to race away.

Well, she wouldn't be running this time. It had taken him too long to track her down, and she owed him for all the wasted years. Her crimes would not go unpunished. They could have ruled the world together and he'd have treated her like the princess she was. Instead, he'd nearly lost everything and she'd hidden herself away pretending to be someone she wasn't.

Working for a stuffy depository of old books? What kind of life was that? It was beneath her. Surely she couldn't have changed that much since he'd seen her last. It didn't matter. She'd either take her punishment and they'd move forward…or not. Having witnessed her stubborn streak more than a time or two, he was putting his money on the not.

"What's happened?"

He didn't notice the young woman until she spoke. She stood next to him, her hands stuck in the pockets of her tight jeans, her long hair hanging free around her face. "Vampire kills," he said conspiratorially, as if he possessed inside information—which of course he did.

Her intake of breath was sharp, frightened. "Again?"

He suppressed a smile and shook his head. He hoped his expression was suitably somber. "It's terrible. I swear the vamps are taking this city over, and the stupid cops can't seem to do a thing to stop it. None of it's right. I don't know what we'll do if the police can't protect us."

He felt her shiver as she crossed her arms over her chest. "This is all so terrible. Can't even take a walk in your own neighborhood lately."

Looking around, he realized the young woman was alone. Not a beauty by any stretch, but she was cute in a bookish kind of way. Her light-brown hair was long and whipped around by a light breeze. She wore nice jeans and one of those hideous hoodie things that all the young people seemed to favor in this decade. Still, she had a freshness about her that he liked, and her clothes, while young and trendy, were definitely expensive, as was the carefree cut to her long hair. All in all, potentially a very nice dinner.

"What's your name?"

She cocked her head and studied him with chocolate-colored eyes. "Meagan," she offered timidly.

He smiled and put a hand lightly on her arm. "Well, Meagan, I don't think this is a good night for a pretty young woman like you to be out all alone. May I walk you home or to wherever you're heading? I'll make sure you get there safely."

She hesitated for only for a moment and then took his arm. The warmth of her hand flowed through the cloth of his shirt. "Okay, I'd like that. It doesn't feel very safe out here tonight. I don't know what I was thinking when I walked down to the market."

"No worries. I'm here now and you're safe with me. Which way?"

"Just on the other side of Embassy Row."

Patting her hand, he started to walk. "Then let us be on our way. The sooner we get you behind locked doors, the better."

As they moved away from the police tape, flashing lights, and crowds, he pulled her a little closer to his body. She smelled good. A light, fresh fragrance that only the young could pull off. He hoped she tasted as good as she smelled.

"You didn't tell me your name," she said when they were a couple of blocks from the crime scene.

He smiled again, this time allowing just the tips of his canines to show. "You can call me Vlad."

❖

Colin, Riah, Adriana, and Ivy were clustered around the table with a laptop booted up. Naomi wasn't sure what they were searching for, but all four heads were tilted toward the bright, small screen. Tory had walked out to the patio off the living room and stood breathing in the air washed fresh and clear by the rain of a passing storm. The motion light mounted on the back of the house glowed, bathing Tory in buttery yellow light and making raindrops sparkle like a thousand diamonds tossed across the deck.

Naomi hesitated, figuring she should join the four at the table but wanting more urgently to go outside. When her hand had touched Tory's earlier, everything inside her shivered. It was almost like touching an exposed electrical wire. The last time she'd felt something like that was with Hannah.

God, how she hated thinking about Hannah. Every emotion it brought up was extreme, the memories painful. Losing someone like that was never easy. She blamed only herself for what happened. She understood completely why they could no longer be together and, painful as it had been, had let Hannah go without a fight. She never looked back because every time she did, she saw that look on Hannah's face and it broke her heart all over again.

To feel the same kind of attraction toward another woman now was not just stupid, it was impossible. Tory was a vampire but that wasn't the real issue. Regardless of how exciting it felt to be around her, the rush meant nothing because nothing could come of it. She would not put herself in a position of vulnerability. Coward that she was, Naomi never wanted to feel that kind of hurt again.

She stood in the living room watching Tory through the open door and listening halfheartedly to the conversation at the table. The chatter faded as she riveted her attention on the woman outside. Even from the back, Tory was hot. She was a small woman, not much taller than five feet, with long auburn hair that Naomi could almost feel running through her fingers. Her hips were slim, her waist small. How easy it would be to wrap her arms around that tiny body and pull her close.

When she noticed Tory's shoulders begin to shake, Naomi moved. All her resolve to stay neutral went out the window…or the patio door in this case. She was at Tory's side in a moment. "How can I help you? Tell me what I can do."

Tory turned, her expression so shattered that Naomi reacted on pure instinct. She put her arms around Tory and pulled her close. Her head rested against Naomi's breasts and her tears soaked into her shirt. Naomi wove her fingers through hair just as soft as she'd imagined.

"I'm sorry," Tory muttered when her tears subsided.

"Don't be." She continued to run hand over the glossy hair. With every stroke, her heart raced.

Tory stepped out of her embrace and gave her a wry smile. "I really am sorry. Tears for a troubled homeless woman."

"Your friend was killed."

Tears welled again. "It isn't fair. Belle never hurt a soul. Why would anyone, human or otherwise, want to hurt her? What kind of sonofabitch would kill a harmless, troubled woman?"

"Stupid as it sounds, life is rarely fair."

This time Tory laughed. "Stupid as this sounds, I actually learned that by the time I was about five years old. Fair never entered into the equation where my life was concerned."

Naomi gave her a crooked smile, grateful for the laughter that seemed to have lifted Tory's mood away from despair. "Sucks to be you."

Without warning, Tory took one of Naomi's hands and brought it to her lips for a kiss at the center of her palm. The sensation sent the electricity shooting right through her again. Keeping that never,

ever resolution wasn't going to be easy when it came to this woman. Vampire, she reminded herself, vampire.

"Yes, it does!" She pushed stray hairs off her face and squared her shoulders. "Enough with the pity party. It's not going to accomplish a damn thing or change anything. Instead of standing out here and watching me cry like a ten-year-old, let's go see if the others can use our help."

Raindrops began once more, falling gently around them. Naomi barely noticed her hair and clothes growing damp. All she could think about was how beautiful Tory looked in the rain. What was happening to her?

With effort, she found her voice, hoping she sounded calmer than she felt. "Okay, we can do that if you're sure you're ready for it." She hated to leave the intimacy of the patio. She liked being here with Tory and wished they could stay here together just a few minutes longer. What could it really hurt? Except with no good excuse to stay outside besides the fact she just wanted to be alone with Tory, they probably should go in and help. She started for the French doors that separated the patio from the living room.

"Naomi?"

She paused with her hand on the doorknob and looked back at Tory, who was a step or so behind her. Their eyes met and again that warm feeling flowed through her body. "Yeah?"

"Thank you."

CHAPTER TEN

The call came a little after three with a jarring ring that put everyone even more on edge than they already were. Naomi slowly replaced the handset and turned to look at her guests. Her heart was as heavy as her guilt. Nathan's warnings rang in her ears. So did his "I told you so."

"It's started."

She was pretty sure the look of dismay on the faces turned her direction mirrored the one on her face. At the moment, her faith was wavering, which was almost as bad as the news delivered by the phone call. Over the last few years she'd been confident her faith was solid and unshakeable. Apparently the universe was sending her another *wake up, sister* call because at the moment she felt anything but solid and unshakeable.

With less than two hours of daylight remaining, they mutually decided that Riah, Ivy, and Tory would stay at the house while Naomi, Adriana, and Colin headed to the Mall. Nathan was already on his way.

Tory resisted at first. Not that she wanted to make the trip to the Mall with them. No, she argued to go home. She wasn't buying their argument that she needed to stay at Naomi's for her own safety, at least until Riah stepped in and convinced her it was a good idea. Naomi understood all too well the power family could have, and in this case, it was family that made the difference. Naomi was glad Tory agreed to remain for more than one reason.

Right now, though, they needed to haul ass over to the Mall. She shuddered to think what they might find, or who they might find. Becoming an unofficial ambassador to the preternatural community had evolved slowly yet, at the same time, solidly. Despite her own violent past, she was the trusted confidant of those who lived on the fringe through no fault of their own. People might think they'd asked for what happened to them, and they'd be wrong. No one that she was acquainted with came into their preternatural state by choice. They were either born with it or cursed with it. The only choice afterward? Accept it or die. She had a great deal of respect for those who accepted it and moved forward.

Through the years, they came to her for advice and even protection. She never said no and did everything in her power to help them. For too long she'd killed vampires, and others, without ever thinking about what had turned them in the first place or why. She'd been filled with blind prejudice that drove her to destroy over and over again without a flicker of conscience. Even after all this time, thinking back on how utterly closed-minded and filled with hate she'd been brought a flush of embarrassment to her cheeks. Not exactly the golden era of her life. More shaming than even that was how forgiving many in the preternatural community were. While she'd been out there blindly wielding her sword in the name of righteousness, and despite all the blood on her hands, they forgave her a mistaken past and accepted her for the woman she was today.

It wasn't as easy for her to forgive herself. She tried her best to make amends because not all that she destroyed were bad. Certainly some were evil and never should have walked the earth. It was those whose souls hadn't been consumed by darkness that she regretted.

So where had she been tonight when one needed her protection? Thinking about how she'd like to run her hands all over Tory's naked body, that's where. She should have been concentrating on the ones who needed her, and instead she was thinking about herself. She'd failed yet again. Maybe she was one of those tragic souls doomed to repeat her mistakes over and over.

As they turned the corner, the street was bare except for the police cars and emergency vehicles that lined one side of the Mall, their collective lights flashing blue and red. Parking wasn't difficult at this time of day, and it sure wasn't hard to spot the heart of the problem. Her stomach rolled the closer they came to the yards of yellow police tape stretched from tree to tree.

"Sorry, folks." A uniformed officer held up a hand to block them from moving forward. "You need to turn around and go back to your car."

"They're okay, Finn, they're with me." Nathan held up the tape so that the three of them could step beneath it. "It's not pretty," he said quietly as they walked toward powerful lights set up near a particularly large tree. The lights behind the branches sent eerie shadows stretching across the grass.

When she was close enough to see, Naomi's breath caught. She recognized the face despite the gore and matted hair. Stretched out on his back, one arm was thrown wide, the hand dark with dried blood. His other arm was wrenched at an odd angle beneath his body. The heavy odor of blood hung in the air.

She stared down at the crimson-stained hand and thought of the beauty it had created in life. Of the vase that she'd so recently saved from a crash to her living-room floor. No more would that hand coax a mound of wet clay into a gorgeous work of art. Never again would she look down from the pulpit to see his head bowed and his beautiful hands clasped together in prayer. Darin Reed was dead and her heart hurt. Tears burned at her eyes and she blinked hard to keep them back. Not here. Not now. Time enough later for weeping.

"I know him," she whispered, still blinking hard against the tears that didn't want to be held back. "I just saw him, talked to him." She could see him in her head as he'd stood in the courtyard, tapping his chest and talking of death. She could see his expressive eyes and how they gazed at her with such truth in them. Just the thought of never seeing them look at her that way again made her want to retch.

"What is he?" Nathan was just as quiet, his lips close to her ear.

"A man," she said, and then quietly so that only Nathan could hear. "A werewolf."

"Why did they do it?" Colin asked of no one in particular. His eyes appraising, he studied the scene, his gaze sweeping over the acres of grass and trees that defined the National Mall. The look on his face was neutral, but Naomi had the feeling emotion ran deep nonetheless. He didn't know Darin, and yet she sensed he was taking this murder as personally as she was.

Why would the good and proper citizens of this glorious city kill him? Her words were bitter. "Because he was different. No one can tolerate being different, even in this age of enlightenment." In this time of knowledge and understanding it seemed insane that prejudice still existed, and yet it did. Horribly so as evidenced by the lifeless body of her friend. Being different was still a crime in the minds of far too many people.

"No," Nathan snapped. "That's bullshit. This happened because he was a killer, not because he was different. Stop being so damn blind." Nathan didn't even try to be sympathetic.

Her words were just as snappy as she stepped away from him. Sometimes his refusal to open his mind was beyond infuriating. "I was blind before but my eyes are wide open now. I'm telling you straight up, Nathan. Darin never hurt a living soul. He wasn't a killer and he didn't deserve to die like this. Whoever did this is more a murderer than anyone I counsel, bar none."

Nathan didn't give an inch. He stood glaring at her, his hands on his hips, his jacket flaring out in the breeze to reveal the ever-present gun at his waist. "You still have blinders on, sister. Ever since you were reborn, you've walked through this city wearing pitch-black shades. That," he pointed to Darin's lifeless body, "is an unnatural thing. Maybe he didn't deserve to be murdered and dumped on the Mall, but at the same time, he shouldn't have been here at all."

How could they be twins and yet be polar opposites in what they believed? "Nathan, that's a crock and you know it."

His dark eyes were hard. "Is it? Don't kid yourself. This is just the beginning. It's going to get a lot worse out here before it gets better. It's going to be open season on preternaturals and you're foolish if you think different. This guy won't be the last one we scrape off the ground."

"Unfortunately, he's right, Naomi," Colin said as he put a hand on her shoulder. She resisted the urge to shrug it off. Who was he to jump over to Nathan's side of the fence? She'd called him in to help *her*, not join the good-old-boys club.

"No, he's wrong. Darin had just as much right to be here as you or me." She couldn't stop trembling, though she wasn't sure if it was from the anger or the sadness. Why didn't they see, they were all in this world together…humans and preternaturals? They had to find a way to live in harmony.

"That's not what I meant," Colin said. "Nathan's right about the fact that it's just getting started. This murder is only the first. It *is* going to be open season before the next sunset."

"Fucking A," Nathan said. "Listen to your buddy here. At least he has a clue, which is more than I can say for my own flesh and blood."

"Not helping," Adriana said softly as she took Nathan's arm and turned him away from his sister. He didn't seem overly happy at Adriana's intervention but walked away with her sullenly, without saying anything else.

"Sometimes…" Naomi's eyes filled with tears. "He can be such an asshole." She was glad Nathan wasn't close enough to see that he'd made her cry. When they were kids, he'd taken perverse pleasure in doing just that. Fortunately, he'd matured a lot and it wasn't quite the game it used to be. Though she was sure it wasn't his intent to make her cry now, she still didn't want to let him see she was even close to tears. She was stronger than that, and all she needed was a minute or so to pull it all back together.

"Can't we all?" Colin raised an eyebrow. "And it's always worse when they're as close to us as, oh, say, a brother."

Her laugh was brittle and uncomfortably close to hysteria. "Yeah, I suppose so, and nobody can push buttons quite like a twin."

"Look." Colin turned her away from the grisly sight of her murdered friend. "Let's head back to your house and see what we can brainstorm. Even if we can't stop the shit storm that's coming this way, maybe we can keep it from hitting with tornado force. Between all of us, we should be able to come up with something helpful."

She nodded and began to walk in the direction of their car. "It's an idea." Not a bad one either. It wasn't serving any useful purpose to stand here and trade barbs with Nathan. Let him do his job and she'd do hers, though it would be a whole lot better if they could actually work on the same side. The ground they could cover together would be so much more if only he would give her and her friends a chance. She knew him well enough to know it wasn't even worth asking.

Adriana caught up with her and Colin, and the three of them continued in silence. A thousand thoughts were rolling through her head, and so far not a single one seemed to catch. Somewhere in the whirlwind was an answer, she hoped.

Nathan came running up to her just as Naomi reached for the car-door handle. "Wait," he said, his hand on her shoulder.

She shook it off. "What now? More indictments on my congregation? More reasons why we should just hang them all and get it over?"

"Meme, I'm sorry." He didn't sound very sorry.

She whirled. "Go away, Nat. You and I are never going to agree on this, so don't even try. This isn't the time or the place." She was going to see Darin's corpse in her head for a long, long time. She didn't need any more stress.

"I'm just doing my job the best I know how." He almost whined, or so it seemed to her, although whining wasn't exactly something he did, ever.

"Your job is to serve and protect *everyone*, not just humans. You don't get to choose."

"I'm trying, Meme, it's just that it's so goddam complicated. Even you have to understand that."

"No, I don't. Everything's complicated, so try harder." She got in the car and slammed the door, her face forward as if he wasn't standing right outside her window.

Adriana reached up from the backseat to pat her shoulder. "Give him a break, Naomi. He's not a bad guy."

"You don't even know him," she shot back.

Her snap didn't seem to faze Adriana. "Ah, honey, I grew up with three brothers who lived right next door. I spent so much time with them, it was almost as if they were my own siblings. Bottom line, I know all about guys. Sometimes they're just plain slow on the uptake, and they're all a pain in the ass most of the time."

"Hey." Colin cut in as he turned to glare at Adriana. "I resent that."

"Nothing personal, sugar," Adriana told him as she patted his shoulder. "But it is what it is, especially when it comes to brothers."

"Humph." He turned back around to stare out the windshield.

Adriana gave Naomi a wink and then settled back against the car seat. Feeling better, Naomi put the car into gear and turned it toward home.

❖

He wasn't happy. After all his fine work, she failed to show up to see. True, he was pleased with the most current result of his assault on this nation's fine capital. An uneasy vibe rippled on every street corner, and people moved about, all the while glancing over their shoulders. Exactly what he'd been aiming for.

Inside Meagan's Mercedes, he watched as people stopped, gawked, and then went on their way. The police were somber and, if he did say so, twitchy. He liked that. He enjoyed the way it made everyone so nervous they scurried about like frightened puppies. Too bad they didn't know what they were looking for or running from.

The dark-tinted windows of the expensive car made it easy for him to study the crowd without being noticed. That and it kept the sun off his skin. Once the sunlight hadn't bothered him. Of course, that was before he'd been locked away and deprived of the very thing that gave him immortal life. He was well on his way to being his new and improved self, but it was still a fair way off. It was going to take a lot more life-giving blood before he could walk in the sunlight again and not feel it burn into his skin. But he was patient. It was only a matter of time before he became the kind of vampire who could walk in both day and night.

He turned his attention back to the activity outside. Where was she? By now she had to have guessed it was all a message to her. He couldn't have made it any clearer if he tried. The book alone should have brought her racing back to New Orleans. Was she getting daft in her old age? Who else did she think would even know the book belonged to her? Everyone else with that knowledge was long gone.

In the backseat, Meagan sprawled, dead—but only for a few more hours. He grimaced and wondered if it was such a good idea to turn her. She was just so cute and, best of all, willing. Reminded him of a great mutt—appealing, though no show dog, and always eager to please. After they'd met on the street, he'd taken her along for a late-night party, fully intending to kill her. The minute she'd wrapped her lips around his cock, he'd changed his mind. Her mouth was absolute magic. So, instead of killing her, he'd given her the most precious thing he had to give.

Now, her shirt gaped, revealing a luscious full breast. He smiled. Yes, it was right to keep her as a pet. He'd been alone since Victoria left him for dead all those years ago, and he knew in his heart that he was never meant to travel the earth alone. True, he was a vampire, which put him above mere mortals. He was also a man and all men had needs. He ran a hand over Meagan's breast and then turned back to study the activity on the Mall.

The dawn was just beginning to break overhead by the time the District police finished scurrying about. The yellow tape came down, the emergency vehicles cleared, and the last of the law-enforcement responding brigade got in their cars and drove away. All traces of the handsome werewolf he'd spent a few hours enjoying were gone. Pity, the werewolf had been a good-looking sort and a fair amount of fun too. But one pet was plenty, and his latest lay in the backseat.

He yawned and ran both hands through his hair. The truth was hard to ignore and he didn't have time to be foolish about it anyway.

Daylight was approaching very quickly, and she wasn't going to show no matter how long he sat here. Might as well get poor little Meagan back to the bedroom where she could turn in dim-lighted comfort.

He could grab a little rest until nightfall and be ready for more fun and games with Meagan before he went on the hunt for his princess again. He reached back, ran a hand across her breast one more time, and then faced forward again. Slowly, so as not to attract unwanted attention, he put the car in drive and left the Mall.

❖

Weariness lay heavy on his shoulders and Colin fought a losing battle to keep his eyes open. For over twenty-four hours he'd been up and on high alert. Now he was feeling not just every hour of it but every last minute. His reserve of energy had finally run out and his tank was dry. Timing-wise, it was okay. After all, none of them could do much until nightfall. Continuing to hang out here sort of awake wouldn't accomplish anything constructive.

For the last hour he'd been in the kitchen inhaling coffee like a drunken sailor, and while it worked for a while, it wasn't doing a very good job any longer in terms of keeping him awake. His mind might want to keep going but his body had other ideas. Actually, the mind wasn't all that sharp either. Trying to keep a solid train of thought was getting more difficult by the moment. Time to get some sleep.

He and Naomi had hashed out all they could for the time being and polished off a full pot of java in the process. Sliding off the stool, he left her sitting at the counter with her hands wrapped around a mug and staring thoughtfully out the window. Truthfully, she needed sleep as bad as he did, but she didn't seem inclined that way. She was a big girl and, like him, this wasn't her first rodeo. She'd sleep when she was ready. He, on the other hand, headed out for a firm bed, soft pillow, and beautiful partner.

The bedroom was dark and silent when he slipped inside and closed the door behind him. Ivy was stretched out on the bed, not breathing and not moving. At first seeing her like that had freaked him out. It brought back memories he didn't want to possess.

That terrible night in the Spokane morgue when Ivy'd been helping to fight a nasty band of vampires on a rampage to destroy Riah, she'd already been his lover. Until the moment the wooden stake she'd used to kill one of the vampires pierced her body as well, he hadn't realized she was more than a bedmate. He loved her and would do anything to protect her. In that moment, it had seemed so simple. All Riah needed to do to save the woman he loved was to share her blood and turn Ivy into a vampire.

Riah hadn't wanted to do it. She'd been "clean and sober" for more than two centuries, and talking her into abandoning that resolution hadn't been easy. He'd wanted to shake her, scream at her, whatever it took to make her see it was the only way. Ivy was her friend too, and he didn't understand how she could stand by and let her perish. Not before or since had he been so blindingly desperate to make something happen.

Thank God, Colin and Adriana were able to make Riah see the bigger picture. It had nothing to do with taking human blood or turning an unwilling victim into a creature of the night. No, it had everything to do with saving the life of her friend and his lover. He'd never been as grateful as he'd been the moment Riah touched her own blood to Ivy's lips.

Even then he'd waited miserably for hours—until the next nightfall—before he was sure she was still with him. He was not likely to forget the feeling of relief the second he first saw her move again.

Still, it wasn't as though she was the same woman he'd fallen in love with. She was the same heart and soul, the same beautiful woman with the jet-black hair and dark, sexy eyes, the same hot, passionate lover. The difference? This woman spent her existence in the nighttime shadows and required blood to survive. And she didn't breathe when she slept. Freaky.

Of course, by now, he was accustomed to the strangeness of sharing his life with a vampire. His own world was so radically different from anything he'd imagined. When he'd come face-to-face with Ivy and her good friend, the vampire, Dr. Riah Preston, he'd been one hundred and ten percent convinced that all vampires were evil. His entire life to that point had been spent wiping every last one of them from the face of the earth. He'd come awful damn close to making it happen too. He'd been the best at his job.

It had only taken one gorgeous Hispanic coroner, one spunky and brilliant black scientist, and one five-hundred-year-old vampire about a week to change his mind.

It had also changed his life. He hung up his sword—so to speak— and began fighting evil in a completely different way. He and Naomi had hunted side by side for a good many years until a traumatic hunt changed her forever. She'd walked away and turned instead to the calling of the church as a lay minister. He'd never understood her decision, not that he'd ever tried very hard. At the time, he thought she'd simply lost her nerve and taken the coward's way out. Hunters did not walk away from the calling, the church, or the hunt. Wrong was only one word to describe what he'd been back then.

To say he got it now was an understatement. The world he'd grown up in was elemental in its embrace of black and white. He'd believed it so completely, it was all but carved in his heart. They were good, vampires were evil. Simple and easy for even the dullest to understand. Hell, if he'd been into ink, he'd have had it tattooed on his ass.

Until he met Ivy. Through her, he came to discover so many amazing shades of gray. He'd never been happier and he was eternally grateful he'd forgone that tattoo.

Colin stripped down to his boxers and lay next to Ivy on the big bed. Even though she didn't move, having her at his side never failed to relax him. She was with him spiritually even if not quite physically, and that was all he needed. The weariness that had pounded him down eased away, and he drifted into sleep easily and quickly.

Consciousness came back like a slow fog lifting over the river. Fuzzy at first, he felt a wonderful warmth seep into his body. As the fog cleared, he smiled. He knew the source of that warmth and never tired of it.

He touched Ivy's silky hair. "Hello," he murmured.

Her head on his chest, she continued to hold him in her hand, coaxing him into hardness. "Sorry I woke you."

His smile grew. He wasn't sorry at all. "Sure you are."

Ivy rolled on top of him. "I know you need your sleep. A hard-working man like you wants his rest so he can be big and strong to fight demons."

Her bare breasts were pressed against his chest and her hips moved suggestively. He didn't really know what heaven would be like, though he didn't think anything could top the touch of her skin against his. Even if God turned him away on Judgment Day, he'd always know that he'd been given a glimpse at heaven when his life was joined with Ivy's.

He turned his head and glanced at the bedside clock. "Well, I got a sweet five hours. Now I'm good as gold."

"Hard as gold too."

He kissed her, his tongue seeking hers. He loved the way she tasted and the way her soft body pressed into him. Her silky hair smelled sweet. "Have I mentioned that I love you?"

"Once, maybe, but it was so long ago perhaps you should tell me again." She kissed his ear, then traced her tongue down his neck.

He ran his hand up and down her back. "I love you."

CHAPTER ELEVEN

Tory came into consciousness with a snap. She shot straight up, her eyes wild, her hands shaking. Where was she? It came to her slowly along with recognition of the sounds and smells. Naomi's house. She sank back on the bed and let out a long breath. Nothing like being a little jumpy.

A door opened with a quiet creak and Naomi stepped into the bedroom from the bathroom. A towel was wrapped around her head and a second around her naked body. Steam followed her out the door, making the room smell of lilac soap and sweet shampoo. The polite thing to do was look away. She couldn't and didn't.

"Oh, I'm sorry." Naomi stopped and clasped her arms around herself. "I thought I could sneak in and out before you woke up. I'm really sorry about disturbing you. I was trying to be quiet."

Tory rolled onto her side and propped her head on one hand. "Please, this is your room, I'm in your way. Do whatever you need to." *Like drop the towel.*

"I just needed to shower and change." The towel didn't drop.

"Well, you certainly look clean and shiny." And delicious. Tory tried to remember the last time she'd really looked at a woman. It had been years, lots of them, like decades lots of them. Even back then, she hadn't allowed herself to feel anything beyond pleasure. Her relationships with lovers were always quick, and not a single one ever knew what she was. Safer for everyone that way.

Whoa…she was jumping ahead of herself just because a sexy, almost-naked woman was standing in front of her. That didn't make her desperate. Anyone would be thinking along the same lines. With a hint of moisture clinging to the swell of Naomi's breasts at the towel line, and her long legs shapely and strong, it was a given that her mind would jump to passion or, rather, sex. In her rather odd existence there wasn't any room for passion. A quick screw now and again, yeah. But anything beyond raw sex that might require an investment on her part? Not a chance. The formula worked for her and she saw no reason to change a thing. Still, Naomi was pretty hot in that towel.

It took a minute to realize Naomi was studying her. "What?" she asked as she swung her feet to the floor.

Naomi shook her head. "I don't know. There's something sad about you, Tory. I don't know what it is or why, but it makes me feel like I should do something. I don't know exactly what that might be, just something."

Tory smiled though she felt no humor. "Sad doesn't even begin to describe me. I'm your worst nightmare, as well you should know. You hunted things like me for a living. You know what we are, what I am."

Naomi, still holding the towel, sat next to her. She smelled fresh and lovely. Tory clasped her hands together in her lap.

"I know what you can be and I know what you are. There are two roads, Tory, and each of us chooses which one to take. Even for those like you, the path isn't set in stone. You didn't let it destroy you."

Again her laugh was bitter. "I didn't? I exist because I'm too scared to let someone like you take my head. I creep around in the darkness because it's more comfortable than having to face the reality of what I am. It would probably be better for all of us if I stepped out of the darkness and let karma do its job."

Naomi put an arm around her shoulders. Her skin was warm, the pressure of her body against Tory's almost unbearable in its tenderness. Her nearly bare breast pressed against the flesh of Tory's arm.

"No," Naomi said softly. "You don't deserve to die. You're right, I did spend a good many years tracking down and killing vampires, and I did it with blind determination. I didn't know any better then. I do now. I know what's right and what's wrong. I know who's evil and who's not."

Tears started to form in Tory's eyes. She got up and moved away from Naomi. "Maybe you've spent too much time in your church and not enough back out in the real world. A monster is a monster, and wanting to believe it different doesn't make it so."

"Maybe you're the one who's spent too much time behind closed walls."

At the door, Tory stopped and gazed at Naomi for a long moment. She was so beautiful. "I don't think so."

She opened the door, walked out into the hallway, and then closed it softly behind her.

❖

His plans for the evening weren't particularly ambitious until he spotted *her*. She slipped into the rear entrance at the Library of Congress, a tall man following close behind. Just the sight of her sent a shot of electricity through his body. She was as beautiful as the first moment he'd laid eyes on her. Still graceful and lovely, still walked with the same determined stride that had caught his attention on the very first day. He'd been so impressed all those years ago by the young woman with the incredible grace that he'd been driven to know more.

He'd done a bit of homework to find out who she was, and it had taken a fair amount of digging even for an experienced researcher. Her entire existence was shrouded in mystery, deep and almost impenetrable—almost. People talked to him, always had. He was just that kind of man. He'd dug and probed until he learned what he'd wanted to know.

He'd been struck first by her beauty, overwhelmed by her pedigree, and impressed by her heart. One beautiful summer evening, he'd introduced himself. She became part of his world and he'd loved her as his own. He believed she loved him too, until that dreadful night anyway, when he became a victim.

What she'd done still cut at him. How she could have betrayed him so completely was beyond his comprehension. Yet, that's exactly what she'd done and forgiveness was not in the cards…ever. She had to pay. He would never be able to reconcile with being a victim.

Besides, he wasn't the one who set any of this in motion. The responsibility for all of it lay squarely on her shoulders—action and reaction, cause and effect. He was simply doing what needed to be done in a very entertaining way. Who was he to deny fate?

He had to be careful tonight, however. The ripples on the night air spoke to him, coaxing him to feed the fever. His body tingled all over and his mind buzzed. Smiling, he began to walk away from the Library of Congress. She could wait a little longer. The time wasn't quite right yet for them to meet face-to-face, and he wasn't ready to let go of the fun.

In the meantime, humans were all around to toy with, meals to be enjoyed and havoc to create. His little Meagan was waiting patiently for her first meal, and he didn't want to disappoint her. Hunting was more challenging thanks to his campaign of fear, but that just made things more fun.

His path hadn't taken him far when he spied an interesting man in one of the ubiquitous hooded sweatshirts all the young people seemed to wear these days, walking with his hands stuffed into the pockets of a well-worn pair of jeans. He smiled and leaned against a tree waiting for his prey. Yes, a very promising night indeed.

As the man drew closer, the faint scent of weed drifted on the air. He smiled. Just the kind of guy he was waiting for. "Sick hoodie, man," he said as the young man walked by.

"Thanks." His voice was muffled as he kept his head down. His step didn't slow, the weed smell now blending with the strong odor of tobacco.

Stepping into stride beside him, he smiled and asked, "Got a smoke I can bum, man? Kinda quiet and boring out here tonight. I'm Vlad, by the way."

"Jim." He offered him a cigarette and finally brought his gaze up to meet Vlad. His eyes were a deep shade of blue with pupils so large the blue was just a ring around the black. "Surprised to see ya out, ya know? Everybody's freaked out about the vamps and sticking close to home."

"Aren't you?" He lit the cigarette and took a long drag, letting the smoke flow into his lungs. Tasty.

Jim straightened up. "Fuck, no. I can take care of myself. No fucking vampire is going to suck me dry. I'll show the motherfucker who's tough."

Glancing sideways at Jim, he grinned, his fangs beginning to show. The guy was high as a kite and didn't have a grasp on the reality of where he was. Definitely not a clue who he was with. "I know what you mean, man. I feel that way too. I wouldn't mind kicking a little vampire ass."

"No shit. Figured I'd see what was out and about. I'm not gonna sit at home and play with my own dick. You feel me? I gotta find some action."

Meagan's hungry face flashed in his mind. He smiled and put an arm around Jim's shoulders. "You don't say. I bet we could find some action together. Twice as much fun."

He nodded his head and grinned, his teeth yellow and crooked. "Sick…let's do it."

❖

When her phone rang a little after midnight, Naomi was positive it had to be Tory or Colin. Earlier, they'd gone back to the LOC to grab the New Testament. One glance at the caller ID and her heart sank. Not a chance Nathan would be calling just to say hello. Did he ever sleep anymore? Sure didn't seem like it. In fact, the last few days, it seemed like all he was doing was calling her or showing up on her doorstep.

"Yeah," she said into the handset, holding it with an uncharacteristic death grip.

"You've got a big problem, sister."

"Me? Why?" The tension in Nathan's voice set her on edge. Apparently this was starting to get to him as well.

"A crowd's beginning to mingle at the church."

A crowd? It didn't make sense. "I don't understand. There's no service tonight. Nobody should be hanging around there this time of night."

"Somebody's let the cat out of the bag. The rumor running through the crowd is that the church harbors preternaturals, and now they want them brought out."

"Nathan, that's crazy. No one's at the church except the security guards. No one ever stays there, human or preternatural."

"Yeah, you know that and I know that, but about thirty or forty people are outside right now that don't, and let's just say they're starting to get restless."

Her hands began to tremble, not exactly a great trait for a big, strong vampire hunter. Maybe there was more than one reason she was an ex-vampire hunter. She could think of only one thing to do. "I'll be right there."

"Don't come alone."

"Who do you want me to bring? Nobody's around right now." Seriously, about the only other people she could call would be the bishop or another of the clergy, and chances were they'd be unavailable. This was Ordinary Time, an uneventful period in the calendar of worship, which was why during the last few weeks only Naomi and one priest had been presenting services. Last thing she heard, the bishop was in California at a clergy meeting.

"Bring the hunter."

"Colin? Are you serious?"

"As a heart attack."

She didn't know what to say to that. Nathan had never been real big on the whole hunter thing even when she was one. It wasn't that he disapproved of the ideal behind the corps of hunters the church employed. No, it was more that he liked to operate inside the normal channels when dealing with anyone, whether they were human or not. It was one of the reasons he always took issue with the hunters' style of justice.

He didn't exactly have to coax her into agreeing to take Colin along. Frankly, she'd feel better with him there. Naomi told Nathan as much, then hung up and turned to look at Ivy, Riah, and Adriana. "I've got to go." She headed for the closet to grab her jacket. "Shit is about to hit the fan."

"We'll go with you." Riah followed her. "You're not going into something dangerous without backup."

Turning, Naomi held out a hand. "No!"

Riah stopped abruptly, looking as though Naomi had slapped her. "What?"

"I'm sorry." Naomi apologized in a hurry. "I didn't mean to snap. But you really can't come with me. An angry crowd's gathering at the church and I've got to go try to talk them down."

"At the church?" Ivy piped up. "Why?"

"They think we're harboring preternaturals inside."

"That's ridiculous." This came from Adriana. "I'll go with you."

Of the three, Adriana was the only one who might be safe. Still human—aside from being born in a parallel world, that is—she would be able to move easily in the crowd searching for those who were not. Still, this was her problem, not Adriana's. The thought of putting anyone else in danger just didn't work for her. "I don't think you should."

"Bullshit," Ivy declared. "We're all going. Don't think for a second we're going to let you go into the fray alone. That's not the way we do things."

"No." Naomi insisted. "It's too dangerous. People are out for blood...particularly vampire blood. This could get out of hand very easily and I don't want anyone hurt...or worse. I've seen it happen before."

Riah and Ivy looked at each other and shook their heads. Riah slipped on her jacket and walked to the door. "I've been hunted before more times than you can imagine. I can deal with it and so can Ivy and Adriana. Now let's get on the road before someone who can't gets hurt."

Nobody seemed to listen to her. It was as if she was talking to a wall instead of a trio of intelligent women. If she couldn't convince a single one of them to stay here, how on earth was she going to persuade a crowd of angry people to disperse? She started to give it one more try but she was alone. All three of the others were already outside.

In the car, Naomi asked Ivy to call Colin. As much as Nathan could be a pain in the ass, right now she agreed with him: having another hunter to back her up was a good idea.

Kind of odd, this turn of events. In the old days, she'd be hunting the preternaturals in her quest to keep the humans safe. She would have been front and center trying to flush out vampires and any other ilk of preternatural hiding so she could put them down. Tonight, her position was a hundred and eighty degrees from that. She and Colin would be keeping the preternaturals safe from the humans.

Funny how things worked out.

It wasn't remotely funny when they arrived at the cathedral. Nathan either couldn't count very well or the crowd had grown significantly since his call. The latter was the more probable scenario, and now the number outside the front doors easily reached a hundred. Fortunately, Tory and Colin pulled in right behind them into the underground parking area. Naomi ushered the entire group into the lower-level entrance door.

Rather than taking them upstairs into the main vestry, she guided them to a room on the lower level. Better safe than sorry. The women protested when Colin and Naomi turned in the direction of the ascending stairs. Riah, Ivy, Tory, and Adriana wanted to go up with them. It wasn't a good idea. This was a battle for humans...period.

Adriana wasn't about to be left behind and Naomi wasn't going to argue with her. Despite her birth into a parallel dimension, Adriana, like Naomi, was human. From that standpoint, she was on safer ground. Naomi's main concern was that Adriana was such a little sprite of a thing, she'd be too easily hurt. How much backup could this delicate woman be? She told her as much and it didn't go over very well.

"Oh, good grief." Adriana scoffed. "I can kick ass and take names with the best of them, so don't you worry your pretty little head about me. Besides, didn't anyone tell you? I'm a kick-butt wizard. My power could come in handy. Now, come on, let's go before this gets any worse."

Colin came to Adriana's defense. "She's right, Naomi. I've seen her put down more than one. She'll be fine and her powers could come in useful. I'm not opposed to having every available weapon at the ready."

She still wasn't totally convinced. Then again, she wasn't totally opposed either. Colin had a point. Weapons came in all different sizes and shapes. "All right." She headed to the stairs. "Let's see what we can do."

CHAPTER TWELVE

Tory paced the hallway outside the small chapel where Ivy and Riah sat quietly talking. Simply sitting around and waiting wasn't working for her. Small talk was even worse, and a waste of her time and energy. She kept thinking about what Viola had shared with her—all this was happening because of her.

Well, that wasn't exactly what Viola had relayed, but the ripple effect was undeniable. If Tory hadn't been here, the crowd outside wouldn't be threatening the District, the murders wouldn't have happened, and this city would still be coexisting peacefully under its unspoken truce. The events of recent days all pointed squarely in her direction. She was the catalyst to the violence and chaos that gripped the city.

Story of her life—one catastrophe after another. It had started with her mother and continued even after they took her head. Tory's birth and survival had been a big bad secret never shared with any but a trusted few. Her presence in the lives of those who helped her was dangerous. She was a liability for anyone and everyone around her. Her family suffered because of it. Her friends died because of it. Now an entire city was reeling because of it.

Somehow it had to stop.

Walking through the darkened hallways, she felt the souls of those entombed here—Helen Keller, Anne Sullivan, Woodrow Wilson. So many others whose deeds of kindness, philanthropy, and dedication made the country, and the world, better. All in stark contrast to what Tory was bringing into this time and place. It wasn't right and it wasn't just this time and place. It was every time and every place since the day she was born. Wherever she went, danger followed and people died.

Perhaps it would be better if she finally just threw in the towel. What was the point anyway? Sure, she knew books. It wasn't like she hadn't had a few hundred years, give or take, to become a respected expert, even if she did have to change her name and identity over and over. It was a rare treat in this incarnation to actually be a version of her true self.

Expertise aside, she wasn't all that special. There was any number of rare-book experts throughout the world who could easily step into her shoes. If she wasn't around any longer, the world would simply continue without her. For that matter, who would even remember her? Special, she wasn't. No one really needed her and few would miss her.

Once upon a time, she'd felt special. Not the creepy, unnatural kind of unique created when she'd been turned. That whole master, novice thing in the vampire world didn't count. Dysfunctional was a far better descriptor for that one. No, the only time she'd really felt special, even loved, was with Roland. For almost a decade she'd caught a glimpse of what it was like to be truly loved.

It all changed again on that awful night, and her rose-colored glasses were pulled from her face and crushed. Reality rushed in and never again did she allow herself the luxury of loving another…human or vampire. It wasn't worth the pain and heartache. As long as she walked the earth, she'd never forget the look in Roland's eyes that night or how she felt in the face of his utter disappointment. Failure was hard enough to live with in a normal lifetime. When that life never ended, it was crushing.

Everything would be so much easier if she just ended it all, except she wasn't strong enough to let go of her life, such as it was. So instead of bringing her existence to an end, she hid like a little girl afraid of the bogeyman. She hit the hidey-hole jackpot here. The Library of Congress was a fantastic place to hide. Huge, with enough work to keep her busy for at least a hundred years, it was perfect for an antisocial, commitment-phobic vampire.

Unfortunately, even with all its undeniable perks, she couldn't stay more than a decade or two. Before too long, she'd have to move on. Leaving, whether she wanted to or not, was an integral part of her existence. This job, like so many before it, only marked time for her. She enjoyed the work while it lasted and then found a new name, a new place to live, and a new place to work. Moving on was what she did.

That's not what bothered her now. She just didn't appreciate being pushed. She wanted to be the one to choose when to go, but tonight it seemed that decision, like so many others in her life, was out of her hands. Others were once more directing the course of her life.

She walked down the darkened hallway until she reached yet another small chapel. Alone, she sank to the kneeling board in front of the altar, dropping her head into her hands. She had to think, had to figure out a way to stop all the madness happening outside. Naomi, Colin, and Adriana shouldn't have to bear the burden of a catastrophe started because of her.

The air was stale down here, the board beneath her knees hard despite the pad designed to make it more comfortable. It reminded her of the chapels of her youth. She'd prayed for guidance in those days, believing God would show her the way. Her hand strayed to her neck and she fingered the black pearls she always wore. The handcrafted silver and black pearl necklace was the only thing she possessed that had once belonged to her mother. Ever since she'd been a child, it gave her comfort.

At the sound of footsteps, she jerked her head up. A woman she didn't recognize walked through the open door and directly toward her. She jumped up and backed away until a wall at her back stopped her. She had no avenue of escape.

"What do you want?" Her survival instincts made her canines lengthen and her focus sharpen. A rush of adrenaline coursed through her body. She was coiled and ready to leap.

The woman stopped, her hands folded in front of her. Her dark hair was parted in the middle and pulled back into an intricately designed head-hugging cap. She wore a simple white dress that flattered her slender figure, a beaded choker from which dangled a gold filigree pendant with what looked like an emerald in the center, around her neck. "I came to talk with you, Victoria." Her voice was soft, and something in her face whispered *familiar* to Tory.

She tilted her head and studied the woman. Her skin was smooth and unlined, so white her dark eyes stood out. The way she gazed back at Tory should have bothered her, but it didn't. Her canines began to recede.

"Do I know you?"

The woman shook her head, her expression suddenly radiating melancholy. "Not really. Once, a very long time ago. You were far too young to remember."

The woman's manner of speaking was odd—too formal and very

soft, as if she was afraid to speak loudly. A little like she remembered her family—the family that had raised her far from the Tower of London, where she'd been born. "How did you know I was here?"

She inclined her head and a tiny smile turned up the corner of her mouth. Her eyes were gentle. "I just knew."

Not exactly an answer. Tory studied the stranger's face. Something...

"You look familiar," she insisted.

The woman's gaze touched on something deep inside her and she couldn't shake the feeling that, whatever it was, she should know. She didn't often forget those she met. Names maybe, but faces, never.

"I suppose I do."

"You said I don't know you."

"No, Victoria. I said you were too young to remember our meeting."

What the hell? "Can you please enlighten me? I'd absolutely remember you if we'd met before."

"Sit." She sat on one of the small pews in the tiny chapel and patted the seat beside her.

Tory hesitated. Even if the woman's presence wasn't threatening, she wasn't impressed with all the vagueness, especially right now. This was not the time for games, except, even neck-deep in the chaos around her, the woman had managed to grab her attention. She was, against her better judgment, intrigued. There *was* something about this woman she recognized at a subconscious level, and she wasn't leaving until she figured out what it was.

"Why do I know you?"

A dark cloud seemed to pass across the woman's pretty face before she said softly, "You were never given the chance to know me. Time ran out for me and you were taken away for your own safety."

Uneasiness prickled at the back of Tory's neck. "You're starting to freak me out. What do you mean we didn't have enough time together? Who the hell are you?"

She took Tory's hand in hers. Silently, she stared into her eyes and the tingle of the familiar became something much more. The enormity of the thought racing through her mind was unbelievable and, even considering everything she'd experienced in her long life, too big a stretch even for her. Still, the truth was right in front of her and denial didn't change a thing.

"Oh, my God." Realization hit like a baseball bat to the head. Her eyes were so like Tory's it was frightening, and that wasn't the end of it. "I look just like you, but how? Why? Why now?"

She inclined her head slightly, still studying Tory's face. "You needed me."

"I still don't understand. I've needed you a hundred times since I was born. You were never there, until now."

Despite her best intentions, tears started to well in her eyes. An ache began in her chest, something she believed she was long over. Time hadn't softened the pain. The reality of her life as an orphan still hurt. She had been fed, clothed, and protected, but she doubted she'd ever really been loved. Everyone had been acutely aware of the danger her presence in their lives presented, so she'd been alone until Pierre. And that didn't count.

"You needed me," she said again. "So I came."

"I always needed you." She hated the echo of a sob that sounded in her voice. Weakness was not something she ever allowed anyone to see or hear. Not even a ghost.

Again the shadow of darkness crossed the woman's face. "I'm sorry, so terribly sorry. I never meant to leave you, and if I could have stayed I would have. I didn't have a choice."

It was too much. Outside the world was fracturing; inside it was her sanity. "Are you as I am?" What other explanation could there be?

She lightly squeezed Tory's arm, her fingers warm on her skin. "No, I am as I've been since that day in the Tower of London."

"When they took your head." She was right; she appeared as young and vital as on the day she died.

The woman nodded and pressed a warm hand to Tory's cheek. Tory pressed against her hand, feeling the warmth of it to her soul. How she'd longed for this simple touch every night as she'd hidden away in her room.

"But I can feel you, hear you, even smell you."

"Yes."

"HOW?" Her voice rose and the panic in her chest almost swallowed her whole. So much for being in control. What was happening at this moment was impossible, even for her. In all her centuries of life, she'd never encountered a ghost.

"Faith." The single word seemed to be her no-questions answer. She continued before Tory could protest. "Please listen, my time is short. He is coming for you, and you must protect yourself and the ones you love."

"He? He, who? Pierre?"

"The one you gave your heart to."

A man? Not bloody likely. Not in this lifetime, or the last, or the one before that. Tory was consistent, if nothing else, and she consistently went for women. She'd never given her heart to a single man. Except...

"You can't possibly mean Roland."

"He is the one."

Well, this ghost was way off base. Tory stood up and, looking away, said out loud for the first time ever, "You don't understand. I destroyed him. No, that's not even right. I didn't just destroy him. I staked him inside a coffin and, for good measure, made sure he was bricked inside an unmarked crypt so the world would never even know his final resting place. I wiped him from the face of the earth."

❖

"This is going to get ugly fast," Nathan whispered in Naomi's ear.

Yeah, well, she'd already figured that out all by herself. Didn't take a rocket scientist to see trouble brewing at an epic level outside the front doors of the cathedral. Naomi just wasn't sure how to quell the simmering violence lurking just beneath the surface of the crowd. Naomi stood one step in front of Nathan, with Adriana and Colin right behind him. The four of them presented a small but solid wall of reason. She eyed the growing assembly warily, searching for any sign of trouble about to erupt. What to do?

A hand gently squeezed her shoulder, and when she glanced back, she was surprised to see Karen. She was in uniform and her face mirrored the worry that creased Nathan's. Naomi didn't know where she'd come from, but she was awfully glad to see her.

"We gotta do something before this gets out of hand," Karen said quietly into her ear.

"I know." She answered just as quietly. "Tell me you've got a brilliant idea."

"Don't I wish, sister."

"Not very encouraging, Karen. You pick up anything at all?" Maybe her sensitivity could give them a glimmer of an idea of how to keep this crowd from going out of control.

Karen shook her head. "These guys are way too alive for my skill set to help. The way things are going, though, it won't be long before somebody ends up in the ground, and then I can help you."

"I'd like to get this stopped before that happens."

"Back at ya. I'm not in the mood for bloodshed tonight. Too much paperwork."

How she loved this woman. Karen wasn't just a necromancer or a cop; she was a light when darkness fell all around her. If only those standing before her could find themselves touched by the magic Karen possessed. Maybe then the frightening mood could be defused.

This wasn't the first time she'd encountered displaced anger and fear. It had been a part of her life for as long as she could remember. Being different had a way of doing that. She wasn't a vampire, a werewolf, a witch, or any other being of enhanced ability. No, she was a good old-fashioned human. What set her apart was her sexuality, and that seemed to rile people up as quick as, sometimes even quicker than, the preternaturals.

That she was a lesbian bothered more than a few. Fortunately, none of them were in her family. There had been plenty everywhere else over the years, including when she was a hunter. Colin had been one of the few she'd trusted enough to be honest with. Not that he'd hit on her or anything like that. On the contrary, they'd become good friends during the years she'd carried a sword.

Others had not been as tolerant as Colin or her family. She'd been called names, shut out of organizations, made to feel something less than human. It had taken her a good many years to find balance, and she found it through God and this place. The cathedral and the church family embraced her and never made her feel anything less than what she was.

The church had rescued her when she didn't feel worthy of being rescued. She'd abandoned what she'd believed was her calling and had lost the woman she'd considered her one true love. The church had saved her and now it was her turn to pay back the favor. It was time to take a stand.

"Please." She shouted to be heard over the growl of the crowd. These were humans, yet the sounds that rippled through the air reminded her too closely of animals. It shot a shiver of fear up her spine. "Please, listen."

Someone yelled back from the crowd. "Nobody's gonna listen to you, preacher. You're protecting killers!"

"Bring them out!" screamed another, and cheers rose in the night air.

Nathan leaned close and whispered in her ear. "I think we need to wait for the special-forces folks to control this crowd. This could get violent really quick, and there's too many of them for us to hold back. We don't stand a chance."

Naomi shook her head and thought of the Book of Luke. Loudly, in order to be heard over the crowd, she began to quote, "But I say to you who hear, love your enemies, do good to those who hate you, bless those who curse you, pray for those who abuse you. To one who strikes you on the cheek, offer the other also, and from one who takes away your cloak do not withhold your tunic either. Give to everyone who begs from you, and from one who takes away your goods do not demand them back. And as you wish that others would do to you, do so to them." The rumbling in the crowd lost some of its intensity as she recited the words.

Taking heart with the change even as small as it was, she continued. "This is a place of peace, a place where all are welcome. You are welcome, all of you, but only if you enter in peace. No blood will be shed in God's house."

"We just want the killers." A deep voice rang from the fringe of the crowd. "Bring us the killers and we all go away."

"There are no killers here." Not quite the truth. Both she and Colin had taken their fair shares of lives, and the vampires in her crypt? Killers perhaps, but not in the context of tonight's chaos-embracing crowd. She doubted anyone in front of her would care about that particular distinction. They wanted blood and not of the human variety.

"You're lying," someone else screamed.

She sensed when both Colin and Nathan tensed behind her. She stepped back until she stood between them, laying a hand on the arm of each. Then she focused on the crowd once more. A low murmur erupted, though no one moved that she could tell. She sent a prayer of gratitude skyward for that.

"I give my word, you have nothing to fear from anyone in this church tonight. All of us," she waved her hand behind her to encompass everyone on the steps as well as inside the cathedral, "want to find and stop this monster just as much as you do. But I tell you again, the person, the thing, you seek, is not here."

By this time, police presence had arrived in numbers sufficient to surround the crowd, and Karen moved away to join them. Black-clad officers with dangerous-looking weapons watched the crowd with rapt attention. Naomi prayed silently the weapons trained on the people wouldn't be used. More than anything, she didn't want blood spilled, either human or preternatural, on the church grounds.

After standing motionless with her hands clasped in front of her for what seemed like hours, to her great relief, the crowd at last began to slowly and methodically disperse. It started with one or two people losing steam and gradually increased until the mob fell apart.

Mutters of unhappiness could be heard as groups of people broke apart and moved in all four directions. Fortunately, nothing more was said or done that might incite a violent reaction from either the crowd or the waiting police. A single misstep by any one of them could trigger an outpouring of violence. One werewolf had already lost his life for no good reason, and she would do anything to make sure it didn't happen to another. Darin was one casualty too many.

For nearly an hour, people slowly wandered away and the four of them stayed on the steps in front of the doors until SWAT loaded up and cleared out as well. When everyone, including Karen, was at last gone, Naomi let out a breath and turned around.

"That was close, but praise Jesus, no one was hurt."

"That was pretty fucking amazing," Nathan said, shaking his head. "I don't know how you did it. If I hadn't seen it with my own two eyes, *I* wouldn't have fucking believed it." He touched her cheek. "Always said you were more than a pretty face."

"Come to church sometime and maybe you'll get it." She squeezed his hand. "Miracles happen all the time, brother. And you bet I'm more than a pretty face."

He snorted. "Yeah, well, that's not gonna happen, sister. This shit might work for you but I'm still a bona fide skeptic. Me and church? Not in this lifetime. Now, why don't you gather your vamps and get the hell out of here before something else blows up. You're on borrowed time as it is."

Even if she wanted to pinch his head off, Nathan was right. They were tempting fate by staying here. She needed to get these people to safety and then they could figure out who—or what—was behind the murders. Sooner rather than later. Patience and calm heads won out this time. She'd be a fool to think the same thing would happen next time.

"Come on," she said to Colin and Adriana. "Let's go get the others."

CHAPTER THIRTEEN

No, no, no."
　　The crowd had pulsed with anger, poised for an incredible outburst of violence. So close to storming the Bastille. Exactly what he'd been aiming for. He'd been licking his lips, ready to embrace the charge. Then that bitch came out on the steps and talked them all down. The whole fucking crowd! Fury turned his vision red, and he had to force himself not to burst through the doors, sink his fangs into her neck, and drain her dry. Would serve the bitch right.

He would find out who she was, and when he did…she'd be done. He wasn't about to give her a second chance to thwart his finely laid plans. Too much time and effort had gone into the planning, and even after this setback, he was far from done. This was going down, one way or the other.

Unfortunately, at the moment his hands were tied. The damage was done or, rather, undone. Until the crowd dispersed there'd been real potential in its collective anger and discontent. Blood should have been pouring down the broad concrete steps, turning them from gray to crimson. At first, he'd really believed the spreading anger was strong enough to keep the crowd intact. His belief was misplaced. The city wasn't quite ready. The mood wasn't quite to the point of explosion, and that's what he needed to flush her out into the open.

Or, more precisely, to flush her out into the open…alone. She'd gone into the Library of Congress with the man who'd also come to the steps of the cathedral with the woman preacher. A hunter. And what was even worse? The woman preacher was one too. He wasn't fooled; he could smell them a mile away. There wasn't a vampire on the planet that didn't spend far too much time eluding the bastards. They were an itch he could never quite rid himself of. Every time he turned around, one was there waiting and anxious to put a stake in his chest and separate his head from his neck. Different cities, different faces, same goal: to destroy him and the few left in the world like him.

Now, here was not just one of the assholes tagging along with his one and only, but two. It wasn't just wrong, it was obscene. Vampires and hunters did not, under any circumstances, coexist. With relish, he'd done his best to obliterate as many of them as he could.

The one disturbing discovery he'd made not long after being freed from his unholy confinement was that very few vampires were left, at least that he could find. When he'd been entombed, many of his kind had roamed the earth, or so he believed. They ruled the darkness and had been free to take as they pleased.

He wasn't sure what had happened in the intervening years. He did know, though, that the number of vampires seemed to have dwindled until he could count them on one hand. There had to be more, had to be. He just needed time to seek them out.

His game now was as much to terrorize Victoria as it was to shake up the vampire world. He wanted them to come out. He wanted them to help him. It was past time for the vampires to stand tall and take what was rightfully theirs. After all, most of them had been around long before the humans who screamed in terror at their mere presence. It was their time to rule, and hunters like the dark-haired man on the church steps or the pious preacher beside him could just go straight to hell. He'd be the first in line to send them there.

As things unfolded, he'd wanted to scream at all of them. But after he took the time to really assess the situation, he had to admit that this was a minor setback. All in all, things were going along well enough. The humans were in an uproar despite tonight's retreat. They'd already taken the life of one. A little nudge here, a little push there, and things would head in the right direction. Before anyone realized what was happening, chaos would reign. It would all work out to his advantage.

The anticipation of her kneeling before him was almost too much. He'd been waiting for so long. She would be sorry for all she'd done and all she'd tried to do to him. Of course, he'd be gracious and hear out her apology. Then and only then would he even consider letting her back into his good graces. First, there'd be punishment. After all, she'd have to pay for the many years he'd lost and the time it had taken for him to recover once he'd been set free.

Yes, she'd have to pay, just not tonight.

Straightening his shoulders, he turned away from the quiet church grounds and began to walk back to his car. About time to help his pretty Meagan find a tasty snack.

❖

Naomi sensed a difference in the air the minute she reached the bottom of the stairs. Granted, the restless crowd outside had made her nervous, but whatever this was, it made her heart race. A cold breeze cut across her face, causing her to shudder. A window open somewhere? Great, that's all she needed, one more problem.

When she turned the corner into the small chapel, Colin moved quickly to Ivy's side and wrapped his arms around her. Likewise, Riah came to Adriana and put her hands on her face, staring deeply into her eyes as if making sure she was still okay.

Naomi stood alone in the doorway, shifting from foot to foot. After a moment, she turned away from the two couples and walked slowly through the passageway. The tender way they interacted with each other was too harsh a reminder of what she'd lost. Better to walk away and not dwell on what was done.

She found Tory in another of the tiny basement chapels. Sitting on a carved, wooden bench, she had her head bowed and her hands folded in her lap. Her long hair fell around her shoulders in dark, shiny waves, and her whole body shook slightly. For a second Naomi didn't understand why. When she did, she didn't hesitate.

She sank to the bench beside Tory and took her hands. "You're safe," she said quietly. For the moment anyway, though, she didn't voice that thought.

Tory pulled one hand away and swiped tears from her face. "Safety isn't what I'm worried about."

Her eyes were bright as she raised them to meet Naomi's. The look in them made Naomi's heart flutter. "What is it, then?"

"You tell her," Tory said, still gazing into Naomi's eyes.

Naomi wrinkled her brow and looked around. "Who are you talking to?"

Tory swept her gaze over the tiny room. "Where did she go?" she asked in a puzzled tone.

Naomi had no idea what Tory was talking about. They were alone. "Who? Colin? I left him down the hall with the others."

"No." Tory's voice rose. "Not Colin, my mother."

"Your mother?" What was she smoking down here in the dark?

Tory nodded, her head bobbing. "Yes."

Naomi looked around the room. No corners to hide in. No bulky furniture to hide behind. No one else in the room except the two of them. Definitely smoking something. "We're alone here, Tory, not to mention that your mother was beheaded a few hundred years go. No one survives that, human or vampire."

Tory was shaking her head adamantly. "No, no, she was here just a few minutes ago. I swear to you, Naomi, she was here. I talked to her, touched her, and her head was very attached."

Okay, this was getting a little weird and it didn't make sense. On the surface, Tory seemed like a perfectly rational vampire. Saying that her mother was here in the church wasn't just irrational. It was impossible.

Only the six of them were here tonight in the lower level, or crypt, as it was called. Stress was evidently beginning to take a toll on Tory. Not that she blamed her. It was starting to fray her nerves as well.

Taking her hand, Naomi spoke softly. "It doesn't matter, we're alone now."

Tory dropped her head on Naomi's shoulder. "I'm not crazy, Naomi, she was here."

"Honey, we're alone. Just you and me."

Tory sighed and murmured, "Sometimes I'm so tired..."

She didn't need to finish, Naomi understood. Probably better than most. Tired was one of the reasons she'd walked away from the hunt. One reason. She tried not to think about the other. This wasn't the time to dwell on her painful memories.

Right now, she intended to focus on the moment, which was a good one, all things considered. The feel of Tory's body so close to hers, and the weight of her hand on Naomi's thigh, was incredible. She wanted to wrap Tory in her arms, pull her close, and keep her safe. She was so small, and she trembled all over. She looked like a lost and fragile woman—not the powerful vampire she really was.

Tiny as she might be, appearances could be so very deceptive. Lessons from her former life came back to Naomi even in tranquil moments like this. It never paid to underestimate the power of a vampire. Tory could probably pick up Naomi and toss her across the room if she was so inclined. But this wasn't about strength or power; this was about the spirit and precisely the reason Naomi had come to the church in the first place.

Even more than spirit, it was about the comfort of another woman.

Finding peace within her soul had taken years. God knows, she'd never wanted to be different. On the contrary, she'd wanted to be the pretty, normal little girl her parents had always dreamed of. For years she'd tried to fit in with those around her. She failed on all accounts. She wasn't pretty, she wasn't little, and she sure wasn't like all the other girls. Nope, when it all shook out, she turned out to be handsome rather than pretty, tall instead of little, and a very less-than-normal vampire hunter.

Her road to acceptance turned rocky early on. This place, this church was the lifeline that ultimately saved her. Her crisis came on a dark, moonless night. Desperate and lost, she'd stumbled through those massive front doors. She'd thought it was the end and it turned out to be just the beginning. Everything changed.

Like now.

What was it about this place? Things happened to her when she walked into the cathedral. Good things.

Like Tory, in her arms.

❖

Colin left the women at the house. Daylight was less than an hour away and Ivy would need to rest. They all would, including him. Still, he couldn't ignore what was building inside and had been since they landed here. Time to buck up and face his past.

His new life was great in so many ways. Some things didn't change, like the fact that he was still hunting evil. But now he fought against dark forces with the one he loved at his side. That she was the very thing he'd dedicated his life to wiping out was an irony not lost on him—he just didn't care. All that mattered was that Ivy was with him each day and each night.

What he was going to do now had to be done alone, even as close as he was to Ivy. She'd argue and want to go with him, which was part of the reason he was going during the day when she was at rest. Less explaining to do.

A great many years had passed him by and yet he'd never gone. Now it was more than just wanting to make the walk; he needed to cross the acres of grass and confront what had changed everything. Being back here where it all started brought up emotions he'd thought long resolved or, if not resolved, at least permanently put to rest. Funny how often he was wrong these days about lots of things.

Bright sunlight washed over Rock Creek Cemetery when he stepped out of his car. A light breeze whispered through the trees, and the smell of freshly mowed grass gave a feeling of life to this place of death.

The headstones he sought were on the other side of the cemetery. He could have driven much closer. Instead, he made a conscious choice to park as far away as possible and still be on the cemetery grounds. He needed the time it took to cross the cemetery to gather his strength. Or maybe it was courage he needed to marshal.

The closer he came to the headstones, the slower his steps became. Nothing intentional about it, more a byproduct of having put this off for too long. Really, it shouldn't be a big deal, yet the nearer he came, the more he hesitated. It was as if a weight pressed down on his chest making it hard to breathe, hard to think straight. He'd had a long time to reconcile with this and would like to believe by now this would be easy.

He was a seasoned vampire hunter who traveled all over the world putting down every manner of evil. He'd seen the worst there was to see and faced it all with courage. Three headstones surrounded by lush green grass, towering trees, and flowering bushes shouldn't make his hands shake and his stomach roll.

A good five feet away from the trio of gray stones, he stopped, shoved his hands into his pockets, and closed his eyes. Tears pricked at his eyelids and it took quite a few deep breaths to back them away. Confident that his emotions were in check again, slowly he opened his eyes and looked at first one, then the second, and finally the third. His father. His mother. His sister.

Tears once more stung his eyes. So much for being in control. At least he had on sunglasses and was grateful for the dark lenses he could hide behind. His trembling hands were stuffed into jeans pockets so that he looked like a man simply visiting the graves, not a son and brother a mere heartbeat away from a breakdown. For a full five minutes he stood and focused on taking slow even breaths. In and out. In and out. Finally, his heartbeat ebbed and his trembling hands quieted.

"I'm sorry," he whispered. "I'm so terribly sorry."

Memories of that long-ago tragedy rushed into his mind as if he were standing on his street again, young and frightened. Terror flooded through him and he began to tremble once more, even as he told himself it was all right. He was transformed into that same kid confronted by an unimaginable horror.

Rationally he understood that he couldn't have changed a thing. He'd been a child and powerless against the evil that destroyed his family. But rationality didn't change how he felt. His heart ached at the memory of that day—how he'd stood helpless in the street watching as his family was brought out of the house, one by one, each in an ominous black body bag. Years of maturity and knowledge couldn't erase the sight and feel of that day.

He walked to the center stone and pressed his palm against the cool marble. He had loved his family, still loved his family. His father, tall and dark, with just a hint of humor in his eyes. His sister, a promising runner whose laugh could be heard all over the house. His mother, a ball of fire who kept all of them on their toes and whose hearty laughter never failed to warm him. God, how he missed them.

Even now he couldn't understand why the vampire had attacked his family. What set their modest home in Georgetown apart from any other? No one else was harmed, no other attacks occurred within miles. Yet he came home to a bloodbath, his whole world destroyed in the blink of an eye. An apparent random attack had left him an orphan. If not for Monsignor, he'd have been lost. Monsignor gave him a home, an education, and, most important, a purpose. He was there for Colin, just like family. Just like a father.

For years he'd been taking his revenge on any vampire that dared to cross his path. He'd hunted them down, nearly wiped them from the face of the earth. With every vampire he turned to dust, he waited for the feeling of satisfaction, the conviction that the murder of his family was being avenged. No matter how many times he swung his sword, that feeling never came. While he'd known his work saved untold numbers of innocent lives, not once did he feel like any of it brought him closure.

Sometimes, the disappointment became almost too heavy to bear. At other times he'd wanted to join those he destroyed but always lacked the courage to take his own life. Perhaps that's why he was so fearless when it came to the hunt. Every time he went into battle he knew he'd win either way it turned out. Vampires would be destroyed or he'd at last join his family.

Then he met Ivy. Just the thought of her brought lightness to his heart and made him believe that perhaps God had a plan for him after all. That perhaps in the dark abyss that was his life, a purpose was hidden. With Ivy at his side, he would find it. Funny how love changed the game.

Smiling now, he sank to the grass. His legs crossed, his arms on his knees, he began to speak quietly, telling his family about his life since that terrible night and about the woman—the vampire—who'd changed it all.

CHAPTER FOURTEEN

S o, do you want to tell me what it is?"
Tory looked up to see Naomi standing in the doorway, one shoulder against the frame, both hands stuck in the pockets of her jeans. Her hair hung loose around her shoulders, and her eyes were intense as they studied her from across the room.

"I don't know what you're talking about." Well, not exactly anyway.

Unaffected, Naomi said calmly, "The big, bad secret that you believe makes you the reason people are dying in my city."

The secret? Like there was only one. She didn't know where to start and wasn't sure she even wanted to. Still, as she gazed into Naomi's eyes, she had the strangest urge to bare her soul...black as it was. What could she lose besides everything?

"You sure you want to hear this?"

"You've got to trust me sometime."

Naomi had a point. Spending centuries trusting no one made her weary, besides making her a coward. Nobody needed to tell her that isolation really was a coward's game. She knew, she just opted not to. Maybe it was time to stop being so afraid.

"It started long before I was turned. Oh, hell, it started before my birth in the Tower of London on February 11, 1554..."

How long could the agony continue? It seemed to Jane it had been going on for days. Strong as she was, her spirit was beginning to wane. Sweat poured from her body, and her thoughts, usually sharp and intelligent, were becoming dull and difficult. She didn't remember what day it was or how long she'd been here. Her sisters at her side, she,

Lady Jane Grey, deposed Queen of England, tried to get comfortable and failed.

Lady Catherine took a cool cloth and laid it against Jane's brow. It cooled her feverish skin and, for just a moment, relief trickled through her battered body. The sensation was wondrous and she prayed it would go on and on. The relief didn't last nearly long enough. In less than a minute, another spasm roared through her and Jane cried out.

Lady Mary laid her lips to Jane's ear. "Hush now, sister, it won't be much longer. Hush or the guards will come."

Jane held Mary's hand so hard she was certain her sister's fingers would be crushed. She didn't loosen her grip. It seemed as though the contact with her sister was the only thing keeping her alive. She had to survive, had to be strong.

"It must end." Jane panted. "It must." She wasn't speaking of simply the pain that had her in its vise-like grip.

Even through the haze of discomfort, Jane felt Mary's tears fall on her exposed flesh and heard Catherine's quiet sobs. She didn't want to leave them or this world. It wasn't the crown she desired—no, she longed for nothing more than a simple life. She'd taken the crown because Henry had decreed it. She'd been groomed to always do the right thing and she rose to the occasion. As Henry wished, she'd been crowned on that lovely Monday in July. What a glorious day it had been too. To be queen was an honor that she did not take lightly.

Nine days later, she lost the crown and had been here ever since. One moment she was a queen and the next a prisoner. Such was her fate. Now her time was growing short. Despite Queen Mary's earlier clemency, the tides had changed once again, and her death warrant was signed. Her life now came down to a matter of hours, perhaps even minutes.

Despite trying to remain calm, Jane cried out as a terrible pain ripped through her yet again. She now held on to both of her sisters. "When will it stop?" Tears rained down her cheeks.

With her free hand, Catherine blotted Jane's damp forehead, wiped away the tears. "Very soon," she cooed.

Suddenly, a pain more intense than any that had come before ripped through her and Jane wondered if her body had just been torn apart.

"Now, Jane," Mary told her firmly. "Push now!"

Jane's scream echoed off the stone walls. At the same time, she pushed and pushed, hoping that finally the pain would stop. It did and, for a moment, silence fell over the locked room. Then a sound began, tiny at first, before building into the full-throated, healthy cry of a newborn infant.

"Your mother really was Lady Jane Grey?"

Tory nodded, not surprised by the obvious disbelief in Naomi's voice. "One and the same. No one besides her close family ever knew of my existence."

"But how? Why? I've never read a thing in any history book about Lady Jane Grey having a child. Did I miss it?"

"No. To my knowledge nothing is written anywhere about me. My existence was a huge secret right up there with the location of the Holy Grail. The family was worried they'd kill my mother even sooner if they knew about the child. Rightly so, I believe. It was a very dangerous time."

"How did they keep you a secret? I mean, they had to notice your mother was pregnant."

"It wasn't that difficult to hide. She was pregnant when they threw her into the Tower of London and, given the styles of the day and the fact she never got very big, no one noticed. After my birth, my aunt, Mary, bless her heart, raised me for the first five years of my life. After that, I was moved from family to family every few years, just to be safe. I was protected but invisible. I was one of the great royal secrets, and that secret saved my life. Well, at least until that bastard Pierre took it away from me and left me with this." She waved her hand in the air.

"Wow, I'm really sorry. I can't even imagine what that was like for you as a little girl."

Disbelief had shifted to a sincerity that touched her in a way nothing had for a long time.

"I didn't know any different and so it was simply my life. Some could say it's a royal curse that I inherited. First Riah, formerly known as Catherine Tudor, youngest daughter of King Henry VII, and then, of course, me, daughter of a queen best known because her reign was a mere nine days. We were forgotten royalty and then we became vampires. Our family was, as they say these days, fucked up."

❖

Last night had been a bust. Now it was time to take it up a notch or twelve—find a way to draw her out, destroy her world as she'd destroyed his. The old lady didn't do it, not like he'd hoped anyway. His other gifts were ignored. Even the lynched werewolf failed to draw her out.

Then again, as he thought about it, last night wasn't a total loss after all. The scene at the cathedral actually held a lot of potential. It might have been defused, but that didn't mean it couldn't still be used to stir things up. The humans were starting to turn against those like him, and that's exactly what he was going for. Of course they weren't going to harm him, no one could. He was just that good. If they killed a few or all of the others, well, their tough luck. Few, if any, came even close to his incredible skills.

The one thing he had to keep a careful eye on was her safety. He didn't want to let her get into a situation where someone could take her. She belonged to him, and only he would dispatch her to hell, where she was definitely headed. He loved her, that hadn't changed despite what she'd done. It also didn't mean she could or would be saved. The way he saw it, he had little choice but to exercise tough love. She had taken it upon herself to act as judge, jury, and jailer in his case. He intended to return the favor but there'd be no jail in her future. No, he would be judge, jury, and *executioner*.

He smiled and ran his tongue over his lower lip. The waiting was such sweet misery. It wouldn't be long now and they'd be face-to-face at last. He could end it all now, except where would the fun be in that? His glorious chess game was progressing so well that checkmate was just in sight. Soon everyone was sure to turn against each other and blood would run in the streets. Stupid humans, they didn't even know when they were being played. The preternaturals weren't much better. A bit disappointing, as he expected more from the superior beings like himself. Of course, he was one of a kind, so expecting others to be on the same playing field was foolish.

When he was first turned, he'd been furious. It had seemed so wrong and against everything he'd believed in. After a little time, he'd reconciled with his fate. No, it was more than that. He hadn't just reconciled to the darkness. He'd embraced it and found a new universe opened up to him. Why he'd never seen the potential before, he couldn't imagine. He was just glad he'd had a chance to live this new life even if she'd stolen years away from him.

Standing in the large picture window of the elegant room, he gazed out over the city lights. Not far away from the hotel, the Washington Monument rose tall and glorious, a beam of bright light in the darkness.

Tourists walked, talked, and laughed, unaware of the danger he posed to them. The city pulsed with life no matter what time of day or night. He liked that about the place, made hunting easier. Even with the current mood of danger and discontent, the city vibrated with energy. The perfect urban jungle ripe for a skilled predator...and one brand new to the game.

He took his jacket from where he'd tossed it across the back of a chair. Slipping it on, he smoothed back his thick hair and smiled. He looked good, he felt good. Time to stir it up, enjoy a bit of excitement, and have fun while he was teaching his newest student the ropes.

Meagan lounged in a chair, one leg slung over the arm. She had the feral, hungry look of the newly turned. She was still cute, only now with a dangerous edge. It appealed to him, at least for a while. Young vampires with their zeal for blood were energizing. He came close and held out his hand. She took it and let him pull her to her feet. He didn't let go, instead pulled her close before kissing her deeply and rubbing his stiffening cock against her center.

She grinned up at him, her eyes sparkling. "Wanna fuck?"

He kissed her quickly and stepped away. A tempting offer but he had a better idea. "A little later. Let's have fun first."

She clapped her hands. "Yay. What do you have in mind?"

"I think a party is in order."

CHAPTER FIFTEEN

Naomi was frankly a bit stunned by what Tory had told her. The daughter of Lady Jane Grey? It boggled the mind, literally. She'd been around enough of the immortals that she shouldn't be surprised, but she was. She'd never expected to come face-to-face with royalty.

It also explained a lot. When she'd first encountered Tory at the cathedral, she found her incredibly attractive and equally off-putting, if not downright arrogant. She'd spent enough time with folks who were way too impressed with themselves, so she sure didn't have to do it by choice. When she got to know her, Tory wasn't any of those things, even with her impressive pedigree.

The attraction she'd initially felt surged back tenfold. Tory's dark hair hung in a silky cascade down her back, and the top she wore clung to her curves. Tight jeans accentuated her slim hips. She was beautiful and sexy and exactly what Naomi didn't need. Standing in front of a window staring out at the darkness, Tory was as still as death and, for a moment, it frightened Naomi. So much so that she put a hand on Tory's back just to make sure she was real.

Both of them gasped at the contact. Tory spun and stared at Naomi, who was as shocked as Tory looked. Slowly she pulled her hand away. Immediately she wanted to put it back.

"I'm sorry," Naomi whispered.

Tory didn't say anything, just took her hand. The spark was still there, only this time she was ready for it. What in the world was happening?

She couldn't seem to move. The feel of Tory's skin against hers was exciting and very, very frightening. Despite her chosen profession and night after night of preaching from the pulpit with people all around her, she was a loner by choice. Companionship and love simply weren't in the cards for her, and spending a lot of time and effort pretending otherwise didn't change a thing. Her destiny was solitude, especially after what she'd done.

This connection with Tory scared her. She'd grown comfortable in her isolated existence and the way it kept her heart safe. Everyone she could help, she did. Still, no one got past the wall she'd erected. Feeling anything beyond empathy or compassion was not welcome.

"Why are you afraid?"

Because I hurt those I care for the most. "I'm not," she lied.

Tory's eyes narrowed. "You asked me to spill my secrets and I did. Your turn to tell me yours."

Naomi wanted to call her on that one. Yes, Tory had shared a secret with her and she appreciated the courage it took to do that. On the other hand, Naomi had spent enough time counseling troubled souls to know the beautiful woman still held more secrets tight in her soul. Sharing only one was a far cry from opening up.

"I can't."

It wasn't a lie. Baring her soul was an impossible thing to ask of her. Owning up to what she'd done wasn't the problem. The repulsion that would undoubtedly fill Tory's eyes if she was to hear the truth was what kept it from passing her lips. The only way Naomi knew how to get from one day to the next was by leaving the truth buried beneath the façade that was her life now.

Tory stroked her cheek with a soothing touch. She should move away. The touch of Tory's fingertips against her skin was so gentle and caring, Naomi leaned into her instead of away.

"Sometimes you have to trust other people."

Naomi closed her eyes briefly. Nothing like having her own words turned back on her. Still, it would take a lot more courage than she possessed to trust. "And sometimes you can't risk it."

"I trusted you and now you need to trust me. I promise, I won't hurt you."

"It's not being hurt I'm worried about."

"Then what?"

Giving up didn't appear to be on Tory's agenda. Painful as it might be, the truth needed to be said. "I don't want you to hate me." She stared at Tory, waiting for the light to dawn.

Instead, Tory's gaze grew soft. She pulled Naomi's head down to hers and kissed her lightly, the gentle brush of a butterfly's wings. Against her lips she said, "I don't think I could ever hate you."

She wanted to believe that and knew better. Her sins were too great, no matter how long she tried to make amends. As much as she'd like to lay bare her horrible deeds and hope for forgiveness from this beautiful woman, it simply wasn't possible. In the real world it didn't happen for people like her.

Beyond the closed door, the rustle of movement almost distracted her. The others were up and about. All she had to do was open the door and walk out. This, whatever it was, would be over. A couple of steps to the door—that's all it would take and she could pretend she didn't feel a thing for Tory. She didn't move.

"Trust me," Tory murmured, her hands sliding beneath Naomi's shirt. "I won't hate you. Not now. Not ever."

Just the mere touch of skin against skin had her nipples hardening in anticipation of Tory's loving attention. Her resolve to stay neutral dissolved and she captured Tory's face, stroking the smooth skin of her cheeks with her thumbs. The kiss deepened and she pushed her tongue past her lips to search and taste. How she could lose herself in this woman. Forget the past and live in just this moment. It would be so easy. How could something that felt this good be wrong?

Her heart beat quickly and it occurred to her she couldn't walk away even if she wanted to. She was drawn to Tory, heart and soul, and while the attraction scared her, the fear no longer stopped her. Touching her, tasting her, was the most natural thing in the world and she wanted more. Even if it was only for this one night, she wanted to love and be loved.

Maybe Tory was right. Maybe it was time to trust. Maybe it was time to listen to her heart.

❖

"Tell me," Ivy said when he walked into the bedroom and draped his jacket over the back of the wing chair in front of the window.

"Nothing to tell." Liar, liar, pants on fire, as his little sister used to say.

He dropped to the bed, meaning only to sit down for a few minutes. Instead, he lay back against the pillows at the same time he kicked off his shoes. They clattered to the floor. Stretched out on top of the bedcovers, he closed his eyes and for the first time in a really long time thought about his family without the deep heartache. Rather than feeling the crushing sadness, he smiled remembering joyous Christmas mornings, summer picnics under sunny skies, and quiet winter nights around a roaring fire built by his father.

Not saying anything, Ivy stretched out beside him and draped an arm over his middle. The feel of her lithe body next to his, the weight of her arm across his midsection was a comfort he didn't think he could ever live without. The tension still in his body began to ease out of him and he pondered the strange way his life seemed to be coming full circle.

"I went to see them today."

He knew he didn't have to elaborate on whom. That was one of the beautiful things about loving another person; they knew most of the other one's secrets. As much as he'd shared with Ivy, though, he still didn't have the courage to reveal a few of his darkest corners.

Her hand moved up to stroke across his chest. Even through the cloth of his shirt, he could feel the warmth of her hand. She smelled wonderful, just a light touch of intoxicating perfume. Her black hair was soft against his arm where her head lay cradled close.

His eyes closed, he told her, "I've never gone before."

"It was time," she said softly, still caressing his chest.

"Yeah, it was. Past time, really. I should have gone before. What kind of son doesn't visit his parents' graves?"

"You weren't ready before, and I know they understand."

"I'm not sure I was ready today. I always thought I'd be able to come here and tell them I killed the bastard who took their lives."

"But you couldn't."

"No, I still don't know who did it. I sure as hell don't know why and then…"

Her hand stilled and he wished he could have stopped the words before they came out of his mouth. He couldn't and he didn't think she expected him to.

"You couldn't tell them you're in love with a vampire." Her words were so soft he barely heard them.

"Yeah," he breathed. "A vampire stole their lives and destroyed my entire family. I spent all of my adult years killing them, all in a vain effort to avenge their deaths. I did it willingly because every vampire had to pay for what one did. You…I never saw you coming, Ivy."

She rose and sat cross-legged beside him, one hand pushing the hair from his forehead. "If I could change what I am and go back to being human, I'd do it in a second. I can't, and even though being a vampire sucks—literally—it has let me be with you. I regret a lot of things but not that."

He took her hand and pulled it to his lips, kissing her palm. "I know, baby, I feel the same way. I stood at their graves today and tried to tell them why I made the decisions I have. I still haven't given up my quest to find their killer, but I don't think I could live without you by my side."

"I know I couldn't," she said, pressing her lips against his. "You make it all okay, even the darkness. And your family, they understand. I believe that with all my heart."

He deepened the kiss, flicking his tongue between her lips. Would he ever weary of the sweet taste of her? No. Even when he grew old and she didn't, it would all still be worth the price they both paid. He'd never imagined having the unconditional love she gave him every day. He would walk through the fires of hell for her.

"I love you," he murmured.

"I love you too. Forever."

❖

He thought about things for hours. His plans hadn't jelled like he wished and needed to be tweaked. So close but not quite there yet. Disappointing really. He'd considered his plan so perfect.

Then again, maybe it was just as well. More fun when things were spontaneous, more exciting. A bit like a cat playing with a mouse and letting the mouse get away just far enough to think it was safe before pouncing and ripping off its head. That's the way it felt to him now. He was letting her believe she was out of his reach, and then when she was all warm and cozy, he'd strike the final blow. It would be sweet.

Tonight called for a little something special, something that would stir things up to the frenzied pitch he'd been aiming for since he arrived in the nation's capital. His casual drop of bodies hadn't produced quite the fervor he wanted. Time to step up the game.

Meagan had turned out to be a great disappointment. He'd brought her out for what he thought would be a nice little hunt before they fucked their brains out, but she'd gone all commando vampire on a guy in an alley not far from the Pentagon. She was a mess, the guy was ripped apart, and it dawned on him that he'd created a monster, quite literally. He really didn't see that he had a choice.

He'd made her. He put her down. Both Meagan and the man she'd attacked were tucked away in a Dumpster a few blocks from the Pentagon. He jumped on the Metro and rode across town. By the time their remains were discovered, he'd be long gone. Next time he had the urge to make himself a pet, he'd be sure to remember Meagan and how wrong that all went.

Alone again, he leaned against the railing at the entrance to the Metro station and watched people come and go. He smelled her before he saw her, a tall, willowy redhead wearing shaded glasses even though the sun was long down. Her slim pants tucked into tall leather boots and hip-length sweater were stylish. The click of her boot heels was steady as she strode up the street in the direction of the National Zoo. She looked as though she belonged here. Nothing about her screamed werewolf, but she was one. Another werewolf. Perfect.

If she sensed him, she didn't let on. Good. He followed her past the zoo, closed at this time of night, and watched her walk up a few steps to a very nice home. The man who opened the door to her was one hundred percent human. Even better.

Now he just had to wait for the perfect moment and then bam, one well-placed little push would put it all into motion. He could feel it in the air. The fear was palpable, thick as a northeastern fog, exactly what he hoped for. Tonight the city was his to do with as he pleased. The puppet master was about to pull some strings.

A bolt of lightning lit up the sky. The air turned heavy and before he ducked beneath the low-hanging boughs of the tree, big raindrops hit him on the top of the head. Electricity rippled through his body. The unanticipated storm was fantastic. Thunder was booming when he crossed the small yard and slipped in through an unlocked rear door. Under the cover of the storm, the screams inside went unnoticed.

Later, when he let himself out the back door of the same house, he was pleased with the results of his patient wait. He vaulted over the fence separating this house from the nearest neighbor and jogged across the tidy green lawn. He stopped long enough to right a ceramic gnome before letting himself out the gate. When he reached the sidewalk he slowed to a casual walk. His shoes were wet from the rain deposited by the storm. It had passed through, leaving the grounds and the streets soaked. The air was washed clean and he filled his lungs with the fresh scent.

In the distance the sound of sirens grew louder, and lights began to snap on in houses up and down the street. The 911 call just before he left the house brought quick results. Emergency services that would be wholly ineffective were mere minutes away. He wasn't worried about being seen. From all appearances, he was just another neighbor out for an evening walk. They wouldn't connect him with what they'd find inside the lovely home. They would, however, know exactly what happened. So would anyone else who got a glimpse inside, and one glimpse was all it would take to snap the fragile thread of calm holding society in check.

The sound of a gunshot split the quiet night just as he started down the stairs at the Metro station. Snap! He whistled a bright tune as he hopped on the Red Line and took a seat next to one of the sliding doors.

❖

Bad timing was an understatement. Tory hadn't felt such an air of barely restrained violence in centuries. Just outside the doors of the beautiful home, a city was on the edge of exploding.

Didn't matter. All that did matter was Naomi, and at the moment she was in Tory's arms. The emotion that she'd promised herself never to feel again surged up as if released from long-term captivity. Her skin tingled, her breath quickened, her fingers itched to run through Naomi's shiny hair.

No. No. No.

She couldn't allow this to happen. She started to step away but Naomi firmly gripped her wrists. Dark eyes met hers and what she saw there took her breath away.

"I know," Naomi said simply. "But it doesn't matter. I can't stop this and I don't think you can either. You might end up hating me, but for this one night, I want to pretend I'm not a monster. I want to love you. I don't want to fight this thing between us anymore."

Tory stopped her retreat. She couldn't argue because she felt exactly the same thing. Freeing her wrist, she touched Naomi's face. Whatever secrets the other woman held in her heart, Tory didn't believe it was anything she could ever hate her for. Of all people, she'd be the last one to cast the first stone…or any stone, for that matter. She shuddered to think about her years as a no-holds-barred vampire. If Naomi had a clue about Tory's ugly past, the woman would be running far, far away.

She wasn't running even in the face of her own obvious inner turmoil. Ghosts had her in their grasp and Tory wondered if she'd ever be free. Old tricks were what she wanted now, ways to tuck those memories into dark, faraway corners so she could savor the beauty of a single moment. Even if it was only for an hour, it was all they'd need, for now.

Time to stop lying to Naomi and to herself. "I want to love you too." She drew Naomi down until their lips met.

She skimmed the soft skin of Naomi's neck, trailing her fingers down to flesh exposed by the opened neckline of her shirt. Naomi sighed against Tory's lips. Any resistance was quickly fading away.

She began with the buttons on Naomi's shirt. One by one they slipped open until she could push the fabric off her shoulders. Suddenly, Naomi pulled away and gathered the fabric to her breast.

"What is it?" Tory asked her in a gentle voice.

A tear slid down Naomi's cheek as she took a step away. "Too ugly," she said, the two words barely audible.

Tory didn't understand. "You're beautiful." She wasn't lying either. Everything about this woman made her blood run hot. Ugly wasn't even in the vocabulary.

Naomi pulled the shirt tighter around her body. "The scars."

It took a second before it dawned on her. Slowly, gently, she took Naomi's hands and freed them from their death grip on the shirt. She slid the shirt off her shoulders and dropped it to the floor.

In the muted light of the bedroom, she tenderly touched the ragged white lines that started above her right breast, disappearing into the top of her bra only to appear again below. She didn't say a word. Instead she leaned close and kissed the top of the scar, kissed her breast through the bra, and then dropped her head until she could kiss it where it lay jagged against Naomi's stomach. Her skin was heated against her lips.

Tory brought her head up and gazed into Naomi's tormented eyes. "Whoever did this to you only marred your skin. They could never destroy your beauty."

"So ugly," Naomi murmured, but this time the dread Tory had heard only moments before wasn't there.

"Beautiful," Tory said against her lips.

"I haven't…not since…"

Tory understood. Scars weren't always visible. Hers were on the inside, and she knew exactly how long it had taken before she could allow another woman to touch her.

She took Naomi's hand and placed it on her breasts. Her touch was hot even through Tory's shirt. "Touch me. Let me touch you. There's nothing wrong or ugly about it."

The dam broke and Naomi dropped her hands to the hem of Tory's shirt, grabbing it and pulling it over her head. Unlike Naomi, Tory wasn't wearing a bra. Silence fell over them as Naomi gazed on Tory's naked chest. The expression on her face brought heat pooling between her legs.

Naomi groaned before dropping her head to suck a nipple into her mouth. The warm sensation of her tongue against her breast almost made Tory come right then. Her head fell back and her eyes closed. She wanted this moment and this feeling to go on forever.

Even as glorious as it felt, Tory wanted more. She took Naomi's hand and tugged her toward the bed. In a rush they both stripped out of the rest of their clothes on the way and fell together on the big bed. As she kissed Naomi, she slid her hand between her legs, finding her hot and wet. She rubbed her fingers over Naomi's clit, satisfied by her low moans.

Shifting, Tory moved until she was between Naomi's legs. Slowly she licked the small nub as Naomi's hips moved. She slid two fingers inside where she was very wet, moving in and out as she licked and nipped. Naomi gathered wads of the bedcovers in her hands as her body strained against Tory's touch.

Naomi came with a strangled cry and Tory continued to lick as her body arched. Spent, Naomi sank back to the bed. Tory smiled and laid her head on Naomi's stomach.

"That was…"

"Yeah," Naomi breathed. "It was."

After a moment, Naomi shifted. Looking at Tory she smiled, her eyes glazed and satisfied. "My turn to return the favor."

And she did.

CHAPTER SIXTEEN

So you guys have to understand, I'm pretty new with this stuff," Adriana was saying when Tory and Naomi all but ran into the room.

The scream that had brought everyone into the living room hadn't been loud, just effective. When he'd stretched out earlier, Colin took the opportunity to doze on the sofa in front of the fireplace, its gas log engulfed in dancing flames, while Ivy sat on the floor in front of him engrossed in some research. Tory and Naomi had been in a bedroom burning off a little stress, he hoped. God only knew where Riah'd been but she was like that. Now, they were all back together and staring at Adriana. For a woman with very dark skin, she was as pale as possible.

"Tell us what you saw." Riah ran a hand soothingly down Adriana's neck, and her touch seemed to have an immediate calming effect on her.

"Let me explain to you folks first." She gave her a small smile. "It's like this—" She turned to look at all of them. "I'm not preternatural, but as it turns out, I've got some nifty powers of my own."

"You're a psychic?" Tory asked.

Adriana shook her head. "Not exactly. I didn't know it until my mother, Sabira, died, but I'm kind of from a different dimension."

Both Naomi and Tory gave her puzzled looks. Colin understood but he'd had a head start. When Adriana had returned from New Haven to announce she was from another world, he was pretty sure he'd had the same expression on his face. He'd never even heard of Tigeran, though it had nothing to do with whether he believed Adriana's story of being a sorceress, the child of a powerful warrior and a beautiful sorceress. He believed because he'd seen too much not to. Since she'd returned from that trip to New Haven, Adriana had been different. Better. And that was saying a lot about a woman impressive enough before she even left. Toss in a few potent powers and she was really something.

"The cool thing is," Adriana said, "that I'm a sorceress. At first I didn't believe it, at least not until I vanquished a really evil wizard who wanted to control this world. That was some pretty awesome shit, if I do say so." She smiled and her eyes came alive. "Having super powers is some kind of trip."

"What do you have for us now?" Colin wanted to know what had caused her to scream loud enough to bring them all running. Adriana was normally unflappable but something had shaken her up. That was bothersome in light of what was happening around here.

"Yeah, well, about that." She looked at Tory, her head tilted, her eyes appraising. "Pretty sure it has something to do with you."

Tory dropped her head and then brought her eyes back up to hold Adriana's gaze. "I'm not surprised," she said in a steady voice.

"I didn't think you would be. You feel it, don't you?"

Tory nodded but said nothing. Colin, on the other hand, wanted clarification. Felt what? Personally, the only thing he sensed was how dangerous it was becoming outside. People were scared, and when that happened, it could turn out badly for everyone.

"What?" Riah, like Colin, was getting impatient.

Adriana brought her gaze away from Tory and swept it over the assembled group. "There's a vampire in town."

"No shit," Naomi muttered, and everyone turned surprised looks her way. "What? You don't think a lay minister knows how to swear? I wasn't always a minister, you know."

Tory shook her head. "No, we all figure a former vampire hunter can swear like a Teamster, but given your current line of work, it's a little surprising."

Naomi shrugged. "You can take the girl out of the hunt, but there are just some moments…"

Adriana nodded. "Got a point, sister, and this is one of them. As I was saying, there's a vampire with a hard-on for you, Tory."

"Can you see him?" If Adriana could give them a face, it would make the hunt easier. Colin hoped her newfound powers let her see who the bastard was.

"Not clearly. He's tall with dark hair and dark eyes. Sound familiar?"

There was a long beat before Tory said, "It's got to be Pierre…my maker. I thought some of yours had destroyed him." She looked over at Naomi.

Colin would have said the same thing. When he'd gone in search of Riah, who he'd known as Catherine Tudor, she'd been one of only a very few vampires known to still exist. The records of the church were extensive and he'd had full access to all of them. Right now, he'd give anything to be able to search those records. He wanted to know definitively what had happened to Pierre.

His leaving the church, walking away from his life as a hunter, forfeited any rights he had to those records. The only way to get back into them would to be to do the unthinkable: apologize to the church and—worst of all—destroy the woman he loved. The church would demand it of him and that was something he could—would—never do. The cost was too high.

"I wish," he thought out loud, "we could access the church's records."

He saw the way Naomi's eyes shifted to slits. She knew something. He didn't know what but he'd find out. She moved her weight from foot to foot and wouldn't meet his gaze.

"What?" he finally asked.

Naomi ran both hands through her hair and stared out the darkened window. "I did something before I left."

"As in?"

"As in, I copied the database."

Was she saying what he thought she was? "Sonofabitch! You have a copy of the records?"

Her lips tight together, she gave him a clipped nod. "Yeah, everything up to the point I walked out."

This was a stroke of genius. He had a good recall of what had happened in the few years after Naomi left, and if she had all the legacy records, they had a gold mine. He could kiss her. "Perfect."

He was thrilled but apparently he was the only one. Naomi's expression could only be described as death warmed over. Knowing the power of what she had on her computer, she should be as pleased as he was.

"What's the problem, Naomi? This is fantastic. I don't understand the long face."

She pushed out a breath and finally brought her eyes to meet his. Tears glistened in them and apprehension rippled through him. He didn't like the look she turned on him. "A file exists in the records with details about the murder of your family."

He stilled, his nerves abruptly alive as if just shot with a blast of electricity. Of all the things he guessed might come out of her mouth, that was the last. "My family? You know who murdered my family?" How could she have possessed that knowledge and not told him? And if she made the copy before she left, she'd had that information for several years. He'd thought she was his friend. What kind of friend withheld the facts?

A tear started to slide down her cheek. "I don't know who killed your family. I only know who ordered it." Her words seemed choked out.

For a second he thought his heart would stop. *Ordered them murdered? My parents? My little sister with her Barbie dolls and bright-purple scooter?* That couldn't be right. It was a random vampire attack. Everyone said so. Monsignor said so. No one could possibly have wanted his family dead.

His voice was strangled as he choked out a single word. "Who?"

Naomi's voice shook and tears spilled down her cheeks. Her voice was so quiet it was barely above a whisper, and yet the single word she uttered held the force of a hurricane. "Monsignor."

❖

He stood in the darkness and listened. The chaos in the Woodley Park area was too far away to appreciate. He'd have loved to stay around and watch the professionals try to control the panic. They'd be lucky if something didn't explode, like an edgy neighbor or a paranoid passerby. The mood was quickly turning with his expert touch guiding the way. He was incredibly pleased.

Back at Union Station, he sat in the massive lobby and looked up at the statues that ringed the area. People milled about, unaware of the blood that had been spilled only a few miles away. He thought about what he could do next and smiled. No sense wasting a good night.

He lowered his gaze from the statues and to the people who walked by him, most hurrying with their heads down, intent on getting where they were going as quickly as possible. Nobody wanted to linger. No one wanted eye contact.

So far nothing that really tickled his fancy had passed his way. The hunting in this city, at least in the brief time he'd been here, had been wonderful. Little satisfied him more than a good variety. From Goth, to professional, to gay, to purity, it was all tasty. His earlier snack on the were and her unwary human friend had taken what started out as a bad evening with the Meagan fiasco and turned it on a high note. Now he needed the perfect dessert.

It walked by in the shape of serious, blond, and federal. Could spot an FBI agent from a mile away. He was good that way. Something about the stoic expression, clipped walk, and dark suit. Not for the first time he wondered if they taught a class at Quantico on how to look the part. He laid odds they did.

He licked his lips and rose, falling into step beside the man, whose cologne wafted in the air. He approved, the scent heady and promising. His cock stiffened. He did so enjoy playing with his food.

"Heard there was another slaughter over by the zoo," he said in a conversational tone.

The man turned gray eyes his direction. "What?"

"The killer, you know the not-so-human kind of killer. He murdered again tonight."

"You should probably go home, then." The man's pace picked up.

"I'm Vlad." He matched his pace and stuck out his hand.

For a brief second, the man stared at his outstretched hand. Then he shrugged and grasped it in his own. "Daniel."

"Feel like a drink, Daniel?"

The gray eyes darkened. "A drink?"

"Sure, you know—scotch, bourbon, vodka—something to take the edge off."

His pace slowed and he took a good, long look. Inclining his head just a little, he said. "Why not? It's been a long day."

Gotcha. He could spot 'em a mile away. "I hear ya, brother. I know a nice quiet place where a couple of guys can enjoy a drink and a little conversation." And a good fuck, but he kept that to himself.

CHAPTER SEVENTEEN

Tory didn't know what this Monsignor was to Colin, but by the expression on his face, it wasn't a good thing. What she did know was betrayal. She'd experienced it. She'd done it. She saw it in Colin's eyes now and her heart hurt for him.

"I'm sorry," Naomi whispered.

He didn't move, didn't say a word. Neither did anyone else. Silently, he turned and walked from the room, his back straight, his head high. Ivy gave Riah a look, then quickly followed Colin down the hallway. Still, no one said a word for long minutes after they left.

"What was that about?" Tory finally asked.

Riah and Adriana turned expectant faces to Naomi. If anybody would have a clue it would be another hunter—or former hunter, in both their cases—and the one who'd dropped what was clearly a bombshell.

Naomi's voice was low as she began. "Colin grew up in this part of the country, not far from here in Virginia. When he was just a kid, he came home from a sleepover to find his family had been slaughtered. The local news made it out to be a home invasion gone terribly wrong."

"But it was a vampire," Riah added.

Naomi nodded. "Yeah, it was a vampire, all right. It was ugly and violent and he saw it."

"How awful," Tory murmured. No one had to paint a picture for her. She was ashamed to admit she'd seen it firsthand. Her heart ached for the child he'd been and how the trauma must have shaped his life.

"Colin was left an orphan and so Monsignor Joseph Warren essentially adopted him. He raised him like his own son and began to train him as a hunter when he was barely in his teens. Most of us came in as young adults who had both the calling and the aptitude. Not Colin. He was years ahead of the rest of us and better than any of us too."

"This Monsignor ordered the death of his family? Is that what you said?" Tory had a hard time believing someone from the church would have the ability to order a vampire attack on humans—or the balls, for that matter. It was contrary to everything the church and its hunters stood for.

Then again, she'd seen enough subterfuge, deception, and outright lying in her time to know anything was possible, even killing an entire family. People, the most surprising people, were capable of terrible things. The real question was why. Sometimes the answer was obvious and sometimes the answer was never discovered.

Again Naomi nodded. "I didn't believe it when I first came across the entry. Monsignor wasn't that kind of man, or so I thought. Then I started to dig and, sure as hell, Monsignor had orchestrated the slaughter. Let's just say I was sick to my stomach."

"That doesn't make sense. The whole mission of the church and its hunters is to save humans, not kill them," Tory said.

"I thought so too but I was wrong. Colin was—is—special, and Monsignor recognized that early on. Colin and his family were in Monsignor's parish at the time. He was just a priest way back when, but he was going places in the church and everyone knew it. I think he was a little drunk on the power that gave him and he wanted Colin as one of his hunters. What better way to ensure that would happen than to make him an orphan?"

Riah shook her head, her expression sad. "He didn't have to kill his family."

"Makes sense in a warped way. In fact, it was perfect. Colin was left all alone in the world and because of the very thing Monsignor wanted him to learn to hunt. I'm sure he chalked up the loss of Colin's family as necessary collateral damage."

"That's fucked up," Adriana muttered.

Tory agreed wholeheartedly. She'd run up against any number of hunters and the holier-than-thou's who pulled their strings, but this… yeah, Adriana had hit the nail on the head: this was fucked up. She ached for Colin. She understood in a way that was too personal. After all, hadn't she been an orphan her whole life? Her own parents had been executed mere hours after her birth. Not literally by a vampire, although an argument could be made that they sure were in a figurative sense. Vampires for power who didn't even blink when it came to killing for the crown had existed for centuries. Her poor mother and father never had a chance. Neither would she, if not for the families that hid her.

"If you knew, why didn't you tell him?" Riah asked.

She wondered the same thing. Why would Naomi not share the truth with him? He had the right to know.

Naomi let out a long breath. "I've thought of him a thousand times since I found that entry, and I just didn't know how to tell him. He loves Monsignor. How do you destroy someone's whole world?"

"How can we help?" Surely they could do something.

"I don't know." Naomi's eyes were troubled. "I knew that someday I'd come face-to-face with Colin again and would have to reveal the truth to him. I sure didn't relish being the messenger in this case, except I'm sure no one else would tell him and, ultimately, he has a right to know."

"And now he does." Tory laid a hand on her arm.

"Look," Riah said as she rose from the sofa. "I think we need to give him space. Learning someone you love has betrayed you takes a huge toll, and sometimes the best thing is a little time."

Tory stared out into the darkness. In the distance, the sound of sirens crackled through the night and unease whispered through the air. Chills rose on her arms. "I don't think we have much time."

Riah stood beside her. "Probably not, but he needs a bit of it anyway."

"Well, we can't just do nothing." Adriana began to pace. "I know Colin needs space, but not too much. We have to do something and soon. Shit's about to hit the fan, I feel it."

"I agree and I think I have a solution. We give Colin some peace and quiet to digest what I laid on him, and in the meantime, we dig into my pirated database to find out whatever the hell we can. Among all of us, we're bound to come up with something helpful."

She agreed. It was a good idea and, really, the best course of action at the moment. "Well," Tory said to the other three. "What are we waiting for?"

❖

Colin was cold, so cold he felt as though he'd been dropped into the center of an iceberg. He remembered feeling this way once before in his life and never thought he would again. As many years as he'd had to prepare himself for uncovering the identity of his family's killer, this possibility had never entered his mind.

Naomi's words echoed in his head until he wanted to scream. It simply couldn't be true. Monsignor? The man who had taken him into his home and treated him as if he was his own son? The same man who gave him love and understanding when he was lost and struggling? The man who gave his shattered life a purpose? No way. No fucking way.

It had to be a lie, yet something deep inside told him it wasn't. Besides the gut feeling another truth stood out: Naomi wouldn't lie to him. She had no reason to. More than once, she'd had his back and saved him from the same fate as his family. She wouldn't save his life only to destroy it with something as cruel as this. No, Naomi had told him the truth. He'd seen it in her eyes as the words left her mouth.

The look of pure pain on her face crushed him. Even worse were the expressions of pity on Riah and Adriana's faces. He hadn't seen Tory's but had no doubt it held the same look of sorrow. He couldn't take it. Only Ivy was different. No pity, no grief. She was the only person who knew his heart, and in her eyes he saw only love. If he made it through this, it was her strength that would carry him.

Now, as he stood in the kitchen, his hands braced on the counter, she came up silently behind him and wrapped her arms around his waist. Her head rested on his back. The tenderness of her embrace undid him.

Not since he was young and confronted with the death of his family had he allowed tears to fall. He'd wept that day for his family and his own terrible loss. Now, with Ivy's body pressed close to his, sobs once again shook his body. He didn't know if it was from pain or fury. Most likely a combination of both.

Naomi's words had triggered a rush of emotion long held in check, and he was powerless to stop it now. A lifetime of being strong and in control slid away. It was as if he was that young, lost boy standing on the street, his world shattering a little more with each body bag loaded into a van.

He loved this bike. It was screamin' fast and bad. All of his friends were jealous because he was the first one to get this model. Dad surprised him with it because he'd just made straight As. He didn't want to tell Dad getting the As was easy, 'cause then he'd expect him to do it all the time. But if he could get cool stuff like this bike, it might be worth it.

He'd kicked Jay's butt yesterday when they'd hit the trails down by the river. Jay was smaller and not quite as strong, but the bike was what really made the difference. He was unstoppable. All night Jay had whined about his bike and they'd brainstormed how to get him one too. Then the two of them would kick everybody's butt.

After talking half the night, they'd slept in, which wasn't good. His parents expected him at Mass—no excuses. When he realized he wasn't gonna make it in time, he'd tried to call home. Nobody answered and he figured they'd already left. He was really gonna get it. The best he could do was haul it home and try to get to church before the service was over. If he was there by the end, they'd never know he was late.

As he took the first corner, he almost laid the bike down. Sweet. He was zooming by the time he rounded the last corner onto his street. This bike was awesome. At this rate, he'd be late, but not terribly. He wouldn't get in too much trouble.

He slowed, his pedals barely moving. Something weird was going on close to his house. Police cars and an ambulance were parked in and around his driveway, his house. Dad's car was still there, blocked by the police. How was he gonna drive everyone to Mass with the police cars parked behind him? Lots of people in uniforms were hanging around but he didn't see Dad. A bad feeling started to wash over him.

Without thinking about what it would do to the perfect paint on his new bike, he dropped it to the pavement and began to run. All he heard was the slap, slap, slap of his chucks against the asphalt.

"Mom, Dad," he screamed as he ran.

A beefy uniformed policeman grabbed him as he charged the yellow tape that surrounded his front yard. His legs kept pumping even though the officer held him airborne. "Whoa, son, you can't go in there."

He struggled against the vise-like arms that held him captive. "I live here. Where's my mom and dad? My sister?"

The grip didn't loosen and his feet still didn't touch the ground. "Just hold on, son."

"Mom! Dad!" His screams had everyone turning to look at him. He continued to fight against the arms holding him.

He stopped fighting only when two men wheeled a gurney with a long black plastic bag on top out the open front door. "What's that?" he whispered, a sick feeling in the pit of his stomach.

A minute later a second black bag came out of the house and, after

*that, a third smaller bag followed. His legs turned to Jell-O and he was
pretty sure he was gonna hurl.*

"NO..."

*Suddenly the vise released from around his body and he was free.
Before he could bolt, another set of arms wrapped around him. A gentle,
familiar voice told him, "I'm here, Colin. You're safe."*

Monsignor held him as he wept.

The last time he'd shed tears was on that long-ago morning.
Monsignor had been there for him, comforted him during the worst
moment of his life. Before his eyes the bodies of his parents and sister
were loaded into ambulances and driven away. His whole world had
shattered in that moment and Monsignor was the one person there for
him. He'd made him feel safe when he was most alone. He'd played
him.

All those memories crashed in on him now, all the old feelings of
sorrow and despair. After a few minutes, he reined them in. Wiping his
face dry with a towel he'd picked up from the counter, he turned and
gathered Ivy into his arms. "This is so fucked up," he whispered against
her hair. "How could he do this to me? Why?"

Her arms tightened. "Maybe she's mistaken."

"God, how I wish that was true. Naomi doesn't make that kind of
mistake. If she wasn't certain, she never would have said a word to me.
It's true."

"So the man who raised you essentially murdered your family."

"You ever have that feeling that you've always known something
bad but couldn't quite nail down what it is? It's like somewhere in the
back corner of my mind I had questions about Monsignor that I could
never put voice to."

Ivy stepped away and put a hand on his cheek. "Yes, I know what
you're saying. I've had my own moments like that."

He took a breath and leaned into her hand. "I never imagined a
man I loved so much could do something so horrible, but in my heart I
know it's true. I never understood why I was spared. Now I do."

"I'm so sorry."

"So am I." No one could ever know how sorry. Rationally, he
knew he wasn't to blame, yet the emotional side of him felt guilty. If
not for him, Monsignor never would have set his family up for death.
They'd all still be alive.

Ivy took his hand and looked up into his eyes. "Now what?"

He squared his shoulders. All right, he'd had his moment of self-pity, his little-boy tears. Time to man up and find a vampire, time enough another day to face the one who'd changed his life—and kill him.

"Let's go take a look at those records."

Ivy's brow pulled together, a small frown turning down the corners of her mouth. "Are you sure you want to do this? We can get this vamp another way."

She had a valid point. The records weren't the only way to take the monster down. It was, however, the quickest way to get what they needed, and the way things were going, sooner was a hell of a lot better than later. Yeah, he was sure.

He leaned down and kissed her slow and long. "I'm going to be okay. Let's go use the best tools we've got, and when this is all done, I'll have a long heart-to-heart with Monsignor. I'll be fine, little vampire."

She smiled up at him, her dark eyes sparkling. This was the face that made his heart sing even when everything around him was crap. "That's my big, strong vampire hunter."

Hand in hand they left the kitchen and went in search of Naomi and her computer.

❖

He stood in the shadow of a large tree and looked skyward, where the moon hung round and golden. Fate was smiling on him. Even when he wasn't trying, the gods dropped presents in his lap.

The werewolf was young and the pull of the moon too strong to disobey, despite the dangerous mood of the city. He'd felt his presence long before he saw him, the smell of the young wolf wafting in the breezy night air.

Red eyes almost glowed in the creamy light of the moon. His youth made him strong, fast. It was undoubtedly what he believed would keep him safe while he satisfied the urges that he couldn't overcome.

Hunting wouldn't be easy tonight, for fear kept most of the residents of the city behind locked doors. He liked that because he was the architect of the rampant terror. Human nature was predictable, though, and despite it all, some wouldn't heed danger signals. For some it was necessity and, for some, the rush of a walk among monsters. He didn't care either way, only that they walked into the darkness. So far, he hadn't been disappointed.

Three groups would venture out despite the danger. The first, those who had to be somewhere, did it as quickly as possible. They didn't veer off the path, didn't waste time. They tried to keep as far out of danger as possible.

The second, like the young werewolf, were compelled to come out and maybe even enjoyed the hint of danger. Still, they paid attention to what was around them because, beneath it all, they didn't want to die.

He counted on the third group the most—the ones who would take justice into their own hands. They trusted no one, felt security existed only when they took control. Volatile, dangerous, they were the storming villagers. Fortunately for him, group three was a large one.

A bit of humidity made the air heavy. Born and raised in a humid climate, he didn't care. In fact, it was a little like an old friend that made him feel at home. He leaned against a tree and listened to the sounds of the city dampened by the violence.

Smiling, he watched and waited. He was confident his wait wouldn't be long and he wasn't disappointed. A muffled scream cut through the night. The young werewolf had made his move. He stepped from the shadows and shifted into his best human imitation. He was very good at it. Wasn't hard. After all, even before his transformation, his whole existence had been about blending in, making those around him comfortable. He was born with the gift and he carried it with him into immortality.

As he drew close to a group of three men with weapons poorly concealed in their clothing, he quickened his step. Group three was about to be deployed.

"Werewolf," he said without preamble and looking suitably disturbed.

"Son of a bitch. Where?" asked a short man with a deep voice.

"I got a good look at the direction he was heading. Follow me, I'm sure we can catch the sonofabitch." He started to jog in the same direction the young werewolf had taken, his scent growing stronger with each step, along with the hot scent of blood. All three men were right on his heels. This was going to play out perfectly.

"I hear something." The tallest of the group, a man at least six four or five, quickened his pace. He was reaching inside his shirt toward the distinct bulge of a handgun.

Though it was difficult, he managed to restrain himself from smiling. Humans were so predictable. His work here was done. With the trio on a straight line to the werewolf, he faded into the shadows. At the sound of the first scream, he started to whistle.

CHAPTER EIGHTEEN

Tory kept thinking about the New Testament and Viola's cryptic words. Somehow, they were tied together, although she didn't know how they could be. That book was on Roland's chest—right next to the stake she'd driven through his heart—when she'd left him to be sealed up in the crypt.

Logically, none of it made sense. Yes, New Orleans had been devastated by Hurricane Katrina and any number of crypts smashed by the fury of the storm. Not Roland's. The cemetery where his remains lay was untouched by the powerful waters responsible for so much destruction. She'd checked. The book should still be walled up inside the crypt.

That left the only other man in her life: Pierre. Again, it didn't make sense. He'd been destroyed, and if he hadn't, wouldn't he have come for her before now? But Adriana's vision seemed to point to her maker.

Viola's announcement that she was at the heart of the current chaos was disturbing. She'd been off the grid for over two hundred years, keeping such a low profile that no one even knew she still walked the earth. Well, that was true a few days ago. It was a new game now since her whole incognito thing was blown to hell. She went from no one knowing about her to being in an odd sort of posse. Even with all of that going on, how could she be at the center of anything?

"What are you thinking about?" Naomi ran a hand down Tory's hair.

She looked up at her and smiled, thoughts of their lovemaking chasing away everything else. "Nothing," she lied. She didn't want to mull over the troubling questions when she could enjoy Naomi's touch instead.

Naomi squatted in front of her and took both her hands. "You do know what I do for a living these days, right?"

Tory laughed. "To be honest, I wasn't really thinking about that."

"No, you weren't, but you were thinking mighty heavy on something else. So tell me. Let me help. You have to understand, Tory, you're not alone anymore. Your days of being isolated are over. You have friends. You have me."

Tory was accustomed to keeping her own counsel. Sharing with someone, anyone, was a foreign concept and something that usually meant danger, both to her and the other person. It was one of the unfortunate side effects of being a vampire. As she gazed into Naomi's eyes, she didn't see anything even remotely dangerous, and Naomi was particularly well equipped to take care of herself.

What the hell, might as well give that sharing thing a shot. "I'm trying to understand how I figure into this whole mess."

Naomi nodded. "I've been thinking about that too."

"It's got to be Pierre. Nothing else really makes any sense, and besides he's the one who'd know exactly how to screw with me. He was a master at manipulation to get what he wanted, especially when it involved me. Getting that New Testament out of Roland's crypt would definitely do it, and Pierre would have no problem grave robbing." She freed a hand and ran it through her hair. "I thought I was free of the bastard and once again I'm wrong."

"You know what? Before we make any decisions on who or why, let's look at those pirated records. Maybe we're missing something or someone."

Tory and Naomi both turned toward the door at the sound of Colin's voice. "Don't look so shocked, ladies. Yeah, Naomi, your news threw me for a minute, but we've got bigger issues than what happened to me decades ago. There isn't time for me to feel sorry for myself. We've got to move forward before anyone else is killed."

"You're sure you're okay with this?" Naomi dropped Tory's hand and stood up.

Ivy, standing behind him, patted Colin on the arm. "I'll vouch for him. My hunter is ready to find out who this asshole is and shut him down."

Adriana came hurrying into the room. "If you guys are done babying the poor little boy, can you get into the office and help me and Riah?"

"Poor little boy?" Colin grinned.

Adriana winked. "Suck it up, hunter boy, we've got some bad boys and girls to catch. No time for memory lane." Spinning on her heel, she disappeared back down the hallway.

"Well, you heard the lady," Colin said, and headed out behind Adriana. "Can't kick ass if we don't know whose ass we're kicking. Let's go find out."

Tory decided she liked this former hunter more and more. He could take a punch and keep going, so she certainly didn't have an excuse for not pushing forward. It might very well be Pierre inciting the city to violence, and if it was, perhaps it was time to get reacquainted... vampire-hunter style. She turned and followed Colin and Ivy down the hall and into Naomi's spacious office.

Riah leaned back in the chair when they walked in, her hands still poised over the keyboard of Naomi's computer. "Wait until you see what our good pastor stole. This is some pretty wild shit. Way to go, Naomi."

Naomi jumped when her cell phone rang. She'd been so engrossed in what she was doing, she'd lost herself in the moment. They'd all been reading through the church records until daylight dawned and everyone but Naomi went to rest. She didn't want to give up, so sure she was going to come across something important. So far it was a bust. She wasn't any closer to understanding what was going on than when she started, and sunset was approaching once again. They'd all converge again and she'd have nothing to show them for her full day's work.

She pulled the phone out of her pocket and looked at the display. Her forehead wrinkled as she flipped it open. "Hello."

"Help me."

The whispered words were hard to hear and she sure didn't recognize the voice.

"Who is this?"

A muffled sob and then, "Karen."

"Karen?" She thought of the handsome redheaded policewoman and frowned. Not once in all the time she'd known the necromancer had she heard Karen sound scared. She was strong and more than capable of taking care of herself. The frightened voice on the other end of the line sent a chill right straight to her heart.

"Help me."

"What's wrong?" She stepped out of the office and walked to the living room.

"Someone narced on me and now my house is surrounded."

"What do you mean surrounded?" She didn't mean to sound stupid, but surrounded? Karen? She was one of the good guys.

"They've got guns and bats and God only knows what else."

It hit her like a brick. Her stomach took a sickening flip. "Oh, my God, Karen. I'll be there as fast as I can."

She snapped the phone shut and ran to grab her car keys. She stuck her head in the kitchen where Adriana was brewing a pot of coffee in expectation that the rest of crew would be rolling out soon.

"I've got to go now."

Tory rounded the corner just as Naomi turned to race out the door. "You're not going anywhere alone."

Naomi shook her head. "You don't understand, I have to. They're attacking preternaturals. They're even trying to kill Karen and she's only a necromancer. I've got to help."

"Who? This Karen?" This came from Colin. Everyone was now in the room.

"No, not just Karen, everyone."

"Fuck. I was hoping it wouldn't go this far." Colin grabbed the jacket he'd tossed across the back of a kitchen chair last night. "I'm going too."

"Me too." Tory started toward the door.

"No." Adriana beat Naomi to the punch. "You three stay here. As powerful as you are, this isn't going to be the time or the place for three vampires. We can accomplish more if we don't have to worry about protecting you too."

Riah looked as though she was going to say something and then simply nodded. She took Adriana's hand, pulling it to her lips for a kiss. "Be safe."

Naomi sighed inwardly. At least somebody got it and for that she was grateful. She didn't want to see any of her new friends hurt any more than she wished harm to befall her old ones.

Naomi touched Tory's face, her skin smooth against the tips of her fingers. "Stay here."

Tory shook her head and Naomi put both hands on her cheeks, holding her face so that she was looking into her eyes. "Do this for me. Please."

A war raged in Tory's eyes and Naomi didn't blame her. She knew how she'd feel if the shoe was on the other foot. "Please," she said again.

Tory closed her eyes and when she opened them again, Naomi saw the acceptance. "For you."

Naomi kissed her. It wasn't simply a peck but long and filled with promise. She wanted more than anything to stop the insanity gripping this city and to spend a thousand nights in the arms of this woman.

❖

In the eloquent words of a man he'd come to know down South, "Fucking A." Things were going even better than he'd hoped. Once he'd turned the three wannabe vigilantes onto the young werewolf last night, all hell broke loose. Literally.

In the space of a mere day, preternaturals were being pulled from their homes and slaughtered in the streets. His own personal brand of genocide.

He loved it.

All it took was a bit of flame to ignite a full-blown conflagration. His disappointment in the earlier results was of little consequence now. Everywhere he turned the fruits of his labors were clearly evident. The police were stretched far too thin to contain the threat. He wasn't all that certain they even wanted to. It wasn't like the humans were being threatened.

Tonight, he sat in the elegant hotel bar and watched the news reports of all that had happened while he rested. Across the city, angry citizens were taking the law into their own hands. So far, three werewolves, a couple of witches, and a fey or two had been slaughtered. How many more hadn't yet made the local news, he didn't know. He hoped many more, with the obvious exception of himself, of course. He was so good at pretending to be human, he wasn't particularly worried. No one would suspect him of being anything other than homo sapiens.

"Quite the night, isn't it?"

He looked up into the pretty face of a woman about forty with short brown hair and a lovely body. Some potential there.

"Quite."

"Do you mind if I join you?"

"Please." He gestured to the chair across from him.

She sat, crossing her legs and giving him a good view of skin. On the prowl or a working girl. He liked that. Nothing like a hotel bar to grab a bit of action, and he didn't mind helping the local economy if the girl appealed to him.

"About time someone did something about those creatures." Her face mirrored the disdain clear in her voice. She picked invisible lint from her slim skirt.

"I couldn't agree more. A drink?"

"Martini, very dirty."

He signaled for the waiter. They sat in comfortable silence until her drink had been delivered and the waiter was off helping another set of patrons.

"I'm surprised it took so long for something like this to happen," she said after she'd taken a hefty swig of her drink, leaving red lip marks on the rim of the glass. "They've been asking for it for years."

"Just took the right motivation, I think."

"I suspect you're right and about damn time. Hate those dirty creatures. I don't know why they were even allowed to live here, taking our jobs and ruining our neighborhoods. So un-American, if you ask me. Here's to motivation." She raised her glass and he clinked the rim of his against hers.

She downed the martini with practiced speed, and he signaled the waiter for another. Definitely his kind of girl and perfect for a night worthy of celebration without having to empty his wallet. By the third drink, his hand was high on her inner thigh. The fourth drink he had sent to his room.

He'd liked the way she sucked his cock and then opened her legs for him. For a couple of hours, he'd fucked her about every way possible. With such a pretty little face, who would have guessed the kink that lurked just beneath the surface? Those dirty martinis were just the precursor to the dirty girl beneath the expensive clothes. The icing on the cake.

All in all, a pretty damned good celebration, if he did say so. Despite her eager participation and skilled enthusiasm for tonight's games, he didn't think twice about it when he sank his fangs into her tender flesh and drained her dry. She was a bigot and he never could abide them. Still, he'd have rather enjoyed her reaction to knowing she'd done all those dirty things with a vampire.

Hunger was the overriding factor. After their vigorous workout, he was starving. He needed to replenish, and since she was handy, he helped himself to the last thing she had to share with him. Her naked body was sprawled on the bed when he let himself out. By the time the housekeeper came to clean the room, he'd be resting comfortably somewhere far away from the hotel. He could hardly wait to see what the rest of the night would bring, but first he had an important stop to make.

Fire usually wasn't a vampire's best friend, unless, of course, that vampire wanted to blow something up. A friend from the IRA had taught him a nifty trick with a bottle, a rag, and a bit of gasoline. It never failed.

As he walked out of the doors of the hotel, he was whistling even louder than before.

CHAPTER NINETEEN

Naomi drove without saying a word, her speed not even close to the limit. Go ahead, pull her over, she didn't care. Her friend was in trouble and, if the bad feeling in the pit of her stomach was any indication, time was critical. She pressed the accelerator harder.

Once they were in the car, she'd tossed her phone to Adriana and had her call Nathan. He might not agree with everything she stood for or what she tried to do, but he was still her twin brother and that had to count for something. Right? She needed his help. Besides, Karen wasn't just her friend. She was also his sister-in-blue. He would come.

Emergency vehicles were already there by the time she brought the car to a lurching halt in front of Karen's house so hard it made the seat belt lock tight against her chest. Any harder and the air bag would have deployed. A couple of marked cars with lights flashing were parked at the curb, and two men in handcuffs were being placed in the backseat of one. They were kicking and screaming—not a good sign.

She threw her door open and bolted from the car, engine still running, without pausing to consider whether she'd put the car in park. No time. Two EMTs knelt on the ground, a prone body between them. They worked, oblivious to the chaos that went on all around. She raced to them and dropped to her knees.

Karen lay deathly still, her eyes closed. The skin around one eye was red and puffy, a line of blood trailing down her cheek. One EMT pressed rhythmically on her chest while counting out loud, and the other held an oxygen mask to her mouth, squeezing every time the first one reached thirty. She couldn't detect any movement in Karen's chest except for that forced by the EMT on the thirty count.

"Is she…"

Neither one looked up or answered; both continued to work on her friend. Time seemed to slow and Naomi wanted to scream. Her friend was in crisis and she had no idea what to do. She wanted to shake Karen, to tell her to open her eyes, to stay with her.

Finally, after what seemed like hours, the two men looked at each other. "Call it," the younger of the two said.

"Nine twenty p.m."

"No," Naomi screamed. They were wrong. They just needed to keep giving her CPR and, in a minute, Karen's eyes would open. "You can't stop now," she pleaded.

"Sorry," the older of the two said as he looked up at her. "There's nothing else we can do. She's gone." He started to put equipment back into a bag.

"No," she shouted. "She's not gone."

"Meme." Nathan appeared out of nowhere and took her by the shoulders. Pulling her to her feet, he turned her away from the two men and Karen's lifeless body. "Let them do their work."

"They're not trying."

"Meme, they did all they could."

"She can't be dead," Naomi said tonelessly. She thought of the many workouts they'd shared and of all the hours they laughed and talked and sweated. She'd looked forward to the time they spent together and didn't want to believe they'd never do it again.

"Honey, she's gone. They could keep working on her for hours and it wouldn't change a thing. I know she was your friend and I'm sorry."

"She was your friend too," she bit out angrily. "You let them kill her."

He touched her hair. "Yes, Karen was one of us and, trust me, I would never have let anyone hurt her. We'll find who did this, I promise."

She wrenched away, turning to stare at Karen's shattered front door. On the sidewalk, a cell phone lay scattered in three pieces. She must have been holding it when they dragged her out of her home.

"Someone told her secret. Not that many humans knew. You did."

His voice remained calm. "I didn't tell anyone, Meme. You and I might not agree on a lot of things, but I would never knowingly hurt anyone, human or not. Karen's secret was always safe with me."

She slumped her shoulders. "I know. I'm sorry. You never would have set her up to be hurt. I just hate this. I hate what's happening. Mostly I hate why it's happening."

This time, he pulled her into his arms and gave her a strong hug. "I get it, I really do. Now, go home, do what you do best, and let me handle this. I'll find whoever killed Karen and they'll pay. I promise you that."

All the argument went out of her. She returned his hug, then let him go and trudged back to the car. Colin and Adriana both stood silent and watchful as they leaned against the front fender.

"We were too late," she told them as she walked past them to crawl in behind the wheel of the car.

Adriana reclaimed her seat in the back. She reached across the seat and squeezed her shoulder. "I'm so sorry about your friend."

Naomi patted her hand. She waited for Colin to get in, then turned the key in the ignition. "Nathan will do what he can to set this right. We need to get back to the house and kick it in gear. I don't want to see anything else happen."

When they walked through the front door twenty minutes later, she could tell immediately something was off. Tory was staring at the television while Riah and Ivy stood silently behind her, Ivy with her hands on either side of her face.

"What?" Naomi asked when the silence lengthened. No one turned to look at her.

On the television a news reporter was standing on the sidewalk, a smoking house behind her. Firefighters were busy working on what was obviously a home fire. Somebody's night was not going well.

"My home," Tory whispered.

"You want to go home?" In light of everything that was happening, she'd have thought Tory would feel safer staying with the group. There was, after all, safety in numbers.

Tory turned tear-filled eyes up to her face. "I can't. It's burning down."

❖

After the shock wore off, everyone was left tired and defeated. It didn't matter that Naomi's stolen file had finally yielded some interesting results. Between the death of Naomi's friend Karen and the news that Tory's house had been firebombed, all of them collapsed. A person or a vampire could only take so much, and that was pretty much everyone's mantra by the time the sun started to rise.

All the women headed to the bedrooms, where darkness and exhaustion claimed them. Only Colin remained awake. He tried to rest. For hours, he tried to sleep, knew he needed it as bad as everyone else. Didn't matter. Every time he closed his eyes, all he could see was Monsignor's face.

When he met and fell in love with Ivy, he'd felt like the universe was finally sending him something good. Then she'd died in his arms and he'd wanted to die with her. Only by making her the very thing he'd sworn his life to destroy could he save her. It had taken about a nanosecond to make that decision. He hadn't regretted it since.

Now the irrefutable knowledge that the man he loved as if he were his own father had lied to him, betrayed him...used him...ate at his soul. It wasn't fair. Of course, fair had never entered into his life. Maybe it never would—not if he let the universe have its way. Maybe it was time for a little of the Colin-style justice, the very kind Monsignor had groomed him for.

With that thought in mind, he headed to the bedroom where Ivy lay stretched out naked beneath the covers. He took off his own clothes and slid in beside her. One hand holding hers, he finally slept.

He came to consciousness slowly, foggily. He was warm, alive with sensation. Very nice sensation. Warm lips started at his and trailed down his body. He knew those lips. Smiling, he wrapped Ivy in his arms and pulled her mouth to his. He kissed her deeply, running his tongue over the tips of the fangs she never let drop when he was with her.

"I love you," he said against her mouth. "I love you, Ivy Hernandez."

"Back atcha, studly," she said in a husky voice.

His smile grew. "Stud, eh?"

She leaned away and studied him, her eyes moving over his naked and very ready body. "Oh, baby, studly is just the beginning."

Her hands took hold of him and moved in agonizing slowness, up and down. He thought he was going to come right then. "Ivy..."

"Shh, I'm just getting started."

Her hands moved from his cock to slide up his body. Her body followed, pressing hot against his. It was all he could do not to explode. He wanted to be inside her when he came, to feel her exquisite softness tight around him. Sex had always been easy for him, women willing and wonderful. He'd taken what he'd needed and never looked back. He'd never had an interest in promises of forever.

Until Ivy. Yes, it was sex in all its primal, satisfying way, but with her it was so much more. Nothing ever felt like this before. Nothing ever felt this good. When he thought about how close he'd come to losing her, he almost got physically ill. He wanted to hold on to her and never let go. He hated being separated from her.

Ivy's teasing now was driving him crazy. With one practiced move, he flipped her over and covered her body with his. She grinned up at him as he moved and thrust inside. She was hot, wet, and ready. She was wonderful.

He couldn't hold it in any longer. Moving quickly he rocked with her until he heard her breath catch, and then he hit the peak that sent them both skyward. It was all he could do not to roar, but that little bit of sense stayed with him so that the rest of the house didn't have to know exactly what they were doing. He doubted anyone would care, but still…

Ivy ran her hand over his hair as he lay with his cheek resting against her breast. She said something very softly in Spanish that, even with his very limited grasp of the language, he understood.

My heart. He would never, ever get tired of hearing those two words no matter what language she said them in.

❖

Big surprise. Nathan was at her door by six. He looked like hell and she told him as much.

"I'm going on twenty-six hours on my feet, so all things considered, I'm doing pretty well. On the other hand, I hate to break it to you, sister, but you don't look so fresh and rosy either. What's your excuse?"

Naomi sank to one of the kitchen stools and rested her head in one hand. "Don't feel like a million bucks either. Unlike you, I actually tried to get some sleep."

"Doesn't look like that worked out so well for you."

"Understatement."

His expression shifted from worried brother to one that screamed cop. "Are you planning to go to the cathedral tonight?"

She nodded. The last thing she wanted to hear at the moment was his undoubtedly many reasons why she should stay home. "I have to." He should know that without her having to tell him.

He shook his head. "You need to be safe and that's the first place you should stay away from tonight. You know what almost happened the last time you and your friends were there."

Closing her eyes, she ran both hands through her hair. Of course she did, and things were far different from the other night. She didn't want to ask and yet was compelled to. "How many?"

Nathan took a big swig of the coffee he'd brought with him. "Seven just in the last twenty-four hours."

"Sweet Jesus," she said under her breath. When she'd crashed she'd known it was bad out there. She'd seen Karen's lifeless body every time she closed her eyes.

"There are going to be more, and if you hold your service tonight, it could be a catastrophe. People know what you do there. You think you're flying under the radar, but that's an illusion. You think because you're human they'll spare you?"

She understood his concern, she really did. But she was one of the few humans her congregation could count on. If she turned her back on them now, what did that say about her? Besides, she had too much to make up for to turn away when things got dicey. She couldn't hide just to protect her own skin, and she told him as much.

His expression darkened. "I've never known you to be stupid, but that's sure as hell what you sound like now."

Resentment rose in her chest, burning and intense. They were twins. He of all people should understand her, yet he never quite seemed to. Made her want to scream and kick him like she'd done when they were six years old. Tamping down the intense surge of emotion, she took his hand.

"I love you, Nathan. I really, really do. You're the best the DC police has, and under any other circumstances I would do what you ask."

His lips thinned. "You're not going to tonight, are you?"

She shook her head. "It would go against everything I stand for. I can't hide to protect myself when they need me. You have to understand that."

"I don't have to understand, and I don't. You don't owe these freaks anything. You never did a single thing wrong."

That's where he was mistaken. What happened that night years ago wasn't just wrong; it was unforgiveable. She'd become a hunter to destroy monsters. It had never occurred to her until the last swing of her sword that she'd become one. What was it that Nietzsche had said? "Be careful when you fight the monsters, lest you become one." Nietzsche knew what he was talking about and it hit awful close to home in her case.

"I…" The ring of Nathan's cell phone interrupted her.

"Detective Rand." He held the phone to his ear. His expression darkened even more, and Naomi dreaded what she might hear. When his gaze met hers, chills ran up her spine.

"I'm on my way." He put the phone in his pocket and took a last swig of his coffee before tossing the cup into the trash.

"Another one?" Naomi asked, even though she knew.

"No, not another *one*. Another *two*."

Chapter Twenty

I can't do this." Tory shoved the chair away from the desk at the same time she slammed the laptop down.

Everyone turned and stared at her. She didn't blame them. They were in Naomi's office furiously finishing their search of the records she'd pirated. They hoped to find more that would point the way, but so far tonight they weren't making much ground.

Her frustration was almost crippling. Tory's throat tightened and she tried to blink back tears. It didn't work. Despite her best efforts, she began to cry. Not her grandest moment.

Naomi came over and put her arms around her. Tory appreciated the gesture even if it didn't help keep her from becoming emotional. Everything welled up inside and she was powerless to stop the avalanche. Every person had her breaking point and apparently she'd just found hers.

"What's wrong?" Naomi whispered in her ear. Her soft breath was warm and comforting against Tory's skin.

"I know," Riah said from across the room.

Tory peered up and saw Riah's face. She did know. She could see the shadows on her face, the same shadows that were wrapping around Tory's heart. They had more in common than just blood.

Riah explained. "You have to understand what we've been through. The years we've survived and how we've had to survive."

Tory nodded and stepped out of Naomi's embrace. "I get what you were trying to do. I even understand the church's so-called mission to cleanse the earth of evil." She looked between Colin and Naomi.

Riah was nodding. "And don't get us wrong, there is evil among the vampires—terrible, terrible creatures that shouldn't be allowed to survive. But they're the exception rather than the rule."

Tory took a breath. "Not all vampires are bad."

Colin leaned back in his chair and looked up at Naomi. "I don't think anyone in this room refutes that. At one time we didn't understand, but we're all on the same sheet of music now."

"We know that," Riah said with a smile. "We wouldn't be here together if we didn't. It's just that going through these files for us is more personal. It's not a case of reading accounts of what happened to some random individuals."

Tory was nodding now. "We knew many of these vampires. Some were even our friends."

Tory's thoughts turned to Becca Sontag. Hers was the record she'd been reading when it finally became too much. Becca had been a sweetheart, a breath of fresh air in a world ruled by darkness. They'd met about a hundred years ago in Sweden. With her light-blond hair and pale-blue eyes, Becca had looked like a beautiful porcelain doll. They'd become immediate friends, and when Tory left for the United States, Becca remained in Sweden. Even though Tory had cut off contact with all her vampire friends, she'd just assumed Becca was still doing well. She never hurt anyone and never, ever fed on humans. She always thought her friend would be fine because she never gave a soul any reason to hurt her.

Now she knew different. One of the church's hunters had taken Becca's head some fifty years ago. The hunter, brand-new to the church, made Becca his first kill. As Tory had read his detailed report, she couldn't miss his pride about his first successful eradication. It made her ill. For him to kill Becca was a bit like taking a lamb to slaughter. She never would have harmed the hunter, yet just because of what she was, he'd taken her head and then bragged about it.

"The hatred in these things," Riah pointed to the computers, "is hard to stomach. We've always been aware of the church and its hunters. We always knew to watch our backs. Reading the actual accounts and absorbing the enormous volume of hate is something quite different."

"Destroying vampires like Pierre and Rodolphe makes sense," Tory added. "But reading about gentle souls wiped out simply because of what they were instead of what they'd done, well, that hurts."

Naomi's eyes met hers and they were filled with sympathy. "There but for the grace of God go I."

Tory's eyes filled with tears again and she nodded. Naomi understood.

❖

In the lovely house he'd commandeered, Vlad rose from the king-sized bed and stretched. He looked forward to tonight's games and he had such plans for his next round. He'd managed to strike terror into the hearts of the humans in the nation's capital, and now it was time to strike a heavy blow into the heart of his one and only. All the groundwork was in place, all the chess pieces appropriately played. His next move: checkmate.

He showered and stood in the closet studying the vast array of choices for tonight's attire. Norman, his reluctant host, certainly did have excellent, not to mention expensive, taste. He settled on a pair of black slacks, a gray shirt, and a pair of black alligator loafers. They fit as though they'd been made just for him. Fortunate for him, not so fortunate for Norman. He smiled broadly.

Speaking of Norman, he walked to the guest room and opened the door. Deathly pale and motionless, Norman was spread-eagled and naked, his hands and legs tied to the solid wood bedposts. Vlad waited for a moment, watching until he saw the telltale rise and fall of Norman's chest. Good. After he'd fucked Norman a couple of times, he'd fed on him. Keeping him alive for snacking was a stroke of genius, particularly when he didn't want to go out for dinner. He had things to do, and finding a proper dinner could take longer than he wanted to spend. Norman made for the perfect solution.

After dinner, he wiped his mouth and made sure he hadn't dripped anything on his clean shirt. Granted, there were plenty of crisp pressed shirts in the closet. He just didn't feel like changing. He liked what he had on.

He made his way through the house to the door leading to the basement. Flicking the light switch, he walked slowly down the stairs. His footsteps, though quiet, brought the anticipated sounds of struggle. Humans were so unsurprising. Didn't take much to wind them up.

The fat one, Vi something or other, was as still as stone—a big stone, that is. Tied to the chair, she stared at him with a gaze black and hateful. From all appearances, Fatty didn't like him much. BFD. It wasn't like he wanted or needed more friends. Ha.

Wasn't good for a meal either. Just the thought of draining her made him sick. Too much fat in her blood for his tastes, and sinking his fangs into her soft, fleshy neck disgusted him. His palate was far more refined; he preferred delicacies like coifed and manicured Norman.

Getting her down the stairs was a huge pain in the ass. To have carried her down would have been way more effort than he'd cared to expend at the time, so he'd ended up simply grabbing her by the shoulders and dragging her down one bumpy step at a time. The bruises on her legs were still a nice dark shade of black and blue. He suspected beneath the mop of mousy hair that should have been cut off a long time ago, her head looked about the same.

Little Red, on the other hand, was a completely different story. That one he'd tossed over his shoulder like a bag of feathers and carried her to the chair she was now bound to. She was in pristine condition, just in case. She was a hot number he wouldn't mind fucking before he drained her. With that flaming red hair and slim, hard body, she was a full-meal deal. He had every intention of enjoying her bountiful attributes before he served her up.

"Ladies," Vlad said as he stood in front of them, legs apart, hands behind his back. "For tonight's entertainment, we will be visiting an old friend of yours. Now, which one of you wants to go first?"

He studied them intently while they both stared back at him with eyes brimming with fear. The gags prevented them from answering, though he thought their eyes told him all he needed to know. "No preference? Well, then how about you?" He took a couple of steps closer to Fatty. *Fatty, Fatty, two by four...*

Red started to squirm, tossing her head from side to side. She struggled vainly against the restraints binding her to the chair. Like she'd have a chance in hell against him even if she could break free.

"Oh, you don't approve?" He moved next to Red and ran a finger down her cheek. She jerked away, the abrupt movement sending her chair over sideways. Her head hitting the floor made a loud thump. She grunted and he hoped she hadn't hurt anything important.

Squatting next to her, he laid his hand against her smooth white cheek. "Don't worry, pretty, I'll be back for you."

Standing up, he stepped back over to Fatty. He untied her hands from the chair back, intending to retie them before he dragged her back up the stairs. Before he could, she lashed out and sliced his face with her nails. The fucking fat bitch drew blood!

He roared, drew his arm back, and backhanded her across the face. Her scream was loud even beneath the tape as she toppled over sideways and banged her head on the concrete floor. She groaned and the fight appeared to go out of her. With satisfaction, he saw blood on her face too. He tied her hands together again, pulling the nylon rope tight enough that it would hurt like hell. Yeah, that was gonna leave a mark.

His grip on her legs was vise-like as he repeated the process so that she was completely freed from the chair but still tied up. He made damn sure while he was doing it she didn't have a chance to kick him in the crown jewels. Even after he hit her, he wasn't convinced the fight was out of her—not until he had her trussed like up a Christmas turkey. Satisfied she wouldn't be able to misbehave again, he grabbed the rope at her legs and began to drag her toward the stairs.

He glanced back and smiled at Red. "See you soon, beautiful."

Red was crying when he turned out the lights.

❖

Naomi had the urge to throw up. Why she had even allowed herself the fantasy that something could come of the attraction between her and Tory, she couldn't comprehend. Bottom line, she knew better. No way on this planet could she ever make her life right.

She'd never achieve atonement, even with all the years of work at the cathedral. Love was absolutely out of the question. People— vampires—could never love someone like her. The best she could hope for was to help the ones she could and make sure she never harmed another as long as she was allowed to live.

If she had any doubts about whether she had a chance for change, Tory and Riah had promptly put them to bed. Of course they would be hurt by what the church had done to them and their friends. As instruments of the church, she and Colin had no right to ask for their forgiveness or even their friendship. Understanding, if they were lucky. Forgiveness, never—it was an unattainable fantasy.

She needed air. Quietly, while the rest were still talking, Naomi slipped out of the office and walked outside to the deck. The evening air was cool and clear, and she propped her hands against the deck railing as she breathed it in. Fireflies danced in the grass, providing a light show she'd normally find entertaining. Tonight it just made her sad. How she wished things could be different.

"What's wrong?" Tory's voice came from the doorway.

Naomi turned and pasted on a fake smile. "Nothing. Just wanted a little fresh air to clear my head. Too much information to process in there."

Tory's eyes grew serious and she put both hands on her hips. "Bull. What's wrong? Spit it out, Rev."

Truth? Nope. When all else fails, lie. Not exactly the best course of action for one who worked for a church but sometimes unavoidable. "I'm just overwhelmed like you are."

Tory walked over and put a hand on Naomi's cheek. "I repeat, bull. Tell me, I'll understand."

Naomi smiled. How many times had she said the same thing to a troubled soul who came to her at the church? "You are an interesting woman."

"You mean for a vampire."

Actually, vampire wasn't anywhere in her mind at the moment. "No, I mean as a woman."

A tiny smile ghosted across Tory's face, gone as soon as it appeared. "It's been a long time since anyone has classified me as simply a woman."

"I don't think you're simply a woman. I think you're much more complex."

"And you like it, right?"

The insecurity rolled up in the question surprised Naomi. Tory always seemed like the ever-confident woman to her. Being so comfortable in her own skin, even if it was hundreds of years old, made Naomi envious. Finding a place of comfort had taken a very long time for Naomi and, honestly, she wasn't so sure she was there yet.

"Of course I do." No lie there. So far she hadn't found anything about Tory she didn't like.

Tory's eyes were a bit haunted. "The hesitation I hear makes me nervous. Did I do something?"

Do something? No. Reveal a painful truth? Yes. But it had nothing to do with Tory and everything to do with the choices Naomi had made through the years.

"Let's just chalk it up to this whole situation. I don't know about you, but I'm feeling really overwhelmed."

"Amen to that, sister."

"Come on." Naomi pushed away from the deck rail. "Let's go finish this thing." Standing out here, hiding essentially, wasn't helping anyone, and she needed to be of assistance, not a hindrance.

"Probably a good idea." Tory touched Naomi's cheek. "Let's go lend our collective hands."

Ivy came running out just as they started to go in. "Hurry."

Naomi picked up her pace. "What's wrong?"

"Adriana's having one of her new psychic moments."

Naomi and Tory looked at each other, then turned and ran to the office right behind Ivy.

Adriana was sitting, Riah's arms wrapped around her. Both of them looked up when the trio ran in.

"We've got a problem," Adriana said ominously.

"Tell us." Naomi didn't like the odd catch in Adriana's voice.

"He's got Viola."

CHAPTER TWENTY-ONE

Tory thought her legs would give out. "What? How?" She couldn't wrap her mind around the possibility that Viola was in danger. Sunny and Viola were supposed to have flown out yesterday. How could he have gotten Viola? And what about Sunny?

"It has to be Pierre." She hated to admit it but she couldn't pretend any longer. Pierre had proved years ago he would use anyone to get to her. Roland was a prime example. If he thought for a second it would upset her to take Viola and Sunny, he'd do it in a heartbeat.

Thinking of what he might do made her sick. Remembering what he did do nearly made her vomit. The most humane thing would be to simply kill them, but he was never one to do the simple or humane. If he turned Viola or Sunny as he'd tried to do with Roland, she would put a stake through her own heart. She couldn't be responsible for yet another's destruction.

"No." Riah shook her head. "It can't be Pierre. I came across an entry for him in 1958. A hunter by the name of Clark something or other. He's long gone unless somebody faked the kill."

"Clark Rockford." Both Colin and Naomi said the name at the same time and then looked at each other. The identical frown on each face didn't instill her with confidence. They knew something about this Clark, and she had a hunch it wasn't a good something.

"What's the deal with Clark?" She wanted to believe someone really had put Pierre down. She wasn't harboring a great deal of optimism, given the grim expression Naomi turned her way.

"Clark is one of the old guys."

"And?" "Old guy" didn't mean anything to her.

"And let's just say that while he was a competent hunter, he didn't always get his man…or woman."

Riah protested. "But I read a rather detailed account about Pierre's destruction."

"Not surprising," Colin told her. "Clark always said he got the vampire even if he really didn't."

"He lied," Tory said flatly. Her nightmare seemed likely to become her reality, her escape from Pierre just an illusion.

"More than once." Naomi shook her head. "Clark has a good heart but he sorta sucked at being a hunter. Top that off with an ego that wouldn't let him acknowledge failure and it all equals unreliable reports. He was one of the old boys' club. Even so, the church retired him after some of his falsified reports came to light."

"So he is still alive and after me." She knew it. Turning Roland hadn't been enough to punish her. He'd tracked her down and was trying to destroy her whole world.

Riah let out a long breath. "That's not a good thing."

"Hey, wait." Naomi held up a hand. "We said he sometimes lied. Not all the time. Pierre could still be dead."

She appreciated Naomi's attempt to keep her positive. Wasn't working for good reason. "Recent events would seem to confirm Pierre's kill as one of the fabricated events. He's still out there and he's after me."

Tory sank to an empty chair and ran her hands through her hair. She had to think, had to outthink Pierre. She'd spent so many years trying to erase him from her memories it was almost painful to let him back in. A cold band seemed to tighten around her heart.

Colin, like Naomi, tried to put a more cautious spin on things. "We don't want to make any assumptions until we know for certain. It might be Pierre, and then again, it's still possible it's not."

"And how exactly will we know that?" Seriously, they didn't have a crystal ball. The closest thing they had to that was Adriana, and given that her skills were newly discovered, she wasn't what Tory would classify as reliable. Her description of a tall, dark vampire certainly fit Pierre, and honestly, she sensed him, had since this whole thing started. Only one other man had been as close to her as Pierre, and given what she'd done to him, that only left Pierre and he had Viola.

She didn't need to be convinced, though it appeared everyone else needed to be. "It's him," she said resolutely. "I'm telling you, it's Pierre. This is exactly what he'd do to hurt me."

Colin was still shaking his head. "There's one way to find out. We'll ask Clark."

Naomi's face registered surprise. "The only one who'll know how to find Clark is Monsignor."

"Yeah," he said grimly, and held out his hand. "Can I borrow your car?"

❖

While his guest rested uncomfortably in the trunk, Vlad drove the dark-windowed Mercedes slowly through the streets. A little quieter than last night but he could still feel the discontent in the air. It was amazing what a few precisely placed bodies could do to a city, along with a careful shove to those with small minds.

Little changed over the years. No matter when or where, people were people, which meant they could be whipped into a frenzy with a little bit of specific rhetoric. Prejudice and hatred always existed, even if covered up by polite society. All it took was the right nudge and it all boiled to the surface like bubbling lava, hot and destructive. That's what he'd done.

He made a large loop around the cathedral after spotting a conspicuous police presence. That was a tad problematic. Not insurmountable but it would require an adjustment in his plans. Knowing that the cathedral hosted the special services, it made sense the good folks of the District would be here on the hunt.

As he came around for the second time, he smiled when he noticed two men with baseball bats swing at a man cornered at a chain-link fence. He wondered what he was, but not because he cared that the humans were about to make hamburger out of him. No, he was just curious.

He continued on his way and was happy when he found a secluded parking spot very near one of the back entrances to the cathedral. He was able to hoist Fatty out of the trunk and put her on her feet.

"Listen," he hissed in her ear. "You're going to walk through the doors of the cathedral like a good girl without making a noise, or I will kill you right here. Then I'll go back and make your friend wish she was dead. You understand me?"

By the way the woman's body began to shake he was confident she understood completely. Good.

"I'm going to free you from the restraints. Don't say a word. Don't try to run. You know what will happen if you do, right?"

She nodded. Satisfied, he removed the gag and untied her hands and feet. From all appearances, they were a man and a woman going into the church for night services. Perfect. The entrance they used was in the shadows, and it appeared they were operating under the radar. As he was sure all the other doors were, it was locked. That didn't stop him. One well-placed kick and the door opened. He never could have done that when he was a mere mortal. They stepped inside and no one noticed. Even better. He liked things quiet when he was working.

Inside, he again saw no one and heard nothing. So far, so good. He led Fatty to a seat quite near the pulpit that provided a straight line of sight for whoever stood there. Perfect for what he had planned. When he pushed her shoulder, she sank to the empty pew and sat with her hands folded in her lap. A proper woman ready for tonight's sermon. He'd give her credit for being able to follow directions. That wasn't always the case and that's when things got messy. He didn't like messy.

Now he smiled, his fangs just beginning to show. Anticipation did that to him even when he wasn't hungry. "Good girl. This will be so much easier if you behave."

"What do you want from me?" Her voice quavered but she still sat tall. Fatty was a proud one.

"Why, nothing really. I just need you to sit here until our mutual friend shows up."

"Then what, you'll kill me in front of her?" Strength was returning to her words.

He kind of liked this show of spunk, and he put an arm around her shoulders, pulling her close. "No, not at all," he said in a low whisper against her ear. "You'll already be dead."

He kissed her ear right before he plunged the small dagger he held in his hand into her carotid artery and then held her snug against him until he felt her go limp. Only then did he stand up so he could slip out of the jacket that now had a bloody sleeve. Her fat-soaked blood had ruined it, so he dropped it on the seat next to her and walked away, leaving her sitting alone and leaning slightly. He intended to exit the cathedral altogether until he noticed how dark the shadows were. Someone could hide there and no one would be the wiser. A nice place to watch them find his little, er, big, present. Leaning against a pillar and shrouded in darkness, he hoped his wait wouldn't be long.

❖

Under any other circumstances Colin would say being here meant he'd lost his fucking mind. This wasn't about him, though. This was about saving lives, particularly the lives of those he cared about the most. Once upon a time Monsignor would have been counted among those people.

Not any longer.

Ivy had wanted to come with him, bless her heart. She was worried that he'd do something stupid. Good call on her part. He was worried he'd do something stupid too. But tonight there was more at stake than settling a score. He couldn't afford to let his personal feelings overshadow what he needed to do. Time enough after the current problem was solved to balance the scales.

After giving himself a few minutes to collect his thoughts and marshal his emotions, he got out of the car and walked up the steps of the modest brick home. Lights were on in a few of the windows, and he knew Monsignor would be up. He always was. When he was a kid and living here, he often thought Monsignor must be at least part vampire because no matter what time of night Colin might wake up, he'd be sitting in his study reading, going over reports, or in later years, working on the computer.

As a kid, he'd found that insomnia comforting. He'd felt protected knowing Monsignor was awake and watchful. Now it made him wonder what the man had really been doing in those wee hours. He'd find out. Soon.

He knocked and stepped back, stuffing his hands into his pockets. He didn't have to wait long. Monsignor Joseph Warren hadn't changed since he'd last seen him. Even after all these years, he was tall and dignified, and age seemed to have passed him by. Yes, there were small lines around his eyes, but he still looked like the same man who'd been at Colin's side since that awful night.

Then again, of course he'd been at his side since that night. He'd created the night to get his hands on Colin. At the thought, rage surged into his chest and he wanted to wrap his hands around his neck, to squeeze until there was no longer a breath in his body. He wanted to take the life that had hijacked his.

He didn't. Not tonight.

"Monsignor." He was surprised how calm he actually sounded.

A smile creased the old man's face and his dark eyes lit up—from all appearances, genuine joy at seeing his adopted son at the door. "What a wonderful surprise. Do tell me you're back." Monsignor opened the door and motioned for Colin to enter.

He hesitated, not sure he wanted to cross the threshold of this house again. Not doing so made it about him, and that wasn't right. He suppressed his own rage and walked through the open door. Colin made his way to the familiar front room. He'd done his homework in this room, watched television, spent hours listening to Monsignor tell stories, fallen asleep on the sofa. This had been his home from the moment everything had changed, his family taken from him. Until tonight it had even felt like home. Now all he felt was cold.

"I'm not back."

Monsignor looked both confused and sad. Then said brightly, "You just came to visit?"

"No."

His brow wrinkled and confusion was clear in his voice. "No?"

No sense dragging this out. Besides, he didn't really feel like spending any more time than necessary under this roof. "I need information. You know what's happening out there."

Monsignor's face darkened. "We have people on it," he said in the firm voice Colin remembered.

"I'm sure you do, but I want to stop it all before any more die."

Monsignor laid a hand on Colin's arm. "I wish you were with us, Colin. You were always the best."

Colin stepped away. "It's not going to happen. Not tonight. Not ever."

Monsignor looked sad and shook his head. "I can't pretend I understand. I don't because I thought I taught you better than what you've become."

"We all have things we don't understand, but suffice it to say that I'll never be back."

Monsignor's shoulders straightened and the man in charge was easy to see. "Well, then you'll just have to be content to let the hunters take care of things. It's what they do."

Colin straightened his shoulders as well. "I repeat, I don't want *anyone* to die."

Monsignor shook his head again before lowering himself into a large leather chair. "I don't get it, Colin. How can you fight for them? You know what they are. You better than anyone know what they've done and what they're capable of."

"That's precisely why I fight for them. I do know them." Even though he tried not to let it, an edge came into his voice.

"I can't help you." Monsignor closed his eyes and ran a hand through his short, white hair. For a second, Colin caught sight of the old man he really was. When he opened his eyes again, that man was gone.

Colin didn't budge. "You will help."

He looked up at Colin with a puzzled expression. "You know I can't."

Blowing out a breath, Colin said slowly, "You owe me." His gaze didn't break from Monsignor's face.

Monsignor tilted his head and looked puzzled. "I owe you?"

"You owe me." Colin said the three words even slower, his eyes boring into Monsignor's. Finally, he saw with satisfaction the moment that comprehension struck. Monsignor's shoulders slumped and a shadow seemed to pass over the man. The old man came back.

"What do you need?"

CHAPTER TWENTY-TWO

Naomi opened the lower-level entrance door to the cathedral with the key only a handful of people possessed. She was jittery and passed it off to everything that had happened over the last few days. Silently, they all entered through the door and she walked to the wall where a light switch was located. The room brightened.

The crypt was as safe a place as any for Riah, Ivy, and Tory. She'd been uncomfortable leaving them at the house with the chaos that was everywhere. Even driving the short distance from her house to the church had her shaking. Now that they were here, she hoped to keep them from harm. Nathan's concerns were not misplaced and she had them front and center in her mind.

In one of the small rooms in the cavernous lower level, she settled the three women at a wooden table. The work to identify the mastermind behind the outbreak of violence in the city had to continue.

"The wireless connection may not work here. These old concrete walls are great for stability but less than optimal for modern technology. It's worth a try, though."

"Do you have a landline available down here?" Riah asked. "If all else fails, I'd like to call some people out there who might be able to fill in some of the blanks."

Good idea. She might have thought of it too if it weren't for the fact that she was terribly rattled. Who would have ever guessed that the skilled vampire hunter Naomi Rand would be all atwitter because of a war outside her door? After all, hadn't she been fighting a war since she was fresh out of college? Despite the years she'd been out of the game, she still knew what the battle would require. She was ready if she had to be.

Even so, this was different. She'd been so idealistic back then, so full of herself. She'd been absolutely convinced there were two sides and only two sides—good and bad. She was on the side of good, all vampires were on the side of bad. No exceptions.

She would have told anyone who asked her back then that she was principled and faithful, that God was one hundred percent on her side. Those were her excuses for living life with blinders on and the church... oh, the church and Monsignor...always at the ready to reinforce her narrow-visioned belief.

The difference between then and now? These days she could admit she'd been full of hate for something she didn't understand. Believing in black and white was easy and, most of all, safe. She'd embraced ignorance and she'd been wrong. All of it came with a very high price tag.

She didn't want to be like that anymore. Despite being terrified right now, she wasn't about to let hate win, even if it meant her life. The world wasn't black and white but many glorious shades that she'd learned to appreciate, even love. She could never go back to an either/or existence, and it might very well cost her life. If she died this night, at least she'd know she tried to stand up for what she believed in and what she knew in her heart was right.

Settling Riah before a telephone, she headed upstairs. Adriana came with her. She didn't think she needed backup, but Adriana had been adamant about watching out for her. It wasn't hard to understand what Riah saw in her. Naomi was going to miss them all when they went home. *If* they went home, but she didn't want to think about that possibility. She planned to hold on to the belief that they would all live through this.

"You think anybody will show up tonight?"

Standing in the nave, Naomi looked around. "Well, attendance will probably be light, but it's important that I be here even if no one comes. The preternaturals have to know they have humans here to help them. It's hard enough for them as it is. I don't want them to think I'm only a fair-weather friend."

"I'd bet my last nickel that nobody considers you that. You kick ass, if I haven't mentioned that to you before."

"Thanks." She appreciated Adriana's words. They went a long way toward lightening the heavy load on her shoulders. "You're very sweet." Adriana gave her arm a gentle squeeze.

"Hey, look." Naomi pointed. "At least one person showed up. The bastards aren't winning yet."

The lone woman sitting near the front of the nave and facing the great choir struck her as odd, and not just because she was leaning a bit as if she were asleep. It wasn't unusual at all to find someone sleeping in the pews. No, this was different. Naomi wrinkled her brow as she studied the woman, noticing the pale-brown hair and ample girth even from where they stood in the back of the church. Hadn't she seen this woman somewhere before?

As she studied her, a sick feeling started in her stomach and spread. With a cry, she took off at a run. "No, no, no!"

Adriana hesitated only briefly before she was on her heels so close Naomi could almost feel her breath on her neck. She reached the pew in a matter of seconds, the metallic scent of fresh blood growing stronger with each step. A sob spewed from her throat as she saw Viola's pale, lifeless face.

❖

Tory attempted to concentrate, but no matter how hard she tried, she kept thinking about her home, or rather the pile of ash it was now. Nobody doubted it was arson, and in true twenty-first-century style, it was fully insured. Certainly she was sad about losing her paintings, sculptures, and the other items she'd picked up along the way, but it wasn't the loss of her things that made her sad. Things could always be replaced.

The threat behind the arson made her feel incredibly vulnerable. Maybe she'd just been deluding herself all along. She'd gotten so comfortable with the life she'd invented here that she'd missed the warning signs. Could be because she wasn't looking, and that wasn't like her. She always knew when she'd been made, or at least that was true in the past.

Someone in DC had made her, and she'd been oblivious. Dangerous didn't even begin to describe what that meant. So far it had only cost her a home. She didn't want to think about what would be next. She worried less about herself and more about the others. The mere fact that they were in her immediate presence could be fatal.

Her eyes were wide open now, and she had a gut feeling that the torching of her house was only a warning. Whoever it was wanted more from her than physical possessions. They'd wanted to shake her to the core and they'd succeeded in grand style.

She hadn't wanted to believe Viola when she'd declared she was at the center of the discontent rolling through the city like an ocean wave. Why would she? For almost two centuries she'd kept her head down and her secrets close. After that night in the cemetery, after what she'd been forced to do to Roland, she wanted nothing more to do with anyone. Caring about people, loving them, only ended in misery. The cost was higher than she cared to pay. Besides, it wasn't fair to put others in such a dangerous position.

For all her careful attention to a state of isolation, she'd failed big—not just for herself either. So far, it had cost the life of a woman who'd never hurt another soul. For as long as she lived, she'd always think of Belle and how just knowing her had destroyed the poor woman. She'd see the image of her stretched out on the steps, her eyes sightless and her meager possessions scattered across the concrete every time she thought of her. The ache would be with her forever.

Tipping her head back and taking a deep breath, she tried to shake off the melancholy. Feeling sorry for herself wouldn't help anyone, least of all her. It wouldn't bring Belle back, and they had to concentrate on finding Sunny and Viola. She wasn't about to let Pierre, or anyone else for that matter, hurt either woman.

"You okay?"

Tory looked over to see Ivy standing in the doorway. "Yeah, just having a little pity party."

Ivy walked into the room and took a chair next the small desk where Tory sat. Her expression was serious, her dark eyes intense. "You're entitled, you know."

"Maybe, but it doesn't accomplish a thing." Didn't even make her feel any better, so it was truly a worthless exercise.

"Did you know Adriana lost her house too?" Ivy asked.

That got her attention. "No. How?"

Ivy scooted a little closer. "Did you ever hear about Riah's first love Meriel?"

Tory nodded. She knew about Meriel. During her early years, the stories were still being told about the two young women. The rich and powerful did love their gossip, even if it was from decades earlier. Particularly when that gossip was all about a love affair between two young, beautiful, and wealthy women. That one of the young women was her relative made the gossip all the more interesting.

"Well, Meriel, or Destiny as she was called by the time we ran into her, blew up Adriana's house."

"She blew it up?" Okay, that got her attention. A little more personal than the fire that took her home, even if it was intentionally set.

"Oh, yeah, kaboom!" Ivy threw her arms up and waved them wide. "Not only did she lose her home and possessions, but everything she had been working on for years went up in a ball of flames."

"Working on?"

"See, now that's the really tragic part. Adriana, Riah, and I, when I could, worked together to try to figure out how to reverse vampirism. We were a regular scientific superhero team."

Tory shook her head. Though she loved Ivy's colorful way of telling things, she'd heard that story a million times. Somebody was always coming up with some magic potion or another that would cure them all. Those that tried the witches' brews were cured all right. Cured right into a pile of dust. She wanted no part of that.

Ivy smiled as she studied Tory's face, her enthusiasm for the story seemingly undampened by the disbelieving look she couldn't hide.

"Be a disbeliever, but you're wrong. You see, Adriana had rushed down to Riah's morgue that night to bring the news that she'd finally found the cure that would release Riah from her prison of darkness. It was incredibly exciting and Adriana was sky-high."

"Seriously?" Despite Ivy's upbeat retelling, she still had a hard time believing the tale. She'd seen and heard of too many cures that ended badly. No one that she was aware of had even come minutely close to actually finding a cure.

Ivy put a hand over her heart. "On my mother's grave. Adriana discovered a cure."

Tory raised one eyebrow. "Your mother is dead?"

A crooked smile lit up her face. "Nope, alive and kicking. But if she had a grave, I'd swear on it. I sure wouldn't lie in a church. Grew up a good Catholic, after all. Don't have any desire to spend the rest of the night saying Hail Marys."

Tory laughed, surprised how good it felt. Some of the darkness lifted. It was hard to resist getting pulled into Ivy's optimism. "Well, I don't want to be the one responsible for making you say a hundred Hail Marys." Tory studied Ivy's face. Could it be possible? "She really found the cure?"

Ivy nodded. "True story. She really did. But when Meriel blew up her house, she also blew up the cure. Adriana's been trying her hardest to recreate it ever since. Until then, you, me, Riah, we're all stuck. But I know our little Adriana. That girl will make it happen again. She's not just a budding sorceress, she's a class-A scientist."

"She could make us human again." The idea was hard to accept, yet at the same time, it sent a thrill through her. What she wouldn't give to live like a real woman once more. She'd never really had her chance at a normal life, and selfish as it might be, she wanted it. She wanted to walk on the beach at sunrise, to find wrinkles around her eyes, to see gray hairs pepper her dark hair. All the things that humans bemoaned, she wanted.

"Damn straight." Ivy stood and patted Tory on the arm. "Now, you get those calls made, missy, and I'll get hustling on my end. Night's a wasting and we've got at least one killer vampire to smoke, if not more."

"You're right, Ivy."

Ivy winked and started to leave.

"Ivy?"

"Yeah."

"Thank you."

Tory turned back to the desk and picked up the phone receiver, looked down at the piece of paper she'd pulled from her pocket, and started to punch in the first number. From above, a sound stopped her hand in mid-motion. It took only a moment to process the source of the sound: a woman's scream. She slammed the receiver down and left the room at a full-out run.

Colin used the cardkey Naomi had given him to gain access to the cathedral's underground parking. During normal working hours, it was open to the public. During the night, it was secured because those who came for the night worship rarely came in vehicles. They preferred to slip in and out of the cathedral as quietly as possible, keeping tight to the shadows. Safer that way even without the current state of affairs.

Like the worshippers, Colin wanted to stay under the cover of darkness. The mood in the city was volatile and that was being nice. In the trip from Monsignor's to the cathedral he'd counted no less than six roaming groups of vigilantes. It didn't bode well for a night free of violence, which, given what had happened last night, was unlikely.

Nothing about what he'd learned so far tonight filled him with confidence that they'd be able to put a damper on the city's troubles. Not that long ago he'd been on track to destroy the last of the known vampires. At that time, he'd been aware of only two that still survived. He was intending to destroy them both and free the earth of an ancient evil. Turned out he was wrong on all accounts.

The path he'd been on had brought him all sorts of surprises. Like, more vampires existed than the church's records reflected. He couldn't destroy them all. Worse…at least as far as the church was concerned… not all of them were evil. Particularly not Riah or his beautiful Ivy. Talk about a paradigm shift. It still boggled the mind on occasion.

He'd walked away from his life as a hunter though he'd still respected Monsignor and what he stood for. Or what he believed he stood for—things like truth, goodness, faith.

Maybe he'd been blind or, perhaps more than blind, naïve. He'd wanted to believe in Monsignor, but it boiled down to good old-fashioned denial. He'd let himself be lulled into believing what was on the surface was the truth. He never took the time to look deeper.

Nothing had brought that home more than tonight's visit. Monsignor hadn't admitted he was responsible for the death of his family, but the truth was in his eyes. In the old days, Colin wouldn't have noticed. He'd have taken Monsignor at his word and called it good. It was as much his fault as Monsignor's.

Tonight, he would have loved to hear the words come from the old man's lips. It didn't happen, at least not this time. Monsignor wasn't giving it up. After all, he'd been trained to keep secrets, and he did it well.

However, Colin did get the information about Clark Rockford that he'd come for. He was fairly certain Monsignor was leveling with him, and while that was a good thing, it didn't answer many questions. In fact, all it really did was bring up more.

Or maybe he was hoping for the easy answers. No such luck. They'd have to do some more digging and figure this out…quickly. Nothing else so far had been easy, so expecting this to be was unreasonable. Still, they had to know one way or the other, and now he did. He just needed to bring the others up to speed.

He opened the stairwell door and had started climbing the stairs when he heard a faint sound echoing off the concrete walls. From this far down, he wondered if maybe he was hearing things, but he had a bad feeling that he wasn't. He waited for a few seconds until the sound came again. This time, he knew exactly what it was.

Taking the steps two at a time he ascended the staircase, then pushed through a door on the main level. The scent, though faint, hit him immediately: blood. The stairwell door slammed behind as he began to run.

CHAPTER TWENTY-THREE

Vlad was very glad he'd decided to stay. The reactions as they came in one after the other were priceless. The holier-than-thou former hunter turned as pale as…well, a vampire! Funny to think she'd been able to take a vamp's head without so much as blinking, but one dead and bloody fatso and she was shaking like a little girl. How the mighty fall and how fantastic it was to be around to see it.

Her little black buddy was upset but maybe not as rattled as he would have liked. A little more gasping and trembling would have been preferable to her calm approach to his special gift. Made him want to sink his fangs into her tender neck and feel the spasms in her shapely body as he drank her dry. Wanted to. Didn't. His work here was done and certain to draw his quarry out. She wouldn't take kindly to the death of her friend, precisely why he'd chosen Fatty.

Wait until he brought out his final gift. He smiled just thinking about the pixie all trussed up and ready for his return. She was going to be fun. No way to lose with her. She'd be a good fuck and a good drink. Top it all off with the reaction from dear Victoria and she had *perfect* written all over her. All the years of waiting and planning were going to be worth it.

He hadn't lain in the cold and dark year after year, trapped and furious, for nothing. He didn't give a tinker's damn about forgiveness. Certainly there was a time when he'd embraced that kind of sentiment. Not these days. Not after what he'd been forced to endure…because of *her*. She'd taken everything away from him and now he was about to return the favor. Soon, his moment would be here and he'd get to see the look on her face when she realized she'd lost everything.

And he was the one who took it from her.

Silently, he moved in the shadows, slipping unnoticed out one of the side doors. Once outside, he scanned the nearby area, smiling when he saw them. Like an actor preparing for his big moment, Vlad ruffled his hair with his hands and put on his most frightened face. Then he jogged until he came to the group of men on the fringe of the church grounds.

"Be careful, guys," he said in a rush.

"Why? What have you seen?" The man talked in rapid-fire words, his hands wrapped tight around a baseball bat. Vlad was pretty sure he had a handgun beneath his light jacket. There was no such thing as being too well armed when it came to violent mobs. When he was a child, they'd come with clubs and axes. These days, it was more likely to be an automatic weapon that served to make even the worst shooter a deadly enemy. He wasn't a fan of this era's weapons; he preferred his kills to be more personal. He *wanted* to see their eyes when he took the life from them. Not that it mattered tonight. If the goal was to incite mindless violence, then he was succeeding. These guys came armed and clueless, a perfect combination.

"Looks like some lady got trashed in there." He inclined his head toward the church.

"Like in dead?" This came from a tall, rather intense-looking young man. He seemed as though he was coiled tight and just about ready to spring. His fingers twitched at his belt and the poorly concealed weapon under his shirt.

"Yeah, real dead. I wasn't close enough to see what killed her, but there sure was lots of blood. I got out of there as fast as I could. I think it might have been a fucking vampire."

"Damn it," the first man said. "We can't let the church hide these monsters. Look what's happening. Now they're even killing good people inside. It's gotta stop. We gotta stop it, guys."

The young man beside him pulled a wicked-looking knife from a sheath at his belt. "You're right, man. Let's go. We'll put an end to this shit once and for all. You comin' with us?" He looked at Vlad. "We're gonna smoke these motherfuckers." A smile twitched at the edge of his lips.

This was a guy who'd been waiting all his life for the chance to take blood. Vlad knew his type all too well and under normal circumstances wouldn't have thought twice about putting the punk down. He didn't like the type. Tonight was different.

He shook his head. "No, man, I'm getting the hell out of here.

I'm gonna lock myself up in my house. I don't want no part of these monsters. I got a family to protect." He thought he pulled that off pretty well, and the part about protecting his family—pure genius, as long as they didn't stop long enough to question why a family man would be here in the first place. But they'd be too intent on drawing blood to worry about those little details. His bet paid off.

"Probably a good idea, man. You better let us take care of this. We know how to deal with it. We have some experience, don't we, Adam?" He looked over to the older man, who smiled grimly and nodded.

"We know exactly what to do. You go on home and keep your family safe." He turned toward the church and motioned for the others to follow.

DC might be a major metropolitan city, home to many of the best and brightest, but it was also home to those who acted on emotion rather than intelligence. This bunch definitely fell into the latter category. The collective IQ was nowhere near genius level, and that was being kind. On the other hand, the emotion level was suitably high for his purposes. It was most likely going to take them a while to figure out the logistics of their assault, which was all right. Short of a ground missile to take out the massive doors, breaching any of the secured entrances to the massive building wouldn't be easy.

He sensed a good combination of determination and balls in the men. They'd get inside even if it took all night, and the damage they'd inflict once they did would be the perfect catalyst to disaster. All a person had to do was put a spark to the right kind of kindling to create a roaring fire. He'd put the flame to it and his little fire was on the way to a five-alarm. It was all falling together perfectly.

Vlad started to jog away toward his imaginary family. Time to put some distance between himself and the cathedral. To be anywhere close when they finally forced their way through the doors probably wasn't a good idea. Pity…he'd like to see it. Later, when all hell broke loose, he'd be able to slip in again and enjoy the fun. For now, let the good old boys do the heavy lifting.

❖

Tory blew through the door and toward the nave, very nearly colliding with Colin, who seemed to appear out of nowhere. She slid to a stop, only keeping her balance by putting a hand on the wall. It wasn't the near collision with him that made her stop; it was the scent on the air. Beneath the ever-present smell of burning votive candles was something too familiar and too intoxicating.

Ivy and Riah, following behind, halted as well. The three of them looked at each other and didn't say a word. They didn't need to. They all knew what that smell meant.

Colin didn't wait for them. He raced to the front, where Naomi and Adriana huddled over the form of a large woman. Tory knew she should follow, only the scent of blood was thick and alluring. As strong as she was, sometimes it was better to be absolutely certain about control before rushing in.

Up front, their voices were just a murmur, too low and far away to make out. What she did catch was the way Naomi kept glancing back at her. That expression made her very nervous. Bad news waited for her up there.

She wanted to scream but didn't. It wouldn't help her or anybody else. Whatever tragedy had struck tonight, she'd have to deal with it. With a second to catch her breath, she was back in control, even after the scent of fresh human blood knocked her off stride.

She wasn't the only one affected by the scent in the air. She turned and looked at Riah and Ivy. "You ladies all right?" she asked.

They both nodded and, while pale, looked okay. With the same visceral reaction to the fresh blood, like her, they just needed a moment to collect themselves.

"Okay, then, let's go see what the bastard has done this time."

She started to walk toward the three huddled just below the pulpit but only made it a few feet when Naomi looked up and began to sprint in her direction. Tory didn't much like the expression on her face. When Naomi reached her, she put a hand on her arm.

"Don't go up there."

She looked past Naomi. Of course she was going up there, except...the hair...something about the woman's hair seemed familiar. A sudden, sinking pain began in her stomach. "Oh, my God, he didn't?"

Naomi nodded and continued to hold her arm. "You don't need to see. Trust me."

She closed her eyes and thought about Adriana telling them earlier that he had *them*.

Riah gasped as all the pieces dropped together. "Viola?"

Naomi nodded, her mouth a thin, grim line. "I'm afraid so."

Tory didn't want to ask. "Sunny?"

"If she's here, we haven't found her. Viola was alone in the pew."

Tory wrenched her arm free from Naomi's grasp and ran to where Colin and Adriana stood. The front of Viola's blouse that only hours before had been a beautiful shade of blue now clung to her ample body, dark and wet. The scent of blood was an overwhelming cloud of aroma that any other time would make her crave the taste. At this moment, it didn't make her hungry, it made her want to retch.

Viola's face, slack and pale, was nothing like that of the vibrant woman Sunny had brought to her home. She wanted that woman back, wanted to see the life and joy that had filled her eyes. She wanted her to take her hands again and tell her the secrets she held in her heart. She wanted her alive. Oh, God, how she wanted her to be alive.

As she stood there, her sorrow shifted and suddenly fury roared through her body and came out in her words. "It's got to be Pierre and I'm going to tear his goddam head off."

Colin spoke up, his words slow and calm. "It's not Pierre."

She whirled on him, fire in her voice and in her heart. "Of course it's Pierre. He's the only son of a bitch who would do something this cruel. Nobody else hates me this much. I'm going to kill him."

He shook his head. "It's not Pierre, I confirmed the kill."

Riah looked at Colin sharply. "Are you positive? I tend to agree with Tory. Pierre would be the one hateful enough to do something like this."

"Yeah. One hundred percent. Pierre was dusted a long time ago. I saw Monsignor's records and actually talked to Clark. He doesn't have any reason to lie and I don't think he did. Pierre is dead and has been since 1958."

Tory stilled and stared at Colin. She didn't believe it. How could she? It had to be Pierre. No other explanation made any sense. "This is the same Monsignor that has lied to you since you were a kid, right?"

Colin nodded grimly, his face stony. "One and the same."

"Well, he's lying to you again." It was obvious—the guy was going to tell Colin whatever he wanted to hear.

"No, he's not lying to me about anything now. What would be the point? I have him in a corner and he knows it."

"How can you be so sure?" Why was he trusting the words of a man who'd been lying to him for decades? She knew what Pierre was capable of and what he would do to scare her.

Colin laid a hand on her arm. "I just am. You'll have to trust me, Tory. Pierre is dead and gone. He's not the one doing all this."

She didn't want to trust anybody. Didn't have to. She didn't care what Colin said or what his precious Monsignor told him. Pierre was still here. He was doing all this to punish her, and that meant it was up to her to find him. When she did, she'd make certain he didn't walk away again. The monster had caused too much heartbreak in her life and she was done with it. No more hiding. No more pretending. It was time to come out in the sunlight, figuratively anyway.

"It's him," she insisted.

"No." Riah put an arm around her shoulders. "If Colin is certain, you need to believe him. It's not Pierre, Tory. It's not. What we have to do quickly is figure out now who else hates you enough to do something like this."

If not Pierre, then who? She'd been cut off from everyone for so long she couldn't think of anyone. Her self-imposed isolation made room for a very few, like Sunny, and that left the pool of prospective suspects very small.

"No one," she finally said. Everyone who might have held a grudge against her was long gone. Her world had grown smaller and smaller as the years passed.

"There's got to be someone. What other vampire do you know who's tall with dark hair? That's the guy I saw in the vision." Adriana looked at her expectantly. "I know I'm new at this vision thing, but I know what I saw. Definitely a vamp and definitely tall and dark. Wish I could have gotten a better look at his face."

She didn't know who it could be. She hadn't even seen another vampire for decades. Top that off with the fact that she wasn't interested in men, and her pool of potential candidates shrank. Pierre still kept popping up as the guy, partly because she'd been such a challenge to him. He'd turned her thinking she'd be his plaything, only to find out she didn't care to play with boys. He'd spent years trying to change her, and his failure was part of what made him so angry.

Tory finally shook her head. "I don't know of anyone besides Pierre. He hated me so much he tried to turn Roland just to get at me. I think he thought I was attracted to Roland, and that made him furious. He wanted me and never got over the fact that he couldn't have me. He was going to make damned sure no one had me either."

"Tried to turn Roland?" Riah gave her a studied look.

She guessed she'd forgotten to tell them about that. "Yes," she said softly. "He knew that's what would hurt me even more than killing him. Pierre was a very vindictive bastard. Not a good trait in a vampire, if you know what I mean."

Riah was watching her intently. "What happened to Roland?"

Naomi put her arms around Tory and she was grateful. It was bad enough confessing what she'd done to Naomi when they were alone. At least with her, she'd felt a little secure. Here in the church and with expectant faces staring at her, she didn't feel so great. "I sealed him inside a crypt in New Orleans," she finally admitted.

"That wouldn't hold him indefinitely. Maybe it's Roland?"

She shook her head. "No." That scenario didn't play out for her.

"Katrina could have smashed the crypt and he'd be free. He could have survived. Others have made it hundreds of years in situations like that. Takes them some time to recover once they're freed, but once they start taking in blood, they survive." Riah sounded authoritative.

"No. Even if Katrina destroyed his crypt, which she didn't because I checked, he could never leave."

"Why not?"

"Because I put a stake through his heart and sealed the crypt with protective spells. Even if the spells failed, no vampire ever survives a stake through the heart."

❖

Colin didn't waste any time. With Naomi's help, they bundled up Viola's lifeless body and got her into the trunk of the car. Under other circumstances he'd be the first one to dial 911, and it wasn't that he didn't trust law enforcement now. No, this had everything to do with the rumblings he heard outside the windows and doors of the church. They were stirred up out there, and it was only a matter of time before someone pulled the trigger, so to speak, and they began to storm the doors.

Back in the lower level, he found the women in a small chapel talking in low tones. Ivy looked up when he walked in and came to him. She put her arms around him and hugged. "I don't think I've ever felt this lost," she said. "What are we going to do?"

He held her and laid his cheek against the top of her head. "It's crazy, that's for sure. Nothing really makes any sense and the only recurring theme is Tory. If she's telling the truth, and I think she is, it's anybody's guess who's got a hard-on for her. There are some crazy bastards out there."

"She's telling the truth." Ivy sounded confident.

He didn't disagree. He really did think Tory was being honest. She had as much to lose as the rest of them, if not more. He saw the way she looked at Naomi and he understood. He had the same expression on his face every time he saw Ivy. It was called love. He suspected she didn't even know yet, but he sure did.

He ran his hand down Ivy's hair as he asked, "Who did she piss off? What did she piss off?"

Ivy stepped out of his embrace and looked up at him. "You've been dealing with vampires since you were a teenager. Think about what you've seen. What kind of monster would do this? You had to have come across someone this violent and evil. What are they like? What would they do next?"

He'd been asking himself those same questions since Naomi called him. He'd seen some real pieces of work in his time as a hunter—about every variety of evil possible. Hell, he'd seen more than a few since becoming part of the Spiritus Group. In the past, he could always discern the pattern and figure out where to go next. Not this time. This puzzle had too many pieces missing and it was driving him nuts. He kept thinking he just needed to concentrate harder.

Or maybe he was distracted. First, he'd finally gathered up the courage to visit the graves of his family. Then he'd found out the heart-wrenching truth about Monsignor. And if all that wasn't enough, he had to go to Monsignor and ask for his help. Yeah, there might be one or two reasons why he was off his game right now.

Thank God for Ivy. Every dark cloud had its silver lining, and in his case it was Ivy. She made all of it worthwhile. Funny to think that the core of his happiness was wrapped up in a tidy little vampire package. The universe had a bizarre way of working things out. Not that he was complaining. He'd take Ivy as a vampire any day of the week. It sure beat the hell out of not having her at all. That was an unacceptable option.

As if reading his mind, Ivy framed his face with her hands. "We'll figure this out, handsome, and soon."

He kissed her and then gazed over to where Riah and Tory talked quietly. Naomi and Adriana had returned to the nave to clean up any last traces of Viola's blood. It wouldn't be long before the worship would begin, and they didn't dare leave a trace of the violence that had marred the church. Even if not a single worshipper showed up, they wouldn't give this asshole the satisfaction.

He took one of her hands and kissed the palm. "Yeah, we will."

The sound of running footsteps made him spin toward the door. Adriana burst through, her breathing rapid. "You guys have got to get upstairs now. Sunny just showed up, and it's a miracle she made it through that crowd outside in one piece. Let's just say it's getting ugly out there and we're running out of time."

CHAPTER TWENTY-FOUR

Tory almost knocked Colin off his feet as she tore by him to follow Adriana up the stairs. Better be right about this or fury might finally get the upper hand. Every pot had its boiling point, and after being kept in check all these years, this just might be hers. It was one thing for violence to be visited upon the preternaturals. Not good, but all of them expected it now and again. To hurt an innocent human in whatever sick and twisted game this monster was playing? Well, that was unacceptable on all levels. The loss of Viola had her on the edge. If he dared to hurt Sunny in any way, she was going lose it. At the top of the stairs, Tory paused. Adriana kept going and disappeared around a corner. Colin was thundering up behind her and she held out a hand to halt him.

"Listen," she whispered. She didn't have to tell him twice. Just as she'd done, he stilled and his head tilted ever so slightly.

The sound came again. Footsteps. Their gazes met and understanding flowed strong between. They were both hunters in their own ways and understood what they heard. Not one but several people had somehow made their way into the cathedral and were attempting to be stealthy. Not a very good attempt but it spelled trouble even if it was amateurish.

"How many," he asked, his focus now one hundred percent on the uninvited visitors.

Listening intently for several seconds, she counted silently. "I think three, possibly four."

He nodded. "That's what I'm getting too."

"We need to stop them."

Colin inclined his head in the direction of the intruders. "Let's make it happen."

"No one dies," she said before she took a single step.

"Only if it's me or them."

"Fair enough."

The confrontation with what turned out to be four men was quick. They were big, they were angry, and they were ready for a fight. What they weren't ready for was a fight with a vampire and a vampire hunter. All four were disarmed and out cold in less than two minutes. It took Tory and Colin longer to find something to tie and gag them with than it did to stop them.

Two minutes after that, they'd secured the door the men had managed to pry open and were racing back toward the nave. The men alive, secured, and out of harm's way, her thoughts shifted once more to Sunny. Her stomach was in a knot worrying about what might have happened to her friend and all because of her. Far too many people suffered because of their friendship with her. It wasn't right on so many levels.

Tory slid around the corner and, despite her best intentions to remain strong, she cried out at the sight of Sunny, pale and trembling, but very much alive, standing in the church. Covering the ground that separated them, she wrapped her up in a tight embrace. The feel of her sturdy body was a blessing she would never, ever take for granted. Sunny was alive, she was okay, and that was incredibly reassuring and real.

"He took Viola," Sunny said against Tory's shoulder. "He took her, dragged her out like she was nothing."

"I know."

Sunny stepped out of Tory's arms to look at her. Tory's breath caught in her throat and she held back another cry. Sunny's wrists were rubbed raw and red, and her face was a mass of black-and-blue bruises. Anger, deep and primal, started to rise and her fangs began to drop. This sonofabitch was going to pay. Nobody hurt her friends like this and lived to tell about it.

"How do you know?" Sunny's voice shook.

The thought of what she had to reveal to Sunny made her want to retch. She'd give anything to spare her from the terrible truth. "He brought her here for us to find."

"Is she all right? I need to see her." Hope echoed in her rapid-fire words.

Tory didn't know how to tell her. How could she explain in any way that made sense that the woman she'd brought to this city to help *her* was now dead, just because she was in the wrong place at the wrong time? Oh hell, that was sugarcoating things for her own benefit, not Sunny's. Viola was dead for one reason only: because of Tory. She told Sunny as much.

She waited for the revulsion to reflect in Sunny's eyes, the hate that she was wholly entitled to. It didn't come. Instead, her eyes filled with tears once more and she enveloped Tory in a hug.

"The bastard. We can't let him get away with this," she said. "Viola deserved better."

"You don't hate me?" Tory was astounded. After everything, how Sunny could even stand to look at her was beyond her comprehension. "I would hate me."

Sunny laid a hand against Tory's cheek, her eyes dark with sadness. "You've always been too hard on yourself. Viola wouldn't hate you for this and neither do I. I hate what he's done, but hate you? Never. I wouldn't give him the satisfaction. Don't you see? He's trying to turn us against each other. We can't let that happen or he wins."

Besides her obvious effort to make her feel better, Sunny made a good point. Tory gave her another hug. There was a very good reason this woman was part of her inner circle.

She stepped back and told Sunny, "You know she was able to get a message to Adriana."

"Viola?" Sunny looked surprised.

Adriana was now standing beside Tory. "She was some kind of mad psychic, Sunny, and that's the God's truth. She got the message to me that this creep had both of you. We just hadn't figured how or where when…"

Sunny touched Adriana's arm and they shared a knowing look. If she'd adored Sunny before, Tory was overwhelmed with love for her now. *Grace under fire* was the phrase that went through her mind. She'd seen much in her long years, but few people truly embraced grace, and it had been a very long time since she'd encountered one. Until now. As she looked around, she felt honored to be surrounded by a group where all of them embodied it. She wished she'd been blessed with it too.

"All right," Riah said as she came around to where the three women stood close together. "No more messing around. It's time to kick ass and take names. I've personally had just about enough of this asshole. We've been playing catch-up since we got here. I say we get ahead of this guy and take him down once and for all."

"Count me in, sister," Adriana said as she draped an arm around

Riah's neck. "You heard what my woman said, let's find this creep." She pressed a kiss to Riah's head.

Tory's mind was racing, trying to get hold of a name—any name—that might figure into this mess. Before she could come up with anything that might possibly help, the doors of the church crashed open and Nathan raced in.

His cheeks were flushed and his eyes dark. "All of you have to get the fuck out of here...NOW!"

❖

"No!"

Vlad rounded the corner of the quiet street he'd been calling home since meeting his fuck-buddy and snack du jour, Norman, only to be greeted by flashing lights, crime-scene tape, and a large gawking crowd. The front door to the house was open and uniformed personnel went in and out, all of them grim-faced and silent.

He stared and considered what to do next. No matter how he came at it, he was screwed. As he watched, though, he was curious why his little sprite from the basement never emerged. Only one body came out of the house, and by the size of the black plastic bag on the gurney, it was the unfortunate Norman, who had finally expired right before Vlad left earlier with Viola. So where was Red?

Trying to blend into the crowd as best he could, Vlad moved closer to the bustling action. Law enforcement and emergency services didn't seem to be taking any chances. He couldn't overhear a shred of conversation. Still, somebody had to know something. If he waited long enough, he'd find out what had gone down here.

"Hey," he asked a teenaged girl with pink hair. "What happened? Somebody die?"

She didn't take her eyes off the house. "Yeah, some guy bit it."

"One guy?"

"That's what I heard. Someone else said some lady was all tied up in the basement, but nobody seems to know where she went."

So Red was still in the house when the cops showed up. Where did she go? He glanced around at the waiting patrol cars. The backseats were all empty.

He turned his attention back to the pink-haired girl. "She dead?"

"Nope, not from what I heard. She just seems to have run off somewhere."

Well, that was inconvenient. He was really looking forward to his one-on-one time with her before he delivered her to Victoria. Now those plans were up in smoke. Maybe. She could run, but she couldn't hide. He'd find her again.

His thoughts turned back to the house and the awesome closet full of clothes he wouldn't be able to wear. "You hear how they found the dead guy?"

"Oh, that was pretty sick. From what I caught from the cops, his sister got all freaked out 'cause she couldn't get him on his cell so she came over to check. Found him all stinky and dead. Pretty gross."

"Hear how he died?"

"That's the really crappy part. A vampire drained him. I didn't even know there were any vampires left. Pretty sick, huh?"

Vlad made a clucking noise. "Yeah. Glad it wasn't me, if you know what I mean."

"No shit, man."

He turned and left pink hair watching the cluster of uniforms do their work. His hidey-hole might be shot to hell but that didn't mean he was. There wasn't a trace of him in that house, or not a trace they could do anything with. He wasn't in any database in the city, let alone the country. He was a ghost.

Losing the house wasn't a problem, even if he did regret losing the designer clothes. There were lots of houses and lots of men and women willing to open their doors to him. That wasn't what had him scrambling now. It was Sunny. Not only did her release deprive him of the fun and games he'd anticipated with great relish, but with her on the run, she could cause him any number of complications.

She couldn't go back to her friend's home. He'd been so delighted with his gift of a magnificent blaze on that one. Was she was aware of the budding friendship with preacher girl? Would she go to the church?

The more he thought about it, the more he decided she would. It was an open secret in the city that the night services were the nearly exclusive domain of the preternaturals. The National Cathedral would be a logical starting point to track down a vampire. With madness ablaze in every corner of the city, corralling the vampires, werewolves, and every other ilk of preternatural beneath the soaring spires was just the sort of party he'd been anticipating since he arrived. Everything he'd been trying to achieve was at his fingertips.

Maybe this wasn't a disaster after all. Maybe this was a blessing.

❖

Naomi whirled at the sound of her brother's voice. The fact that he was as loud as a herd of cattle didn't bother her, but the tone of his voice did. She heard fear, something rarely present in Nathan's words. Even though she'd been a hunter and had gone up against some of the most ruthless creatures to walk the earth, Nathan was stronger than she was. If she was a rock, he was a mountain.

He was also the guy who always put his head down and plowed forward. He never let anything get in his way. Nothing stopped him, which is what made him one hell of an investigator. Nobody stood a chance against him.

That he'd just crashed her front doors like he was running from the demons of hell, well, that had her scared. For a second, she had an urge to run home and dig out the tools of her previous trade. She might have given up the sword, so to speak, but that didn't mean she'd actually gotten rid of it. So much of her life was tied to those weapons, she'd found it impossible to part with them permanently. Besides, a little whisper in the back of her mind had made her hang on to them and right now she wished she had them. Maybe this was exactly what the little whisper was all about.

"Nathan." She rushed to him and grabbed his arm. "What's happening?"

Before he could answer the doors banged again, only this time it was Angie Oberman, dressed in her blue slacks, white shirt, and blue blazer. It was as close as she got these days to her old Capitol Police uniform. Angie stumbled, but instead of the crisp, clean attire Naomi was accustomed to seeing her in, her shirt was partially untucked and, most disturbing, covered with blood. Her face was blanched a disturbing shade of white. The woman who could leave Naomi in the dust on a run was barely able to stay on her feet.

"Help me," Angie said weakly as she crumpled to the nave floor. Blood dripped on the tile.

"Fuck," Nathan spit out as he rushed over and knelt at her side.

Naomi dropped to the floor and felt her neck for a pulse. Angie was so pale and wasn't moving. Beneath her fingertips, Naomi finally felt the whispery throb of life.

She swept her gaze over Angie's body, trying to figure out where the wound was located. A disturbing flow of blood was gushing from somewhere on her body. "Where's she hurt?"

Nathan pulled open the top of Angie's shirt, revealing a bloody wound just above her left breast. He slipped out of his jacket and, putting it over the wound, applied pressure with both hands. "We've got to stop the bleeding."

"Thank God," Naomi whispered. "It missed her heart."

"Yeah, but she's gonna bleed out if we don't get this stopped. Looks like she's lost quite a bit already. Call 911, Meme."

Naomi locked gazes with her brother over Angie's inert form. "What's happening?"

"All hell has broken loose. Armed crowds are everywhere. They're shooting first and asking questions later. You guys gotta get out of here, Meme. There's a crowd on the way here planning to kill any preternatural in the church, and nobody is gonna be safe. You have to leave. Call 911 and then get the fuck out of here."

Naomi rocked back on her heels. "I can't just leave. What if I'm needed here? Where would these people go?"

"They're not people, Meme, they're creatures. You used to destroy them, remember?"

Yes, she remembered, and the thought made her feel ashamed. She couldn't, wouldn't leave. This was God's test, and this time she wouldn't fail. She looked down at Angie and her resolve hardened.

"I can't leave."

"You have to."

She didn't even try to argue with Nathan. They'd hashed and rehashed everything so many times already that it was pointless. She wasn't going to change his mind. He wasn't going to change hers.

His eyes grew dark. "Meme, I know you feel you have to help. I even understand, at least a little, why you feel you owe it to them, but if you stay, they'll kill you. There are too many of them and we can't stop them."

From behind her, Tory's voice cut in. "He's right, Naomi, you have to leave."

Naomi looked up into Tory's face and felt something tighten around her heart. Love? Couldn't be, it was too soon. Still, the feeling was intense, deep—something she'd never felt before.

"I won't leave you." She was talking to Tory now.

Tory's voice was as hard as Nathan's. "I'm not asking you to…I'm telling you. I will not have you hurt because of me."

Resentment bristled. "This is my church."

Tory didn't miss a beat. "And this is my fight."

"The hell it is. Maybe somebody out there wants to hurt you. No, scratch that. Someone definitely wants to hurt you for whatever twisted reason. Doesn't change a damn thing. By threatening those I counsel, he makes this as much my fight as yours."

Tory ran her hand over Naomi's hair. Her caress was soft, loving, and Naomi leaned into her touch. "The warrior preacher."

"You can take the fight out of the girl…"

"But you can't take the girl out of the fight."

Naomi nodded. "Damn straight."

Nathan was still trying to staunch the flow of blood coming from Angie's angry wound. "I hate to break it up, ladies, but I need some help here. 911, please."

Colin came over, took one look at Angie, and yelled, "I've got a better, quicker idea. Ivy, I need a doctor. Get your pretty brown ass up here ASAP."

Ivy was already rounding the corner, a first-aid kit in hand. "Move aside, ladies and gentle…"

Colin raised an eyebrow.

"Ladies, gentleman, and butthead," Ivy said sweetly.

"I love you too," he said as he stepped back to let her tend to Angie.

When Ivy took control, Nathan stood and wiped his hands on a towel that Naomi handed him. She felt for him as he tried to get the blood off. When he handed the towel back, it was damp with the fresh blood but his hands were still stained red.

His eyes held hers. "I can't change your mind?"

She shook her head. "Have you ever been able to change my mind?"

He shrugged. "Not just no, but hell no."

"And it isn't going to happen now. I say let's get to fortifying the church before it gets attacked in force." Her earlier feelings of fear slid away, replaced by an overwhelming sense of determination. She wasn't staying simply to protect Tory and the others. Not at all. This was as much about herself as anything. It was her hour to stand tall and face evil head-on.

The truth was right in front of her and had been for a long time. She'd used the church to hide herself away. Oh, she'd helped as many as she could and with all the right intentions. She'd done the right thing.

To deny that she'd also secluded herself here was pointless. Her time of self-serving penance was over. No more hiding. No more pretending. She was back in the fight, and she was damned ready to be there. For the first time since she'd walked away, she had something to fight for. This time, it was for the right reasons.

CHAPTER TWENTY-FIVE

Getting back in turned out to be far more complicated than his earlier exit. Vlad only had himself to blame for that one. After all, he was the one who set the dogs on the church, and being ever so obedient, that's exactly what they'd done. The little group of men he'd pointed to the cathedral had multiplied in the short amount of time he'd been gone. It was almost like a horde of grasshoppers. They were coming from everywhere and converging on the tidy green grass that surrounded the church. If he wasn't so convinced Red would come here, he'd be miles away. She was here, though, he could feel it, and besides, the little bit of danger the crowds presented just made it more fun.

It took a fair amount of stealth to ease in unnoticed. Then again, he was exceptional at blending into the background. Best of all, he had the look. The years spent inside the hallowed halls during his time as a human came in particularly handy now. He could talk the talk, and he could sure as hell walk the walk. If it looks like a duck and quacks like a duck…

No one gave him more than a passing glance and that's all he needed to slide into one of the lower-level doors undetected. He was inside with the door closing silently behind him before the crowd picked up full steam, barely. Even from the crypt he could hear the pounding on the massive doors of the main entrance. He quickly stepped into the shadows as someone zipped by to secure the door he'd just entered through.

A scent wafted through the air and he stilled. He knew it. A smile blossomed across his face. Patience and good planning were going to pay off. At long last, they were about to come face-to-face. Excitement rippled up his spine, making his fingers tingle. He ran his tongue across his lower lip.

This was the night he'd been waiting for and he intended to enjoy every second. By the time it was all done, he would mostly likely destroy her and then watch the city destroy itself. When it was finished and the dust settled, he would be back in the city of his birth—and rebirth—and he would be king. No one, human or preternatural, would question his power. He hadn't waited, imprisoned in that hell on earth, all those years to be just a common vampire. He would be the king and all would bow to him.

When he brought her to her knees, when he destroyed all that she loved, he would give her one last chance at redemption. He would give her the choice she never gave him: come with him and live at his side or die. The choice seemed obvious to him, but she'd surprised him before. He could very well be returning home alone and he could live with that.

Her footsteps were quiet, quick as she moved from door to door, barricading them against the crowds that circled the massive grounds looking for any way in. He had to give himself credit for the skill with which he'd handled the humans. He'd pushed the perfect buttons and now the frenzied masses were exploding throughout the city. Always did have a way with people.

Finally, her footsteps, which had faded away as she went from door to door, grew louder as she made her way back in his direction. He listened to the delicate *tap tap tap* of her shoes and thought about what he'd do. So many choices and plenty of time. In fact, they had forever—if she made the right decision.

Vlad stood at the edge of the tomb of one of the many dignitaries buried in the cathedral. Smiling, he waited. He didn't care who the hotshot was in this particular tomb; all he could concentrate on was her. She was so very close now he had chills. Once again her unique scent filled the air, and for a moment memories of another time and place filled his mind. He'd loved her, as humans do, and had protected her, as humans do. His home had been her home. They'd been happy in those days, or so he'd believed. No, those weren't just idealistic memories. They had been happy together until she ruined it all.

Now he understood what lies she'd told him, how she'd made him believe something that was all an illusion. She'd used him and then, when he'd needed her most, she'd turned her back on him, leaving him to an unthinkable fate. Even now he couldn't understand how she could have betrayed him like that.

She owed him and she would pay.

Her breathing was rapid as she approached, yet as she neared, her pace slowed. His smile grew. It was true, old bonds didn't break. She instinctively knew he was here and could feel him just as he could feel her. The realization made his pulse race. He'd been waiting for so long. He stepped from the shadows and directly into her path.

"Hello, Victoria."

Only one, strangled word came from her lips as she stopped and stared at him. She was visibly trembling as she whispered, "Roland?"

❖

Adriana was helping Ivy clean and bandage Angie's wound when she jumped to her feet and looked around wildly. "He's here."

Colin squinted, drawing his eyebrows together. "Who's here, Adriana?"

"Him, whoever the hell him is. The bastard who's been knocking people off. He's here in the church."

He didn't like the sound of that. "Outside?" He hoped the vampire responsible for all this was still outside the church. From the loud echo of pounding on the doors, it wouldn't be long before whatever and whoever was outside would make it in, and then none of them would be safe anyway.

She was shaking her head hard. "No, the bastard is in the building somewhere and he's got Tory."

He really didn't like hearing that. "Are you sure?"

Adriana gave him a look. "Look, I'm relatively new to this whole psychic thing, but I know what I know. I'm telling you he's here and we've got to find Tory now before he hurts or, worse, kills her. This is not a nice guy."

Naomi, Nathan, and Riah managed to get Angie up off the floor and onto a pew. It wasn't perfect, but considering where they were, it was the best anyone could hope for. Naomi started toward the stairs as soon as she had Angie settled. Colin stopped her.

"Wait," he said, his hand on her arm.

"No." She shook off his grip. "I have to help her."

He got that. He'd been the same way when Ivy had been hurt.

That had been in the heat of battle, though, and this was different. The church was huge and this guy had the advantage. They didn't know who he was. They didn't know what he was. Worst of all, they didn't know where he was. This was going into battle blind and that sucked.

He gripped her arm again, his fingers firm. "Hang on a second. Let Adriana work some of her newfound magic. We need any edge we can get."

Silently he was chanting, *find her find her find her*. Adriana had been awesome before her return from New Haven. Afterward, well, she was turning into a powerful weapon in the Spiritus Group arsenal. Time to put that weapon to good use.

"Okay, you guys," Adriana said to all of them. "I've got an idea I'm hoping will help us kick ass. Let's try another round of that magic we made happen when the werewolf tried to kill Kara."

Kara Lynch, a hereditary witch born in Ireland and raised in Spokane, had recently managed to break a centuries-old curse by using the power of seven. Though not one of them here tonight was a witch, it sure didn't hurt to try the power-of-seven philosophy. At this point what did they have to lose, and trying anything that might help was a good idea.

Naomi and Nathan looked confused as Colin joined Adriana, Riah, Sunny, and Ivy in clasped hands.

"We're gathering power," Adriana explained as she waved Naomi and Nathan over. "Grab a hand and we'll make a power circle."

While Naomi hurried to join them, Nathan just stared. "Seriously? This is what you think will save Tory? No, this is stupid. We've got to do something, not just stand around holding hands and singing 'Kumbaya.'"

"Two minutes," Colin said to him. "Man to man, trust me on this, Nathan. Give Adriana two minutes and then run with your Glock if you think it will help. We've seen the power of seven work before and it's worth a try right now."

Shaking his head, Nathan reluctantly joined the circle. "You're all nuts but I'll give you that long. Then I *am* going to use my Glock."

"It's a deal, man. And if it doesn't produce something, I'll be running right behind you. I don't have a handgun but I'm pretty damned good with a knife."

"Deal," Nathan said as he joined hands with Naomi and Ivy.

Colin looked down at Ivy and squeezed her hand. She squeezed back. His words to Nathan were big and confident, more big and confident than he actually felt. Sometimes half the battle was putting on a brave face.

He hoped to hell Adriana could pull a rabbit out of her hat.

❖

Shock had Tory rooted to the floor. Not in a million years did she ever expect to see his face again. When she drove the stake through his heart on that horrible night, it should have been only a matter of time before he crumbled into a pile of dust.

There was nothing dusty about the man in front of her now. Roland Lyle stood before her in the flesh and blood, and Tory wondered if, after all these years, she'd finally lost her mind. How could this be? How could he be?

As she studied the face she'd so loved in life, shivers raced up her spine. His dark eyes that would come alive as he stood in a pulpit and shared God's word were black and bottomless. Once, long ago, they'd looked on her with warmth and love. Now they were filled with an evil that made her flesh crawl. This was Roland in body. It was a stranger's soul that reflected in his eyes.

"How?" she asked, unable to get more than a single word to pass her lips even though a thousand questions roared through her mind.

His laugh was bitter and his eyes grew even darker. "You, my pet," he ran a finger down her cheek, "are a lousy judge of anatomy." He patted his chest. "You missed my heart, sweetness. Oh, you pinned me to that miserable casket all right and I was stuck there for all eternity— not dead, not alive, and sure as hell not able to move. You sentenced me to limbo and then walked away as if I meant nothing to you."

"I missed your heart?" She thought of that awful night and of how she'd taken the stake, placed it on his chest, and, with everything she had, driven it into his body. Then as she replayed it in her mind, she recalled how she'd turned away in sorrow and in shame. But before she did, she'd witnessed his eyes open, the change just beginning to give him immortality. The look of malice she'd seen had chilled her and hardened her resolve to set him free. She'd done her best to protect his soul and to send him to the heaven he deserved, but she hadn't stayed around to see the results of her labors.

How could it all have gone so terribly wrong?

"Definitely missed the heart." He spread his arms and bowed. "As you can see, I'm alive or, rather, undead, and well. It's taken me some time to track you down, angel, but you know me. Once I set my mind to something, there's no stopping me."

It was true. She did know him—or the man he'd been before. He'd always been determined, and once he started a task, he carried it through to the end. Back then, he'd done wonderful things and helped so many people. She shuddered to think what that meant now.

"What do you want from me, Roland?"

He smiled, and his face wasn't warm or friendly, as she remembered. The change frightened her. "I sent you a gift, a little calling card, you might say."

"A gift?"

"Come now, Victoria, you were always a bright woman. Don't dumb down on me now."

The lightbulb finally hit a hundred watts. Her breath caught in her throat and it took her a second before she could finally say, "The New Testament."

His smile grew, the demonic expression it created even more alarming. "A stroke of brilliance, if I do say so? But you always did say I was a brilliant man, and I always liked it when you praised me. I deserved it but it was still nice to hear."

"But how…" The cemetery where his crypt was located was still intact. Even if she hadn't killed him, he'd been unable to free himself from the crypt with the stake piercing his body and embedded in the casket. By all rights, he should still be inside those stone walls, not standing in front of her like a visitor from hell.

"Did you not pay attention to anything, my sweet? Vandals. Blessed vandals did what the waters of Katrina could not. They took advantage of the chaos and came looking for treasures. Certainly got a surprise when they stepped inside my little home. They managed to set me free before providing me a long-overdue and lovely meal. Those young men set me on the path to the greatness you tried to deny me."

"The protection spells I put in place. You shouldn't have been able to cross them. I was very careful."

He shrugged. "The boys did a good job of breaking those too. By the time I drank them dry, the path out the crypt door was clear. Walked right on out."

"Why are you here?" Nothing about this Roland felt right. He never would have talked this way. Not a single narcissistic bone in his body. This man—thing—that stood in front of her now was evil. She didn't see a single hint of the man she'd loved in his face. Her Roland was gone.

He shrugged. "I thought it would be fairly evident. You have to pay, of course. What you did certainly can't go unpunished. What kind of example would that be? It's the old eye-for-an-eye thing. You remember, Old Testament stuff."

"You want to make me pay because I tried to save you?"

His face darkened, his eyes mean. "Save me? You didn't do a damn thing to save me. You tried to kill me. You took my choices away from me before I even knew what it meant to be immortal. In all our time together, you never told me how incredible this is or how everything becomes yours for the taking. The world is mine, and everyone in it is just waiting to please me. You didn't share any of that with me and then tried to take it all away before I had the chance to enjoy it."

Her heart ached for the man he once was. "It's not a gift, Roland. It's a curse."

He shook his head. "Perspective, my dear Victoria, it's all in one's perspective. You're looking at it all wrong. See it through my eyes. It's glorious. If I'd have truly known, I'd have made you turn me much sooner."

"You're wrong. What you are, what I am, is wrong and always has been. Pierre only turned you because he knew it would destroy me. He knew I would never allow someone I loved to be turned to darkness. I tried to save you from this sentence."

"NO. You tried to rob me of what was mine. You. Had. No. Right."

In that dark and musky crypt, she had driven a stake through Roland's chest, but this wasn't the same man. All she'd wanted to do that horrible night was save his soul and she'd done the only thing she could. She understood now with a sinking certainty that she'd lost. She was looking hell straight in the eyes.

"You're not the Roland I loved." Tears gathered in her eyes though she kept her back straight and proud. She wouldn't give him the satisfaction of knowing how much she hurt.

"That's where you're right, precious. I'm so much better than that pious old coot, and I plan to show you exactly how much better."

He grabbed her arm, pulling her roughly against his chest. His head lowered and he kissed her hard, his tongue darting between her lips. After her initial shock at his bold touch, she felt only a great sadness.

He pulled back, his hands still like vises on her arms. She couldn't move. His eyes bored into hers and the nothingness she saw there chilled her to the bone.

"I should rip your head off," he said on a growl. "But even as bad as you've been, you're still my Victoria. You're mine and always have been. You belong to me and so I'll give you one and only one chance to live through this night."

She trembled, fearing what would come from his lips next. Nothing he could say to her would change a thing. Roland, her Roland, was dead, and no matter what this man asked of her, she wouldn't do it.

"Come with me. Be at my side, in my bed, and we will conquer the world together. Say yes and live. Say no and I'll kill you and your friends. The choice is yours, Victoria. What will it be?"

He hadn't really given her a choice and she suspected he knew as much. This was just an exercise, a game where the ending had already been written. She was going to die this night, and after all her centuries of life, after everything she'd known and seen, only one thought floated through her mind.

Naomi.

Chapter Twenty-six

Naomi felt Tory's touch as if she were standing right next to her. The shock of it made her stiffen and gasp. She broke the circle, her hands flying to her face where she'd felt Tory's fingers brush her cheeks. They all turned and stared at her. Six faces with surprised expressions.

Without explaining she simply said, "She needs us."

Adriana was nodding. Apparently their combined forces had helped clear her vision and Adriana waved them all in the direction of the lower level. "She's near that fancy carved casket or whatever the hell it is down in the crypt. Come on," she waved toward the staircase door, "we don't have much time. This fucker's like a firecracker about ready to explode."

Naomi wanted to take off at a run but reason prevailed. She understood Adriana's reference to the casket and knew exactly where it was. If they paused long enough to formulate a quick plan, they'd have a better chance for surprise.

"Okay, there are a couple different ways we can handle this."

Nathan was next to her, his gun at this side. In his typical cop style, he began to marshal their meager troops. "Meme, you're with me. Colin, you take Riah, Adriana, and Ivy."

"What about Angie?" Riah asked. "We can't just leave her. What if someone gets in? They've already tried to kill her once."

Riah was right. The pounding on the exterior hadn't quieted, and the only thing keeping the angry masses out was the sheer strength of the massive doors. Even as strong and thick as they were, they wouldn't hold forever, and the crowds outside didn't appear to be giving up.

"I'll stay with her," Sunny said. "I'm not a fighter, and I think I'd be more help if I stay here with Angie."

Naomi agreed. Besides, it made her feel better not to leave Angie all alone while the rest of them searched the church.

Quickly, they all worked together and moved Angie to a storage closet with large doors. Angie wasn't small but they managed to carefully lay her on the floor. It wasn't ideal, though it would hopefully keep her safe. Her breathing was even, and for brief moments she'd float into consciousness. She was alert long enough for Naomi to make her understand what they were doing and why. Her eyes were closed when they shut the doors on the cabinet, leaving both Angie and Sunny in the dark.

Loud bangs came again and again from the main doors and Naomi shuddered. If they kept this up, the doors would be destroyed relatively quickly. The thought of the beautiful carved doors being shattered into worthless piles made her sick. The thought of someone hurting Tory made her even sicker.

In fact, it did more than that. She put a hand on Nathan's arm, feeling the tension that had him wired and on alert. "Give me your backup."

Nathan stared at her, his eyes full of concern. He didn't move to unholster the gun. "Meme, are you sure?"

"Give me the fucking gun," she spit out between clenched teeth. No, she wasn't sure she could actually use it. No, she didn't want to hurt anyone. She'd sworn never to take another life but this was different. Tory's life was at stake here and that changed all the rules.

Nathan leaned down and pulled up a pants leg. Strapped to his ankle was a small holster. He took a Walther out of it and straightened back up, handing her the little gun.

"You know this isn't going to kill a vampire, right?"

She raised an eyebrow and expertly palmed the weapon. "I haven't been out of the loop that long."

He was right, though. They were hunting a vampire and a bullet wouldn't kill him. In her old life, she'd carried a gun very similar to this one, except hers was always loaded with silver rounds. Though her primary focus had been the extinction of vampires and her weapons of choice fire, wooden stakes, and a sword, the silver bullets came in handy when faced with an out-of-control werewolf. It happened more than one would think and she'd used her gun whenever necessary.

Tonight she needed stopping power more than anything else. Silver rounds were not loaded into this gun and no werewolves posed a threat to anyone here. No, this was all about the bastard who had Tory. A well-placed shot to the chest would temporarily slow down the vampire holding Tory, and that could mean the difference between life and death for her. She would take any and all advantage she could because she wasn't going to let anything happen to the woman she loved.

The banging outside grew louder. Time was running out; they had to get a move on for more reasons than one. Naomi and Nathan hurried to the stairwell nearest to them while Colin and the women headed to the far side. They were going with the divide-and-conquer strategy. It had to work.

"Be careful." Then Naomi realized how unnecessary her warning was. Colin had been a hunter long before she ever joined the ranks and was still doing it when she left. On a night like this, there was nobody better to have on the team than him.

His backhanded wave was the only response. She should have known as much. He was in hunter mode. She'd seen it in him before and was incredibly grateful to see it now. The bastard with Tory didn't stand a chance.

She and Nathan were almost to the bottom of the stairs when they heard a sickening crash. For a second, she didn't put it together. Then it hit her. One of the front doors had just given way. Screams and shouts filled the air, and the sound of feet thundering through the church above was deafening. They were out of time.

"Hurry," she said to Nathan.

❖

Tory thought about her mother and wondered how she'd felt the day they'd led her from her cell in the Tower of London. Did the same thoughts race through her mind that were going through Tory's right now? Was she scared? Did she say a prayer for the safety of those she loved? She'd like to think so.

Lady Jane Grey had been nothing but a pawn in a sick game for power. Her daughter was now in the same position. From all accounts, her mother had remained proud and dignified through it all, and Tory tried to believe she could do the same. She'd never had the chance to know her mother or her father yet still hoped she could make them proud. No matter what Roland did to her, no matter how hard he tried to humble her, she'd never bow to him. Like her mother, she'd go to her death with dignity.

Roland Lyle had changed in the two hundred years since she'd known him as a man of God. If she looked hard enough, she could still see traces of the familiar in his face, and her heart ached. Nothing else of her Roland remained, which made her heart ache even more. How could such a good man change so drastically? How could everything that was decent and noble be wiped away as if it never existed? It wasn't right.

The man from her past no longer existed, and the one before her was nothing short of a monster. He had stolen lives and terrorized a city. He had hurt innocents and played them all. For him it was all a sick game of revenge in which he alone knew the rules. Her Roland never would have done something so heinous. He would never have been that cruel.

And then she wondered. Had she really known the man at all? Had she seen only what she'd wanted to see? Had she made a saint out of a man better suited as a sinner? Love could so easily be blind, and she had loved him with all her heart.

As if reading her thoughts, Roland smiled. "You're getting it now, aren't you?" His eyes almost seemed to sparkle with merriment.

She did get it and the sickness that washed over her was horrible. "Pierre didn't attack you."

He winked. "Good girl. No, not an attack precisely. Let's just say that from all you'd shared with me during our cozy years together, I suspected he'd come for you sooner or later."

She closed her eyes and could picture the night, the sounds, the smells. "And you just happened to be in the right spot at the right time. A lamb waiting for the slaughter. You *wanted* Pierre to turn you."

"Ding, ding, ding, the lady is a winner." He clapped his hands in a mocking sort of applause.

Opening her eyes, she stared at him, gazing at a man she'd never seen before. "Sweet Jesus."

"The Son of God can't help you tonight, beautiful. It's just you and me. It's been a long time coming, and I, for one, am really looking forward to it. Either way you go, it's going to be a treat for me."

The bottom dropped out for Tory. All her sins were coming home. God must have a twisted sense of justice. She didn't doubt she had a debt to pay and she was willing to pay it. Had it been a few days ago, it wouldn't have hurt so much. Learning the awful truth about the man she'd so loved made her physically ill. If that was the end of it, she could go to her death without looking back.

Except that wasn't it. For the first time, she had so much more at stake, and she didn't want to leave this world. She had a great deal to live for. She would lose more than just her life tonight. Having found Naomi, touching her, loving her, she found the loss unbearable.

He'd asked her to make a choice and she knew what it had to be. It broke her heart but it couldn't be any different. "I won't go with you, Roland."

He shrugged. "Your loss, but frankly I'm not surprised. You always were a little holier-than-thou. Maybe it's your heritage, that royal blood and all. Always did think you were better than the rest of us. I mean, what's worse than a woman of royalty? A vampire of royalty." He laughed heartily.

"That's not true and you know it. I never treated you any different."

He waved a hand in the air. "Of course you didn't. Keep telling yourself that if it makes you feel better. Doesn't matter anyway. It's over now."

Tears gathered in her eyes and once more her thoughts turned to Naomi. She could almost feel the silky strands of her hair as they flowed through her fingers, smell the light scent of lavender soap on her skin, taste the sweetness of her lips. If she held those memories close, she could take them with her. He could end her life, but he couldn't erase her memories.

"Ah, now, don't cry. I'm not going to kill you."

Tory was confused. What else did he want from her? He was going to kill her, he'd told her as much. Hadn't he?

In a lightning-fast movement, he had her in a vise-like grip, his lips close to her ear. "Oh, no, pretty Victoria, I have no plans to kill you at all. I told you I was going to destroy you, and that's what I plan to do."

He dragged her backward until he reached a small wooden chair. With one arm still around her body, he used the other to pick up the chair, swinging it hard against the wall. The chair broke into half a dozen pieces. He picked up one of the legs, tapered and long with a ragged edge. He straightened back up and turned the piece in his hand.

"Oh, yes, Victoria, this will do nicely. Don't you think?" The smile on his face was chilling.

She stared first at him, then turned her gaze to the wooden chair leg in his hand. Then realization dawned.

❖

A sense of urgency propelled Colin down the stairs as fast as his long legs could take him. The women were right behind him. Of course, Adriana was muttering "hurry, hurry" the whole time, which only served to increase the horrible feeling of dread that had all them caught in its web.

He wished he was better armed. The small knife strapped at his waist wouldn't do much. Riah had a few weapons on her, as did Ivy and Adriana. Naomi and Nathan had guns, for what little good those would do. Among all of them, they were a long way from being fully armed.

This vampire had managed to start a war on the streets of this massive city, and as it stood, he felt like they were about to go into battle armed with toys. He'd never wished more for his sword than he did at this moment.

The sound of running feet echoed overhead and he prayed the crowd wouldn't find Angie. He prayed just as hard that the violence-seeking mob wouldn't discover the stairwells and come in search of them. The humans in the group might stand a chance, but the vampires? The hysteria gripping the mob gave them the collective strength to break down the cathedral doors. Once through, they would likely destroy all of them. Whether or not they were human wasn't going to matter.

Why in the hell did he ever let Naomi talk him into coming here? He could deal with anything that might happen to him. In the big picture, he didn't matter. Ivy was a different story. If any harm came to her, he'd never forgive himself. She wouldn't be here if not for him. Neither would Riah. Oh hell, he even liked Tory, and that put him in the hot seat of responsibility for all three of them.

He put a hand up and stopped, halting the women as well. "Adriana," he whispered. "Are you getting anything?" He could feel a change in the air, a heaviness that didn't bode well. If he could feel it, surely Adriana could too.

She stopped behind him and closed her eyes for what seemed at least five minutes. Probably more like fifteen seconds. When she opened her eyes, she met his gaze, nodded, then turned and pointed down a hallway. "That way but be careful, he's close. This guy is dangerous."

"Riah?" Colin said as he stared down the empty hallway. Somewhere down here Nathan and Naomi had to be working their way toward this room too. He didn't see them, didn't hear them. That left their band of Spiritus Group hunters to make the call.

She stepped up and put a hand on his arm. "What are you thinking?"

He was thinking a lot of things, like how he could get them the hell out of here in one piece. Turn and run was the first thought. The second was how it wouldn't work even if they tried. Danger waited for them no matter what direction they fled. The best course of action? Take on one bastard of a vampire and go from there.

"Let's rush him from both sides."

She studied the hallway and nodded, seeming to follow his train of thought. "I think you're right. Let's do it. Adriana, you stay with me."

"On your six, beautiful."

He smiled, thankful for Adriana's irrepressible spirit. If he wasn't so in love with Ivy and if Adriana wasn't gay, well, he could definitely fall in love with her. He had no trouble understanding why Riah had fallen hard.

Flanking each wall, the four of them made their way carefully toward a large room that housed the final resting places of several of the rich, famous, or honored. The closer they got, the more clearly they could make out the quiet sounds of movement. His heart began to race and his pulse pounded. This wasn't the first difficult fight they'd been in. It was the stakes that distinguished it from the others. Tonight, failure meant death for all of them.

At the door, they paused and he looked over at Riah, where she and Adriana stood shoulder to shoulder on the opposite side of the open doorway. Neither of them had a psychic bone in their body, but he could swear he could almost read her mind. She nodded and they pivoted as one into the room side by side.

He thought they'd have the advantage but he'd underestimated their opponent. In a flash, they were thrown off balance as a man, tall and dark, rushed them. Colin didn't get a very good look at him other than to register that he was alone and covered in blood.

CHAPTER TWENTY-SEVEN

Naomi's shot went wide. As the man rounded a corner and blew past them, she only had a millisecond to react. Years of training and experience kicked in, and she pulled the trigger on instinct. It wasn't enough. She'd gotten rusty in her years at the cathedral. Once, a vampire would never have made it past her. Now she had to play catch-up.

Like her, Nathan had taken aim and, also like her, missed. Naomi screamed in frustration, knowing she sounded like a spoiled child and not caring. This monster had Tory and now he was getting away. She took off at a run.

Naomi didn't get a clear look at his face because her attention was riveted on his shirt and the deep crimson stain that spread across it. Blood and lots of it. Nobody needed to tell her whose blood soaked the white fabric. A searing pain sliced through her heart and her breathing became rapid, shallow. She was too late to save Tory, but she wasn't too late to destroy the monster that had killed her.

Reaching out to snag her arm, Nathan tried to stop her. He didn't even slow her down. His fingers barely touched her as she ran by. She raced through the church, heading for the stairwell door in time to see the man begin a powerful sprint up the stairs.

Now she was breathing hard and her muscles screamed in protest. Her heart pounded so loud it seemed to echo off the stairwell walls. Still she didn't slow, and up and up she climbed. He wasn't going to get away.

Once long ago, she'd made a horrible mistake. She'd used her sword to sever the head of a vampire she believed was taking the lives of young women. She'd rushed in to take the vampire's head only to discover she was the one who was wrong. The vampire hadn't been trying to kill the young girls at all. This vampire, Anna Meade, had been saving them from lives of slavery and prostitution.

Anna had dedicated her eternity to spiriting misguided and lost girls away from pimps and abusers. She did so to help those girls escape their tormentors and to start a new life. She did it to give those young women hope, and Naomi took it away. The worst part of all, Hannah had witnessed everything. Naomi would never forget the look of horror in her eyes or the way she recoiled when she tried to comfort her. The sights, the sounds, the smells of that night were forever etched in her memory and carved into her scarred heart.

That night, after Naomi killed her, she'd laid down her sword and sworn never to take another life. She didn't want to ever make that kind of mistake again. She'd been paying for it ever since.

Tonight all bets were off. Yes, she'd been wrong to destroy Anna Meade, so caught up in a web of intolerance and narrow-minded focus that she couldn't see the truth through the smoke and mirrors. Tonight had nothing to do with intolerance or blinders. She knew what this vampire was and what he'd done, and she couldn't allow him to live. He was not going to walk away. He was not going to kill again. She'd personally make certain.

That she'd made it to him seconds too late to save Tory was a heartache she'd have to endure forever. For a wisp of a moment, she'd thought that perhaps love wasn't lost to her after all. After Hannah had left her, she really believed her chance had come and gone—until Tory walked into the cathedral. He had taken that second chance from her.

She would learn to live with the heartbreak but not the reality that she'd done nothing. Even if it was her last act, she was going to avenge the woman who had given her hope that she could love again.

She tore up the stairs two at a time, emerging through the open door. Ahead of her she saw a flash of red as he rounded a corner, the sound of his running steps echoing in the huge building. Good, she was gaining ground. Though she'd given up the hunt, she hadn't given up the physical stamina that had come with it. For five years, she had run more days than not, cycled every chance she got. She was strong, toned, and ready. He might have his preternatural abilities on his side, but she had experience and practice on hers.

He took another turn and she followed, losing sight of him. Powering after, she caught sight of him again as he headed to the shattered main doors. Suddenly, she stopped, breathing hard. It came to her in a flash of profound understanding. She didn't need a sword or a stake. She could end this monster's reign of terror with a single word.

In a voice as loud as she could summon, she pointed and screamed, "Vampire!"

Like gasoline poured on a raging fire, the crowd of vigilantes that had stormed the front doors of the cathedral turned en masse and fell upon the fleeing man.

She stilled and murmured the words of Galatians: "Do not be deceived: God is not mocked, for whatever one sows, that will he also reap."

❖

The sheer force of the frenzied mob made Colin freeze. He'd just made it to the nave when he heard Naomi scream "Vampire." Everything after that one word happened as though a macabre taskmaster had choreographed it. Even if he hadn't been shocked into inaction, it wouldn't have made a bit of difference. From the moment the mob fell on the vampire, it was a done deal. He needn't have worried about their lack of proper weapons. They didn't need them after all.

With screams of triumph and amid hearty cheers, the crowd dragged his headless body out the doors. Behind them came two men holding his head aloft between them like deer hunters showing off a five-point buck. It was not a scene he would ever care to witness again. Yes, an evil creature had met a fate he'd earned. At the same time, he'd witnessed mankind at its worst.

At the triumphant kill the frenzy seemed to fade from the crowd. He thought there'd be trouble, that the taste of blood would incite more violence. Instead, the crowd seemed to move as one body away from the cathedral and back toward the heart of the city. Cheers followed with it, the sounds growing ever fainter the farther away it got. All he could hope for was that this kill would satisfy the crowd's bloodlust.

"Nice way to turn it," he said to Naomi. "A sacrificial lamb is exactly what we needed to ebb the flow of violence."

Her eyes were bright when she spun toward him. "That fucker was no lamb."

Colin's eyes widened. One thing that had always set Naomi apart from the rest of the hunters was the grace of her speech. He was famous for throwing the f-bomb, but not Naomi. He guessed if she was ever entitled, this was it.

"Figure of speech, Naomi."

Her eyes sparked, her body so tense she was ramrod straight. "Bad one," she snapped.

He put a hand on her shoulder, feeling tension there. He'd been so wrapped up in all that was happening around them and keeping Ivy and the rest of them safe, it hadn't clicked. Now it did and his spirit sagged. "I'm sorry. I wish we'd been a minute sooner. We could have saved her."

All the fight seemed to go out of her. "Story of my life, Colin. For a minute I thought God was going to forgive me, but I guess my sins are too great."

"Bullshit."

If she wanted to talk sin, he could spend a couple of days detailing his. There was a really good reason he'd never been a choirboy. The black and white of his world had molded him into an unforgiving and inflexible man—at least until he'd met Ivy. He'd been given a second chance and cherished it. He knew damn well Naomi deserved one too. He told her as much.

Her smile was sad, pain reflecting in her dark eyes. "You're a good man, Colin, and I appreciate what you're trying to do. I really thought Tory and I might have a chance at something special. I was wrong. I can't make up for what I did, and the universe has a funny way of showing us that. Tory paid the price for my failure, and that's not fair."

He opened his mouth to argue but stopped when Nathan raced up to them. "We can't find Tory." His face was pale and drawn.

"What do you mean you can't find her?" That didn't seem right. He'd seen the man's bloody clothes. She had to be down in the crypt somewhere, at least what was left of her.

He was shaking his head. "I mean she's nowhere in sight. Some blood on the floor and then nothing."

He looked at Naomi, whose face mirrored his confusion. "That can't be," she said.

"No shit," Nathan snapped. "Adriana says she's still in the church, and you know, I might have been skeptical before but I'm not now. If Adriana says she's still here, I'm betting on her. We just gotta find her."

Colin saw hope flash on Naomi's face. "Come on, let's do it."

The three of them raced back downstairs to join Riah, Ivy, and Adriana. Ivy came to him and put her arms around him. She felt so good. "You okay?" she asked.

He nodded and squeezed her. He was not just okay; he was great now that he was holding her. "What's up with Tory?"

She shook her head, frowning. "Don't know. We've looked everywhere and can't find a trace. Adriana is positive she's still here somewhere."

"Adriana, what have you got?" Adriana stood next to Riah, her eyes focused as if she was concentrating on something intently.

She finally looked up and swept her gaze over all of them. "She's still alive, I can feel it here." She patted her chest. "I just can't find her." She paused and looked around again. "You know..." she said slowly. "It worked earlier, so what do you guys say we give it another go?" She held out her hands.

He knew what she wanted except for one thing. The power of seven wouldn't work with only six of them.

"We're one person short."

Adriana studied him with a serious expression. "You know, I always thought that the Old Ways were more suggestions than rules. I might be new at all this stuff, but I'm pretty sure the six of us can kick up a shitload of power. What do the rest of you think?"

Why not? They had nothing to lose if it didn't work and a whole lot to gain if it did. "I'm game," he said, and took Ivy's hand.

One by one, they joined hands until they had an unbroken circle. Riah looked around and smiled. "Come on, ladies and gentlemen. Let's give the girl some power."

❖

Awareness came very slowly, accompanied by a sharp pain in her chest. Tory was surrounded by a darkness so thick it was like being in the outer regions of space. Not a single sound penetrated the dark. Everything hurt. Nothing made sense.

A twitch at her eye made her try to raise a hand to her face. She couldn't. Nothing moved—not her hands, not her legs, not her head. For a second she couldn't figure out why. But when she did, all of Roland's cryptic comments earlier made sense.

The pressure in her chest was massive, all-consuming, as if a three-hundred-pound man was sitting on top of her. Beneath her back, stone, cold and dank, pressed against her spine. Even though she couldn't move her hands to check, she knew with certainty that above her face she'd find solid, unmoving stone.

Roland Lyle had kept his promise by sentencing her to a hell only he could understand...and recreate. As she'd unintentionally entombed him inside that stone crypt with a misplaced stake through his chest, he had indeed returned the favor. Only this time, he'd meant to entomb her and had placed the stake through her chest carefully. She would lie here not dead, not really alive, sentenced to exist in limbo with only her regrets.

Her heart hurt to realize she'd never really known Roland. For two centuries she'd mourned a man that didn't exist. Maybe she'd been blind to the reality of his soul because she'd longed so deeply for something she'd been denied. Loss had been integral to her from the moment of her birth. It was all she knew. When Roland came into her life, he gave her a chance at the kind of normal life she'd only dreamed about. Looking back now, she realized she'd seen only what she'd wanted to see. Her fault, not his, but it didn't make it hurt any less.

Tears began to gather in her eyes, sliding down her cheeks and falling to the stone beneath her head. It was all so senseless. It didn't have to be this way. Even in the midst of Roland's betrayal, she could have found a way to accept it because something miraculous had come into her life: Naomi.

She'd never believed it would happen for her—the kind of love that forevers are made of—yet this woman had walked down the center of a church and into her heart. All gone now.

This church, this monument to the heart of the nation's capital, gave her the gift of hope, and for that she'd be forever grateful, even when she languished here year after year, hidden away from the world, from Naomi. It was the perfect prison. He couldn't have picked better. Naomi could walk by the tomb a hundred times and she'd never know Tory was mere inches away. And Tory would still be here, still thinking, long after Naomi left this earth.

Eternity was fucked up.

CHAPTER TWENTY-EIGHT

It's really, really dark." Adriana opened her eyes and looked over at Naomi. "Really dark. There's not a speck of light or even sound. Where around here would be pitch black and completely silent?"

Where indeed? Even if the power went out downstairs, emergency lights would come on. A total catastrophe would be the only thing to knock out all power and the backups at the cathedral. It would be hard to find somewhere that inky.

The silence thing was puzzling too. Naomi had wandered the halls and back rooms many, many times. Sure, it got quiet, but total silence, never. Seemed like there was always a whisper here or there, a tiny noise, a creak or a groan. The church had its own soul, and it wasn't above letting those who walked inside its walls know.

So where could Tory be in total silence and total blackness?

"I don't know," she said finally, her tone flat. She rubbed her hands over her face at the same time she silently prayed for strength. Tears stung at the back of her eyes and she hoped she wouldn't break down, especially in front of Nathan.

"Think, sister," Adriana snapped. "She needs you."

Naomi dropped her hands and stared at Adriana. Granted, she hadn't been around Adriana much, but she had the distinct impression that the edge in her voice wasn't normal.

"I'm the last person she needs." Surely they all had to see that. If not for her, Tory wouldn't be in this mess. She'd brought her here, right into the hands of the psycho.

Adriana rolled her eyes and put her hands on her hips, the edge still in her voice. "Oh, for God's sake. Somebody slap that woman up alongside the head. You're the one person she absolutely needs, so stop feeling sorry for yourself. If you love her, and I'm pretty damn sure you do, then get to thinking. Where the hell could she be?"

They were all looking at her and panic started to well in her chest. She didn't know. If God really had her back, he would give her something. "I don't…"

A thought occurred to her, as out there as in Out There. Still, maybe? "The tombs," she said hesitantly. "She could be in one of the tombs." As she said the words out loud her suggestion jelled. Maybe God was still on her side.

Colin's brow furrowed and he turned to look in the room adjacent to where they stood. "You think?"

Honestly, she didn't know for sure. It was a gut feeling. Even though she was far from certain, in a weird way it made sense. Dark, silent, hidden. Pretty much the perfect description of a stone prison.

"Yeah, I think." She felt more confident now, a little hopeful.

"Well." He looked around. "What are we waiting for? Divide and conquer?"

Absolutely. Then she had another thought. "Look for a broken seal. If he was able to open a top and get her inside, the seal beneath the cover will show cracks. It should speed up the search."

They all nodded and turned in different directions. Ten minutes later, she found it. Her heart was racing as she saw the hairline cracks in the mortar that had been applied on the day the elaborate tomb was sealed with a body inside.

"I found it," she yelled at the same time she put all her strength into pushing the cover out of the way. It moved by inches. This was it. Tory had to be inside. Her heart started racing. "Help!" she screamed.

Colin and Nathan were the first to make it to her side, followed by Riah and Adriana. Ivy came tearing around the corner a minute behind the rest. With the help of the men, they were able to slide the cover over far enough to see inside.

The smell of old decay and dust wafted up as the interior was revealed. So did the smell of fresh blood. As the overhead light illuminated the interior of the tomb, Tory's pale face came into view.

"About time you got here," she said in a hoarse whisper.

Naomi burst into tears. Her hands were shaking so badly, Nathan reached around her to pull the stake from Tory's chest. He threw it across the room and got out of her way so she could gather Tory up in her arms. Holding her close, she carried Tory out of the crypt.

EPILOGUE

Colin held Ivy's hand as they walked together across the lush green grass. A full moon hung in the star-studded sky above, sending a warm, buttery light down on the headstones. It was a clear, beautiful night, perfect for a lovers' walk, except lovers didn't usually stroll through a cemetery—unless it was time to meet the parents.

"This is my family," Colin told her. "My mom, my dad, my sister."

The pressure in his chest and the sorrow in his heart that had been his constant companion since the loss of his family weren't present tonight. He would always feel a deep regret that they'd been sacrificed because of him, but he also knew he wasn't responsible. Monsignor was.

Colin had wanted to kill him, to hurt Monsignor as he had hurt him, yet somewhere between the time Naomi had revealed the truth to him and now, that murderous desire had faded. Too many people had died, and he didn't want to be responsible for one more, even if that one deserved it.

He thought about his parents and how they had tried to raise him in the short years they'd had together. He pictured his bright and beautiful sister, thought about his friends, and most of all, he thought about Ivy. Before her, he'd been little better than a monster himself, one that hid behind righteousness and justified his actions as acts of war. He didn't want to be that man anymore.

He wanted to be free from the past because the future held so much more. If he killed Monsignor the past would be forever carved on his soul. Escape would be impossible. He might not have believed it a year ago, but he did now: he was better than that.

Funny how he'd considered himself a loner who would never

depend on another for anything. From the day he lost his family that had been his mantra. No one but him was responsible for his happiness. But life just didn't work that way.

Ha. He'd been one stupid son of a bitch. Or maybe embracing the loneliness was a good thing—it had made him ready when Ivy rocked his world. She made him happy. She made him feel alive. Without her, he was only half a man. With her, he was everything.

Ivy placed the roses she'd insisted on bringing along at the base of headstones. Red for his parents, pink for his sister. In the moonlight, they looked beautiful. Leave it to Ivy to know exactly what to do.

He gathered her close and kissed her. "Thank you for coming with me." He swore he could feel his mother's smile as he held Ivy in his arms. Mom would have been thrilled by Ivy. His sister would have adored her. Dad would have whistled and given Colin the thumbs-up. She would have found a place in the hearts of his near and dear, just as she filled his now.

She smiled up into his face, her dark eyes intense. "Thank you for letting me."

"I just…"

She laid a finger against his lips. "You don't have to explain. I know."

And she did. Only one of the reasons he loved her.

❖

Naomi thought she was dreaming and it was one awesome dream. Her body was warm and relaxed as fingers stroked feather-light across her breasts and her stomach. Her eyes flickered open and suddenly she realized it wasn't a dream.

She knew that touch and it made her smile. "Oh," she breathed. "I thought you were sleeping."

Tory rolled on top of her and smiled down. Her long hair was loose and brushed against Naomi's bare breasts. The whisper touch of Tory's silky hair made her nipples grow taut and hard.

"Plenty of time to sleep, preacher girl, and besides, I'm not tired." She leaned down and kissed her.

Naomi returned the kiss, sliding her tongue between Tory's lips. She stroked Tory's back, lower and lower, until she held her lovely rounded ass. Would she ever grow tired of the taste and touch of this woman? No. No. No.

Tory's head dropped and she took a nipple into her mouth. Naomi arched into her. God, it all felt so incredible. When Tory's hand slipped between her legs, Naomi thought she might come right then, but Tory wouldn't let her. With exquisitely slow movements she made Naomi tingle from head to toe. She'd take her to the peak and bring her back. It was sweet torture. She cried out when she came, Tory trailing kisses up her body, stopping at her lips for one long, tasty kiss.

When she caught her breath, she flipped Tory over onto her back and returned the very lovely favor. Tory's body arched now, and she cried out. Naomi smiled. Yeah, love was a gift she'd never, ever take for granted.

She lay next to Tory, her body covered in sweat, listening as Tory's breathing started to return to normal. They were in their own special place, wrapped together in passion, love, and contentment.

It was time. She'd been thinking about this since yesterday when Riah had put it out there. That woman was incredible—beautiful, smart, and sneaky—and she sure knew when and where to strike.

Naomi didn't reach her decision lightly and wondered what Tory would think. Then again, she wasn't the only one who had a zillion things to think about, decisions to make.

Seeming to sense the direction of her thoughts, Tory lightly touched her bare breast and asked, "What have you decided?"

She loved the feel of Tory's light caress and the slow, wonderful arousal it evoked. Surprised how quickly she'd come to depend on her, how important she was in her life, she said, "I think we should go."

Tory raised herself up on one arm. Her expression was soft and maybe even a little excited. "Really?"

"Yeah, really." She gave a wry smile. "Really."

After Naomi had taken Tory back to the house and attended to her wounds, they'd all listened as Tory told them of her encounter with Roland. It was the stuff of a pretty good B-movie. After it was all said and done, Riah had surprised both of them with a proposition: come to Spokane with her, Adriana, Ivy, and Colin. Join the Spiritus Group and fight evil.

The spark in Tory's eyes when Riah had first suggested the move wasn't lost on Naomi. She got the distinct impression that Tory was ready for a change. Still, she hesitated.

Born and raised in this area, she considered moving across the country a huge deal. And then there was her family, her twin. Could she leave Nathan? Tory had traveled all over the world, but this was home for Naomi. Even when she was a hunter, she'd always come back to DC. Was she really ready to move to the other Washington?

After Roland's graphic demise, the city roiled a little longer and then peace once more began to settle. The relationship between humans and preternaturals had suffered a setback, though Naomi was confident that, given time, the wounds would heal. The city would once more find a rhythm that allowed both factions to live harmoniously.

The church wasn't as much a concern to Naomi. As she'd turned the mob on Roland, she realized her life belonged not to the church but somewhere else. At that moment, she hadn't exactly been sure what that meant. Until now. Slowly, it dawned on her that God was working in mysterious ways in her life. Not only had she been given a second chance at love, but her way in the world had been revealed too.

She didn't know what the future held for her, but she did know two things: she was moving to Washington state, and she was going to spend the rest of her life loving Tory.

About the Author

Sheri Lewis Wohl grew up in northeast Washington state, and though she always thought she'd move away, she never has. Despite traveling throughout the United States, Sheri always finds her way back home. And so she lives, plays, and writes amidst mountains, evergreens, and abundant wildlife. When not working the day job in federal finance, she writes stories that typically include a bit of the strange and unusual and always a touch of romance. She works to carve out time to run, swim, and bike so she can participate in local triathlons. Sheri is also a member of a local K9 search and rescue team.

Books Available From Bold Strokes Books

The Princess Affair by Nell Stark. Rhodes Scholar Kerry Donovan arrives at Oxford ready to focus on her studies, but her life and her priorities are thrown into chaos when she catches the eye of Her Royal Highness Princess Sasha. (978-1-60282-858-2)

The Chase by Jesse J. Thoma. When Isabelle Rochat's life is threatened, she receives the unwelcome protection and attention of bounty hunter Holt Lasher who vows to keep Isabelle safe at all costs. (978-1-60282-859-9)

The Lone Hunt by L.L. Raand. In a world where humans and Praeterns conspire for the ultimate power, violence is a way of life…and death. A Midnight Hunters novel. (978-1-60282-860-5)

The Supernatural Detective by Crin Claxton. Tony Carson sees dead people. With a drag queen for a spirit guide and a devastatingly attractive herbalist for a client, she's about to discover the spirit world can be a very dangerous world indeed. (978-1-60282-861-2)

Beloved Gomorrah by Justine Saracen. Undersea artists creating their own City on the Plain uncover the truth about Sodom and Gomorrah, whose "one righteous man" is a murderer, rapist, and conspirator in genocide. (978-1-60282-862-9)

The Left Hand of Justice by Jess Faraday. A kidnapped heiress, a heretical cult, a corrupt police chief, and an accused witch. Paris is burning, and the only one who can put out the fire is Detective Inspector Elise Corbeau…whose boss wants her dead. (978-1-60282-863-6)

Cut to the Chase by Lisa Girolami. Careful and methodical author Paige Cornish falls for brash and wild Hollywood actress Avalon Randolph, but can these opposites find a happy middle ground in a town that never lives in the middle? (978-1-60282-783-7)

Every Second Counts by D. Jackson Leigh. Every second counts in Bridgette LeRoy's desperate mission to protect her heart and stop Marc Ryder's suicidal return to riding rodeo bulls. (978-1-60282-785-1)

More Than Friends by Erin Dutton. Evelyn Fisher thinks she has the perfect role model for a long-term relationship, until her best friends, Kendall and Melanie, split up and all three women must reevaluate their lives and their relationships. (978-1-60282-784-4)

Dirty Money by Ashley Bartlett. Vivian Cooper and Reese DiGiovanni just found out that falling in love is hard. It's even harder when you're running for your life. (978-1-60282-786-8)

Sea Glass Inn by Karis Walsh. When Melinda Andrews commissions a series of mosaics by Pamela Whitford for her new inn, she doesn't expect to be more captivated by the artist than by the paintings. (978-1-60282-771-4)

The Awakening: A Sisterhood of Spirits novel by Yvonne Heidt. Sunny Skye has interacted with spirits her entire life, but when she runs into Officer Jordan Lawson during a ghost investigation, she discovers more than just facts in a missing girl's cold case file. (978-1-60282-772-1)

Murphy's Law by Yolanda Wallace. No matter how high you climb, you can't escape your past. (978-1-60282-773-8)

Blacker Than Blue by Rebekah Weatherspoon. Threatened with losing her first love to a powerful demon, vampire Cleo Jones is willing to break the ultimate law of the undead to rebuild the family she has lost. (978-1-60282-774-5)

Silver Collar by Gill McKnight. Werewolf Luc Garoul is outlawed and out of control, but can her family track her down before a sinister predator gets there first? Fourth in the Garoul series. (978-1-60282-764-6)

The Dragon Tree Legacy by Ali Vali. For Aubrey Tarver time hasn't dulled the pain of losing her first love Wiley Gremillion, but she has to set that aside when her choices put her life and her family's lives in real danger. (978-1-60282-765-3)